"In *What the Sea Horse Told Me*, author Mary Knight delivers another captivating narrative that seamlessly intertwines spiritual beliefs, nature, and the complexities of modern-day adolescence.

Leaving the hollers of the Appalachian Mountains in Eastern Kentucky from Knight's debut novel, *Saving Wonder*, this novel travels to Hawaii—embarking readers on a profound journey of self-discovery and acceptance through the eyes of a dynamic twelve-year-old protagonist. Sophie Kai, with a little inspiration from a seahorse, offers a refreshing perspective on themes of identity, belonging, and the importance of embracing one's unique talents.

The novel transcends genres with readers being drawn into a journey where the ordinary and the extraordinary coexist, inviting them to ponder what is truly possible. While rooted in Hawaiian spirituality, the novel speaks to universal truths about the interconnectedness of all beings and the power of intuition, perception, and friendship. It challenges readers to see and feel beyond the limitations of the physical world, encouraging them to embrace their inner selves. *What the Sea Horse Told Me* is sure to resonate with readers, igniting deep and thought-provoking conversations—an experience that I am eagerly anticipating sharing with the students in my class."
—*Jesse Fawess*, middle school ELA teacher, Long Island, NY

(continued)

"The story masterfully explores how grief changes individuals within a family and the interpersonal dynamics of the family group. It's an especially accurate depiction of how children take on responsibility for death losses and how challenging it can be to rewrite those narratives of guilt and self-blame. Sophie Kai's process of finally talking with her mother about their loss was beautiful and a powerful model for how honest conversation can completely transform family connections and create space for healing."
—*Leila Salisbury, founding director of The Kentucky Center for Grieving Children and Families*

"Exquisitely beautiful! Knight's writing took me on an emotional journey of protagonist Sophie Kai's healing and transformation, and her themes of friendship, family, love, empathy, justice, mercy, and compassion spoke volumes as to why this novel needs to be in the hands of our young people. Thank you, *mahalo*, Mary Knight for sharing this book with the world!"
—*Rosie Sansalone,* middle school ELA teacher for 27 years

"Mary Knight uses strong language and descriptive sentences to bring the book to life. Readers will feel Sophie Kai's troubles and victories as she finds her special place at camp and finds her love for the island animals. I couldn't stop thinking about Sophie Kai from the moment I opened the book to flipping the last page shut. Every middle schooler should read What The Seahorse Told Me!"
—*Elsie Fricke,* 6th grader

"This book is amazing! Parts were sad, happy, funny, helpful, and the biggest one is *friendly*. I give it 5 stars!"
—*Hunter Tigar,* 6th grader

WHAT THE SEAHORSE TOLD ME

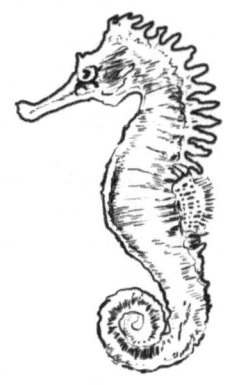

Mary Knight

MIDDLETON BOOKS

Text copyright © Mary Knight 2024

This paperback edition:
ISBN: 978-0-9601243-0-5

ALL RIGHTS RESERVED

No part of this publication may be reproduced or transmitted in any form or by any means, electronic or mechanical, including photocopying and recording, or by any information storage or retrieval system, except as may be expressly permitted by the 1976 Copyright Act or in writing from the publisher. Requests for permission should be addressed in writing to: Middleton Books, 832 Dana Drive, Coatesville, PA 19320

MIDDLETON BOOKS
www.middletonbooks.com

This book is a work of fiction. Names, characters, places, and incidents are either the product of the author's imagination or are used fictitiously, and any resemblance to actual persons, living or dead, business establishments, events or locales is entirely coincidental.

First edition 2024. Printed in the USA.

Cover and book design: Jonathan D. Scott
Cover portrait photography: Sarah Mullins Creative
Cover seahorse in aquarium: Adobe Firefly

 Lexile reader measure 790L

Library of Congress Control Number: 2024936745

Juvenile Fiction/Science & Nature/Environment
Juvenile Fiction/Hawaii/Culture
Juvenile Fiction/Social Themes/Death, Grief, Bereavement
Juvenile Fiction/Social Themes/Self Esteem & Self Reliance

Summary: At a summer camp for young shamans, a twelve-year-old girl learns to use her telepathic powers to help save some of Hawaii's most vulnerable creatures.

*

A Note to My Readers

One of the greatest joys about writing this story was incorporating the Hawaiian language. Although learning Hawaiian words and their pronunciations may be challenging, it will also bring you closer to the spirit of Hawaii that I've tried to convey within these pages.

We have included a **list of characters' names on page 282** (with pronunciation as needed) and a **glossary on page 284** that contain definitions and pronunciations for most of the other Hawaiian words in the text. Each Hawaiian word except for proper names is italicized when it first appears in the novel. Although I tried to offer each word's meaning within the context of the story, the glossary is an additional aide.

This book is dedicated to my readers, who are
teaching me how to be a better writer,

and to Milo and Zora,
who are teaching me how to be a better person.

I am forever grateful.

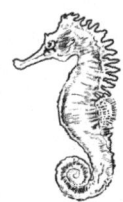

"Seahorses wear their skeletons on the outside," the old man in the booth tells me. "When you dry them out, they hold their shape!" He sounds excited, like this is the greatest news since the invention of the cell phone.

But I'm suspicious. And bored. And *pooped*. I mean, my parents and I have been trying to have fun and "be a family" in Sarasota, Florida, for the entire week. It's exhausting. And now, before heading back to Seattle, Mom insisted on making one last stop at this pathetic, beachside flea market where some guy is trying to sell us his over-priced souvenirs.

"What a way to make a living," Mom says to Dad under her breath, dragging him off to the next booth. "Come on, Sophie, let's go." I'm about to follow, but the vendor keeps yacking.

"Here, little miss ... wanna hold one?" Before I know it, I'm holding a bleached-white seahorse in the palm of my hand. I stare at the weightless frame of this delicate creature that once had a life, when suddenly everything goes black.

Later, they'll say I started shrieking at the top of my lungs, but all I remember is this white-hot, searing pain, like my skin had been dipped in acid and was melting right off the bone. Next, I'm running with an armload of seahorse souvenirs, heading for the ocean, tourists scattering every-which-way. When Mom and Dad finally catch up with me, I'm belly-deep in ocean water, as tiny, ghost-white skeletons in the shape of S's float in and out with the waves.

They do not sink.

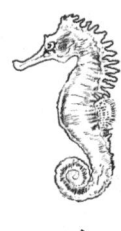

1.
Camouflage

A seahorse alters its color, texture, and even its shape, to blend into its surroundings.*

The incident in Sarasota wasn't the first time this kind of freaky thing happened. Usually, when I touch a live animal, I can sense what they're feeling. If I had known my psycho-telepathic-weirdness happened with dead things, too, I would have avoided that seahorse skeleton like the plague.

I started Googling seahorses as soon as I got home. It didn't take long to figure out why I lost it. According to Wikipedia, about a million seahorses are harvested from the ocean every year for souvenirs like the one I held in my hand. While the seahorses are still alive, they're often left out to dry in the boiling hot sun. That feeling must be so intense for them, that somehow the memory of it gets stuck in their bones and remains there even after they die, which would explain why I felt that searing hot pain when I held those skeletons in my hands. Not fun.

* This excerpt and all the other excerpts are from the sixth-grade report, "Getting to Know the Seahorse," by Sophie Kai Bender.

With live animals, it's usually not so awful. Whenever I touch the neighbor's cat, for instance, all kinds of pictures and feelings zip through me—mostly skittering mice and flitty birds and a twitchy feeling of being on high alert—or, if he's basking in the sun on a cool day, I might feel a flood of warmth settle over me like a fuzzy blanket. It feels like knowing an animal from the inside out.

The first time it happened was four years ago when I was eight, a few months after my baby sister died. I was at my friend Ashley's house, and we were passing her gerbil back and forth. I remember how happy I was to be there, especially since everyone at my house was always so sad. Every time it was my turn to hold the gerbil, the room looked all rounded and blurry, like I was seeing it through a bubble, and it felt like I was being tickled on the inside.

"Here!" I giggled. "Take him! You've got to feel this!"

"Feel what?"

"The tickle. It makes you want to run."

She looked at me like I'd grown two heads.

"He wants to run in his plastic ball," I said quietly. "Can't you tell?"

"Einstein doesn't talk," she said, and shoved him back into his cage.

That's when I knew I was a freak.

The only other time I really lost it was in front of my classmates on a third-grade field trip to a dairy farm. I reached out and started to pet one of those poor, miserable cows who were being milked by a machine inside this stinky old barn. Her mind was all darkness and mud—no green, no sun—just this big empty missing, and I began to cry. Fortunately, Dad was there as a chaperone to settle me down, even though he had no clue what was going on. In fact, I've never told my parents about my weirdness. I don't want them to worry any more than they already do.

When we discussed our field trip the next day, our teacher told us how the farmer takes a cow's calf away from her soon after its birth, so the milk she produces for the calf can be sold to us humans instead. That's when it hit me—why I felt that big empty sadness.

"She's missing her calf!" I blurted out, and everyone started laughing.

For days afterward, the mean boys in my class would come up behind me and shout, "Moo!" or tease me on the playground with moaning cow sounds.

Never again.

From that moment on, I promised myself I'd never touch an animal in front of other kids. That also meant I could never have a close friend. A friend might find out about my psycho-telepathic-weirdness and next thing you know, it's all over school. No, from then on, I hid my weirdness and anything else that might make me stand out.

For the most part, it's worked. Everybody's forgotten about the cow incident, and I get along fine now with most of the kids in my sixth-grade class. I don't accept invitations for sleepovers or birthdays, though. You can never tell what memories someone's pet might be holding onto, and if I accidentally touched one of them? Well, like I said, you never know…

I also tend to agonize over the fate of the poor animals or insects I see along the road, like the butterflies that hit our windshield in spring. Mom's always telling me, "You're being overly sensitive, Sophie," and "You've got to learn to toughen up, Sophie."

Dad's a different story. He never tells me to "buck up" like Mom does. No, whenever I'm having a hard time about something—like that incident in Sarasota—Dad tries to make it up to me somehow. Which is why I'm sitting in my living room in front of an aquarium at this very minute staring at a live seahorse.

And I think he's pregnant.

That's right. I said, "he."

Weird, huh?

When my teacher, Ms. Lovejoy, found out how obsessed I was with seahorses after spring break, she suggested I write a report on them. "Dive into your obsession!" she said. "Write what inspires you!"

This is how I came to know that seahorses are one of the few species where males carry the young. A female will shoot up to 1,500 eggs into the guy's front pouch where he fertilizes them and carries them to term, anywhere from two to four weeks. When I came to that part in my class report, one of the boys said,

"Eeeewww … that's gross," but Ms. Lovejoy said, "Hey, it's science and I think it's cool!"

Anyway, a few hours ago, I had just come back from my grandparents' house where I'd spent the first week of summer vacation, and there was Dad, his chest all puffed out with pride, standing by the aquarium in our living room. Nothing special about that. The aquarium's been there for as long as I can remember in the home entertainment space between the bookshelves. "Better than watching TV," Dad used to say, when the tank had water and fish in it.

When my baby sister died, Dad lost interest in the aquarium, which is why I couldn't imagine what had him so excited. Mom's always hated that "slimy, sloshy thing" in her otherwise neat and tidy, black and white living room. After the last of the clownfish died, I figured Dad was getting ready to sell it.

"So, you got me some seaweed?" I said, trying to sound happy. I could tell he'd redone the interior with some new plants and a few pieces of orange coral. The filter hummed and gurgled, creating water currents in an otherwise empty tank.

"Look closer," he said, rocking on the heels of his feet.

I got down on my knees, pulled a chunk of hair back from my face where it always seems to be in the way, and peered into the aquarium. I expected to see a fish hiding in the weeds, but nothing was swimming. Dad bent down to look with me, and I could see our reflections in the shiny glass—two moon-shaped faces with thick dark hair and large, brown eyes. Unlike me in that moment, however, Dad was still wearing that goofy grin of his, so I kept looking for my "surprise." Maybe it's a bottom feeder, I thought, as I searched the tiny pink pebbles along the floor of the tank. Still nothing.

Out the corner of my eye, I felt more than saw the tiniest flick. And there he was, all greenish brown and curved and bony (except for his extended belly) with a long snout and a knobby tail curled around a strand of seaweed. There were spiky things sticking up all over his head like one of those punk rockers Dad likes to watch on the music channel. One of his round, bulging eyes was fixed on mine. Or so it seemed.

"Oh, a seahorse," I breathed. "Hello."

He didn't answer back. And he didn't blink (no eyelids). But I could have sworn he nodded his horsey-headed snout ever so slightly in my direction.

"Thanks, Dad," I whispered, as my brain fired up that flashback from Sarasota I wish I could forget.

"I hope you like it." Dad straightened up, stretching. "I thought it might help, you know, make another memory to replace the bad one."

"Sure, Daddy. You're the best." I stood up and gave him a big hug. It's been a long time since I've called my father "Daddy," but I just couldn't help it. I knew what he was trying to do.

Unfortunately, it isn't working.

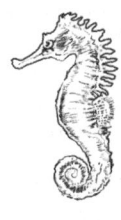

2.

My Brain on Seahorses

The scientific word for seahorse, hippocampus, was coined by Pliny the Elder in 78 AD. It is also the name for a part of our brain that stores short-term memories and emotions.

"Hey, Sydney." I gently tap on the glass.

I've been sitting here on the plush white carpet in front of the aquarium for the last hour, trying out gender-neutral names to see if one sticks. In addition to Sydney, I've tried Alex and Riley, but his tail stays tightly coiled around that same, single strand of seaweed as it has for the last few days, ever since Dad gave him to me.

His stillness makes me sad. Only his filmy, dorsal fin flutters near the base of his spine—I guess to keep him upright—but other than that, nothing else moves. He just keeps looking straight ahead, or rather, straight sideways. I think he's missing his mate.

According to SeahorsesGalore.com, when seahorses pair up, they tend to stay together at least for the mating season. Even after the guy gets pregnant, he and his partner continue their courting rituals. They start their spiral dance first thing in the morning, turn all different colors—like neon orange to red to green—and flirt for up to an hour. Ms. Lovejoy loved that part of my written report. She gushed all over the margins with her purple pen: *Awesome! Great use of details! Fascinating!*

I think she wants to be a seahorse.

Not that I'd recommend it.

"Precarious" is how one website describes a seahorse's life right now, a nice word for "endangered," which is another nice word for being on the brink of being gone for good.

"My father means well," I tell our captive. "I know that doesn't help."

My stomach churns as I think about how it's all my fault that this helpless seahorse was torn from his mate while he was still pregnant. If Dad were here, he'd say, "Oh boy, here we go again with the All My Fault game"—something I've been doing ever since my baby sister died a few years ago. Here's how the game goes:

- If I hadn't lost it with the seahorse skeletons in Sarasota, Dad would never have felt sorry for me.
- If Dad hadn't felt sorry for me, he wouldn't have gotten me a seahorse to make me feel better.
- If he hadn't tried to make me feel better, the seahorse would still be with his mate.

If the seahorse were still with his mate, he'd be doing a spiral dance rather than hanging out here on a skimpy piece of seaweed—pregnant and alone.

Like I said, it's all my fault.

"Where do I even begin to make this better for you, bud?" My nose is less than an inch away from where he floats, tethered to his weed. "Hey! What about 'Bud?' or 'Buddy'?" Not gender-neutral, hardly even a name, but I could swear he turns his snout ever-so-slightly in my direction.

Was that a nod?

Yes, definitely. That was a nod.

"Okay, then. 'Buddy,' it is."

I think maybe we're getting somewhere. If only I could touch him, maybe I could tell what he's thinking. I roll up my sleeve, but just as I start to reach into the water, the memory of what happened the last time I touched a seahorse sends this electrical charge straight down my spine. Maybe this isn't such a good idea. Then again, maybe I can learn something that will help me help him. Buck up, Sophie, I say to myself. Certainly, he's not carrying a memory nearly as painful as the last seahorse I touched. I mean, this one's still alive.

I test the water with my fingertips. It isn't as cold as I expected. I guess Dad has the temperature controlled to be like the ocean. I slowly slide my arm into the water up to my elbow and let it hang there for a while, just an inch from Buddy's perch, letting the seaweed stroke my skin. It feels soft and soothing, and I wonder if it feels the same way to him.

"Hey, Buddy," I say, looking down at the top of his curved head. "I'm not going to hurt you…" but then I think, Gee, what if

I *do*? What if the shock of my touch causes him to go into early labor or something? I'm just about to withdraw my hand when Buddy zooms across the one-inch distance between us and hooks his tail around my little finger.

Oh my gosh! Buddy came to *me*! I want to shout and jump up and down, but I don't dare move a muscle. I swallow my excitement to make room for what Buddy wants to show me.

Out of the thrill I feel in my gut, another feeling blooms: a feeling of fullness, like a balloon that has stretched its skin to the max, not with air, but with … squiggles. Hundreds of squiggles all smooshed up tight and ready to pop. There's also a sense of waiting. But waiting for what? His babies? Oh. He doesn't know *why* he's waiting. He just feels full and that something's coming.

Just then, the mail slot clanks open and shut at the front door of our townhouse.

"Sophie," my dad calls out from his studio. "Would you get the mail please? My hands are covered in paint."

And my hand is covered in seahorse, I want to yell back, but don't.

"Sure, Dad!" I gently wiggle my pinky. Buddy slips back onto his favorite seaweed, and I head to the hallway to get the mail.

My dad, Al Bender, is a painter, the artist type. He works in acrylics—bright, splashy, tropical colors—and *big*. Wall-size big. His Hawaiian-inspired paintings show in galleries all over Puget Sound. He's been looking for an invitation to an upcoming exhibit, and I might get to go with him if Mom's swamped with her law practice, which she usually is.

I sift through the mail. My heart beats double-time when I see a large, white manila envelope addressed to me in flowing pink cursive:

Sophie Kai Bender
4288 Alki Court #3
Seattle, Washington 98116

There's no return address, just a faded red postal seal that reads *Captain Cook, Hawaii.*

Hawaii? What's in Hawaii? My dad was born there—Alika is his Hawaiian name—but Mom and his friends call him "Al." He and his family eventually came to the mainland when he was fourteen after their house was torched by a lava flow. My dad's Tūtū, his grandmother, died before the family left. That's who I get my middle name from. Kai. It rhymes with "bye" and means "from the sea." Wait. I look at the address again. How do they know my middle name? I rarely use it, not even in school.

I hold the envelope up to my face. It smells like those flowers they make Hawaiian leis out of. Plumeria. I recognize the scent from the leis Dad always gets Mom for Mother's Day. There's a promise in that scent. It tugs at me like I could fall right into the envelope.

It says, *You'll be glad.*

3.

Such a Deal

From the moment seahorses are born, their parents have nothing more to do with them. They're on their own.

My hands are shaking as I tear open the envelope and the contents tumble out: a letter, a full-color brochure, and some registration forms. The kids on the cover of the brochure are all swimming in the ocean, dancing hula, jumping off cliffs, or peering into a lake of hot flowing lava. My feet prickle at the thought.

I collapse cross-legged onto the tiled floor of our foyer as I scan the letter. Even though the tile feels cool on my bare legs, I'm breaking out in a sweat.

Aloha, Sophie Kai!

Congratulations! We are so happy to inform you that your essay, "Getting to Know the Seahorse," has qualified you for a full scholarship to our world-renowned Camp Koa, right here on the island of Hawaii. Camp begins June 27th and runs for three weeks. Incidentally, "Koa" means "courage" in Hawaiian—something we know you have!

Your essay was submitted to us by your teacher, Ms. Lovejoy. Here are just a few things she said about you: "highly curious ... knows her own mind ... cares deeply about the natural world ... tenacious," and so much more.

You are just the kind of camper we want here at Camp Koa!

Please tell your parents to contact us with any questions they may have. We know you are precious to them, and it may be difficult to let you go.

Aloha, Sophie! We hope to see you soon!
Malia Jones, Founding Director

I take a few deep breaths to calm myself, a technique my school counselor and I worked on after I came back from spring break. I remember Ms. Lovejoy asking my permission to enter my report in a writing contest, but never in a million years did I think it would lead to this.

Gosh, most kids would be jumping up and down by now, high-fiving everything in sight, but all I feel is dread. It's a familiar feeling. I try to keep it all nice and neat and packed away deep inside, but sometimes, like when I'm confronted with something new, it leaks.

The thought of being away from my parents for three weeks terrifies me. A lot can happen in that time—not just to me, but to them. Come to think of it, Mom's been acting funny lately, kind of run down and picking at her food, which isn't like her. What if she's sick with something like cancer? What if I get seriously injured when I'm three thousand miles from home, and my parents can't get to me in time to say goodbye?

See what I mean?

I run my hand over the glossy cover of the brochure. Man, what I wouldn't give to climb those rocky cliffs. That is, if I could still climb.

Heights. That's something else that terrifies me, although it didn't used to, if the stories my family tell about me are true. Apparently, I climbed a tree when I was four. Dad had to climb up to get me. He used to call me his "brave little soul." After Baby Girl died, something happened to the brave part of me, I guess. Maybe even the soul part.

Don't get me wrong, I still get the urge. There's this tree at Alki Beach just a few blocks from us. Its branches shoot off from its trunk like arms, a perfect climbing tree even for beginners. Dad caught me staring at it a few weeks ago and said, "Go ahead, Sophie … if you want," but then I started feeling that leaky dread. "Nah," I said, "maybe another day."

My counselor calls this my "push-pull." She says we all have it. The push often comes from curiosity or desire, she explained. It urges us to take risks, to jump into our lives, carefree. To illustrate her point, she leapt from her chair and flung her arms out like she was flying. "And the *pull* comes from our fears, like maybe we're afraid of falling, or failing, or—"

"Dying," I said, filling in the blank.

"Right. And then it tugs us back into a place we feel safe." She flopped back into her chair. "Nothing wrong with that," she added. She's always telling me I'm fine just the way I am.

I take the rest of the mail to Dad's studio, where he flips through it quickly, no doubt looking for that invitation to the art exhibit. He frowns when he doesn't see it. "Anything else, Sophie?" I guess he sees the papers from Camp Koa I'm holding behind my back.

"Nah, just some stupid advertisement," I say. I need a little more time to think.

Back in my room, I sprawl out on my bed and stare at the Camp Koa brochure with all the kids laughing and smiling in their Camp Koa T-shirts, and I can feel that push-pull doing its tug-of-war in me. What would it feel like to be a part of something like that?

But then I think about poor Buddy.

I watched a video once at the Seattle Aquarium on a seahorse giving birth. It felt kind of embarrassing, watching something so personal. In a rocking horse kind of way, the daddy shoots the fully formed, teeny-tiny baby seahorses called "fry" out of his pouch. Heads over tails, they come out spinning into the watery world a bunch at a time until the father's pouch is empty. Labor can last up to twelve hours. Problem is, less than one-in-a-thousand fry born in the wild survive to adulthood. Survival in captivity is even trickier.

I already feel guilty about Buddy being ripped away from his mate. No way can I leave him now. He and his babies are going to need all the help they can get.

I let the brochure drop to the floor but read the invitation one more time. One thing's for sure, this Camp Koa lady got that last part right about my parents and how hard it would be to let me go. Make that *impossible*; they are so over-protective. I don't even know why I'm getting so worked up about it. Yeah, Mom is the one who's always telling me to toughen up, but she's also the one who hovers, way more than Dad. I guess she has that push-pull thing going on in her, too. The one time they took their eyes off me (you know, in Sarasota), well, Mom said, "never again." Ever since Baby Girl died, Mom and Dad have watched me like a hawk.

Baby Girl. That's what the three of us called her. Her real name was Mālani, Hawaiian for "she who is from the sky." Like my middle name, *Kai*, my sister's name came from our great-grandma. I guess it took two of us to honor her.

Anyway, Baby Girl never got the chance to grow into her Hawaiian name. She was only five months old when she died. The doctors called it SIDS or Sudden Infant Death Syndrome. I've got another name for it, though. Sister Is Dead and it Sucks.

Dad used to carry her everywhere against his chest in this dark blue pouch. He'd even paint like that sometimes until she woke up and needed her diaper changed. Afterwards, Dad, Baby Girl, and I would play on the floor. I'd dangle her bunny in front of her and make her laugh.

I remember one morning at breakfast when the whole family was together. Mom was getting ready to go back to work. I patted the tight, rounded back of my sister strapped to my father's chest as he walked by dishing out eggs. He had to reach extra far to get around the bulge.

"Just like Mommy when she was pregnant!" I giggled.

Mom reached over and scooped me up in her arms. "Yeah, Honey," she said, looking up at Dad, "now it's your turn!"

Those were the kidding-around days, the come-here-and-cuddle-with-me days.

Anyway.

I've been an only child ever since. Make that an only child with a dead sibling. That multiplies the OCE (Only Child Effect) by about a zillion. There's no way my parents are going to let their only remaining daughter fly across an ocean to a place she's never been with people they've never met to participate in God-knows-what-activities like hot lava gazing or jumping off cliffs. I mean, come on. A person could die doing stuff like that.

I decide to wait until dinner is over to tell them about the letter. That's when Mom and Dad are both itching to dart off to their corners of the townhouse to do what they love best—*work*. Dad goes to his studio and Mom to her office to review her latest case.

While Mom is rinsing dishes and Dad's pouring his last cup of coffee, I take a deep breath and mumble at breakneck speed:

"So-I-got-this-thing-in-the-mail-today-and-it's-for-some-lame-summer-camp-in-Hawaii-and-they're-saying-I-got-a-scholarship-but-if-you-ask-me-the-whole-thing-sounds-too-good-to-be-true-which-is-something-you've-always-warned-me-about-so-I-guess-it's-just-some-kind-of-weirdo-timeshare-summer-camp-scam-and-we-can-forget-the-whole-thing." And then, I toss the envelope into recycling and scoot toward the door.

"Whoa, whoa, whoa," Dad says, setting his cup down on the granite countertop. *Clink.* "What was that about a scholarship?" He leans over and picks the envelope out of the bin.

Dang. I *knew* I should have left that part out.

You see, there's nothing Dad likes better than a good deal—which is why we do most of our shopping at CostSaver, which is why we rent an extra storage space in the townhouse's garage, which is why Dad's studio is jam-packed with good deals on things like toilet paper, outdoor solar-lighting kits, patio furniture, boxes of Belgian chocolates, and factory closeouts of every kind of hiking boot you can imagine. It's like playing a game of "Where's Waldo" every time you stick your head in his studio door, which is about all there's room for once Dad's in there, too, considering he's six-foot-four and well, substantial.

Here's another thing I didn't figure on: Mom's good at reading fine print. No surprise there. I mean, as a lawyer, she gravitates towards fine print like a seahorse to seaweed. So, when she wipes her hands on a dish towel and Dad hands her the brochure, she goes right for the back page—a letter to parents. Mom clears her throat and reads aloud:

Dear Parents,

Does your child seem overly sensitive? Do you sometimes wonder how she's going to get along in the world? Camp Koa will help her find her inner strength, a new sense of confidence in herself and her gifts. You'll never regret sending your child to Camp Koa and neither will she.

Mahalo!

The Kūpuna (the elders)

A chill runs straight through me when she's finished. These elders, or "kūpuna" as they call themselves, are talking my mother's language. It's as if they're writing just to her. And what's worse, my normally suspicious mother is standing there staring off into space as if she's mesmerized or something.

"Yes, look, Clare. Right here. It says she has a scholarship," Dad says, studying the letter that came with the brochure. "I've always wanted Sophie to know her Hawaiian roots."

If ever there were a final shoe to drop, that's it. Every so often, Dad gets on this kick about taking the three of us back to live on the island so that I can know my heritage, but Mom always nixes it before it gets out of hand. She has no interest in a laid-back lifestyle, she says. But *now*, she and Dad are giving each other that "look," the one that means something's already been decided between them. I can't believe it.

Where are the hovering, over-protective parents who watch my every move?

"Hey, you guys know they've got cliffs over there, and like … hot lava?" My voice sounds weak. I can barely get the words out.

Dad stifles a laugh. "Come on, Sophie Kai. How many times do I have to tell you, Hawaiian lava moves as slow as molasses?" He nudges me with his elbow. "You'll have plenty of time to run."

"Not funny, Dad. We don't even know who these people *are*."

Mom wrinkles her brow, then pulls me into a stiff hug. "Sophie, sweetheart, we wouldn't think of releasing you into the care of strangers without first finding out everything we can about them. Look, I'll have my assistant at the office research this organization. We'll make sure they're not hiding something." She pats me on the back, like everything's going to be just fine.

"Okaaaaay," I finally say, shrugging out of her arms.

Some dirt's bound to show up on this Camp Koa, right? At least that's what Mom's always saying when she's prosecuting criminals. It's hard to imagine grandmotherly thugs, but hey. These days, you just never know.

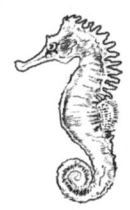

4.
When Push Comes to Shove

The seahorse's tail clamps onto objects so tightly, that it's almost impossible to tug it loose—unless, of course, the seahorse wants to let go.

Dad and I are hanging out on the balcony, our feet up on the railing soaking up the late afternoon sun, when Mom gets home from work and reads us her "findings." Turns out, Camp Koa has a five-star approval rating with the Better Business Bureau and 100% customer satisfaction.

"Not a speck of dirt found," Mom concludes as she slips the report back into her briefcase. "Not even a cliff-diving accident." She makes this last point as if she were delivering closing arguments to a jury. "See, Sophie. Camp Koa is perfectly legit."

Legit. One of Mom's favorite words—sharp and edgy.

"So, I guess you guys will be sending me away then." I drop my feet from the railing with a thud.

It's been a few days since I showed them the invitation, and the thing that's been bugging me the most is how much they've been hoping this whole Camp Koa thing works out. It's almost as if they're excited to get rid of me. Up until now in my life—at least since Baby Girl died—it's always been the three of us against the world. Now it feels like two against one.

"Look here, Sophie Kai." Dad gently tugs at my T-shirt. "We're not going to send you anywhere against your will."

"Good," I say, "because I'm not going." My chair scrapes against the concrete patio as I try to make a quick exit.

"Sophie, *wait*." Mom grabs my arm. "At least, think about it, okay? It's your decision, darling, *of course*. It's just that your dad and I … well, we think it's time to let you live your life a little, you know, maybe make some new friends. You're a tough girl, Sophie. Tougher than you realize. We think this camp will be good for you."

"Oh, I get it. So, the 'toughen up, Sophie' side of you has finally won?"

Mom studies me with those clear, blue eyes of hers. She shakes her head and laughs. "Maybe so. But I'd like to think 'what's best for Sophie' has won, and I'm finally getting out of the way."

"Whatever." It feels awkward seeing Mom lose her edge like this.

"Hey, I'm still working on this mother thing. It's a work in progress, you know?" She reaches for my hand, but I don't know what to do with it.

"Yeah, well, let me know when it's done."

I cringe as soon as the words leave my mouth.

"Sophie!" my father snaps, as shame consumes me.

"Wow," Mom says quietly. "Now that's *tough*."

Later that evening, I'm scrunched up in my sleeping bag in front of the aquarium, staring at Buddy, when Dad walks in. I've stationed myself here for the last couple of nights, hoping to be awake when Buddy starts his labor.

"Hey, Dad," I say without looking up. "Sorry about all the drama earlier."

He sighs. "Yeah, well, you might want to tell your mother that."

"I will."

Dad shoves his hands deep into the front pockets of his jeans. "Look, Sophie, there's something that showed up in your Mom's research into Camp Koa we thought you ought to know." He clears his throat. "Turns out my grandmother knew the camp's founder, Malia Jones. In fact, she was Malia Jones' *kumu*. That may have something to do with your being invited."

"Kumu?"

"Yes, teacher. My *tūtū* taught her things."

"Like what?"

"I don't know ... probably from the old Hawaiian arts, like how to identify certain plants for their medicinal purposes or how to communicate with our ancestors."

"Communicate with our ancestors?" I can't believe Dad's getting all woo-woo on me.

"It's not a big deal, Sophie Kai. Many traditional Hawaiians are in touch with their ancestors through stories, wisdom sayings and the like. That's something it wouldn't hurt you to know more about. It's where you're from."

"I'm *from* Seattle," I say, still feeling a bit testy from earlier.

"Right." Dad drops his chin to his chest. "And … you also come from a long line of Hawaiian shamans … *kahuna*."

"Wait, *what*?" Now I'm getting goose bumps tingling up and down my arms and neck, what Dad and other Hawaiians call *chicken skin*. "Don't kahuna practice witchcraft or something?"

Dad laughs. "Not in our family. Our ancestors inherited special talents, shall we say, talents they used for the good of their community. Tūtū used to say such talents were natural, God-given. But now that technology has taken over the world, most people call them 'magic.'"

"So, do you have a special talent?" I ask, barely able to form the words. What if he has the same weirdness I have? What if it's inherited?

"Well, I guess you could say my talent is art. These natural powers we receive from our ancestors express in different ways."

"Do you think I have a special power?" I hold my breath, wondering if he knows.

"Well, for one, I think you have a gift for getting your way, but you probably get that from your mother." He laughs. "Seriously though, sometimes I think your talent is *caring*, like the way you care about Buddy. Not a lot of people use that talent anymore. It's like they're afraid of it. But not you, Sophie Kai." His voice gets really soft, when he says my Hawaiian name.

"Gee, Dad, thanks." I wonder if he'd get choked up like this if he knew the truth about me.

"Anyway, Sophie Kai, I have a good feeling about Camp Koa. You should go."

"Okay, Dad. I'll sleep on it," I say, still holding out for my right to decide.

Actually, all this talk about my Hawaiian ancestry and special talents has me even more scared to go than before. I'm not going to tell him that, of course. He'd just try to make it sound normal when it doesn't feel that way at all. I wonder if any of the other kids going to Camp Koa are freaks like me. What if I'm not the only one? What if I *am*?

"One more thing, Sophie." Dad walks over to the fish tank and peers in. The light from the aquarium casts a bluish-green glow on his face. "I hate to see you losing sleep over this Buddy thing. Chances are zero-to-none that you'll be able to save any of his babies."

"I know, Dad, I know." I raise myself up on an elbow.

"I just don't want you to get your hopes up, Sophie Kai."

He's right to worry, of course. In an aquarium like ours, the newborn fry tend to get trapped in the air bubbles on the surface.

It's like they drown on the air. My plan is to shut off the filter when the babies start coming out, giving them time to find a tailhold on some seaweed before starting the current going again. At least that's my hope.

Hope. Exactly what Dad wishes I didn't have. His face has fallen into a scowl, not because of me, I know, but because of the situation. It seems he's always trying to save me from some disappointment or other, and yet here's another time he's bound to fail.

"I get it, Dad. This is something I just need to do."

He nods, kisses me on the forehead, and without another word, leaves the room.

I'm dreaming about walking on a river that turns into hot lava, when I wake up with a start. Dang it! I let the droning hum of that filter lull me asleep again. Dad's still in the room, but why is he standing over the tank with a fish net? Wait. I thought he left hours ago. I rub the sleep from my eyes. He's quietly dumping something out of the net into a small bucket.

"Daddy?" I struggle out of my sleeping bag and crawl to the tank.

"Oh, sweet pea. You don't need to see this."

"The babies?" I whisper, as my stomach sinks.

"Yeah," he sighs, skimming the surface one more time. "I was hoping I could get this done without waking you up."

I look into the bucket. Tiny transparent curls lay motionless in a heap, all intertwined like links on a fine-chained necklace. Buddy's babies. I wonder if he knows they're gone.

Considerably less inflated, he's floating as usual, tail curled around his favorite frond of seaweed. His bulgy eyes are turning every which way, independently, like he's searching for something. Up, down, right, left. I lean my palm against the cool glass, wishing I could touch him, to feel what he feels. But then with a jolt, a feeling comes to me anyway. It's not sadness, exactly. It's like how I felt looking into Baby Girl's crib the morning after she died, when I still expected her to be there.

Empty.

Nothing but empty.

After Dad goes back to bed, I sit cross-legged on the living room floor in front of Buddy and open my laptop, where it bathes me in its pale white light. The bucket is gone. The babies are gone. The filter continues its soothing, uninterrupted hum.

When I was working on my seahorse report, I discovered there are these farms that raise seahorses for the aquarium market. Some conservationists think they help reduce demand for wild seahorses, while others think farms make the problem worse by making seahorses more desirable in general. Honestly, I don't know what to think. All I know is I'm desperate. I can't stop thinking about how it's all my fault Buddy lost his babies. You know, that same old drill.

I type "seahorse farms" into the search engine and scroll down the list to see if there are any farms within driving distance of Seattle. There aren't. I'm about to click on "Next Page" when an entry bearing my middle name catches my eye. "Kai House, Home of the Seahorse." How amazing is that? If I believed in this stuff, I'd say it's a sign. It even has a five-star rating with Trip Hound.

I click on their website. Kai House must be its commercial name, because underneath the larger heading, is its Hawaiian name: "Hale o ke kai, house of the sea." Apparently, the "house" is more like a farm that not only breeds seahorses, it offers tours. They even let you touch them. There are pictures of kids my age—their hands stuck into water tanks—with seahorses curled around their fingers. "Not to be missed!" one reviewer says.

"Oh, my gosh," I say out loud to Buddy, half-expecting him to answer. "It's on the island of Hawaii where Camp Koa is."

I don't know if he's zapping me with the tingles or if they're coming directly from inside me. I bookmark the page and slap the computer shut.

Go.

This one, simple word reverberates from somewhere deep inside me. Is that Buddy? Or is it that "push" in me, urging me to take a leap into adventure. A scary adventure. On a plane. Over 2,984 miles of ocean. (Yup, I looked it up.)

Go.

There it is again. That push to "just do it" no matter what. But where's the pull? The part that says, You're out of your mind.

Go.

I lean toward the aquarium until I'm an inch away from Buddy's snout with only a pane of glass between us. The air from my nose makes a little cloud of mist that appears and disappears with every breath. Buddy stares at me with one riveted, black-dotted eye.

"Listen, Buddy. I love my parents, I really do. Dad wants me to go to this crazy camp to get in touch with my Hawaiian roots, and Mom wants me to go because she wants me to get a life, but neither of them have asked me what *I* want."

He waits.

"I mean, sure, it would be nice to be *warm* on a beach for a change. And I'm sure nobody's going to make me climb a cliff or walk on hot lava or do anything I don't want to do, right?"

Go.

"But I'm scared, Buddy. I'm terrified of being in a strange place. Away from my family." A single tear tickles my cheek. I wipe it away. "What if nobody likes me?"

Buddy's long spiny body releases a micro-shiver from the tip of his snout to the tip of his tail. I touch the glass near him and put the other hand over my fast-beating heart. "Do you feel that, too?"

Buddy floats in absolute stillness—no nod, no shiver, no big booming "yes"—and yet, something in me *knows*. Our connection works both ways.

Adrenalin surges through my veins as I realize I'm about to take a leap. For the first time in about five years, I'm about to let that *push* in me win. I take a deep breath.

"Okay, Buddy, here's the deal. I'll tell my parents I'm going to Camp Koa and that will make them happy. But between you and me? The only reason I'm going, is to make this up to *you*."

He nods like he knows what I'm about to say next.

"I'm going to find you a friend."

We stare at each other, nose to snout.

Go, I feel him say.

Find friend.

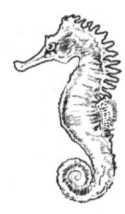

5.
Mission Buddy

Seahorses are often the subject of ancient myths and legends. Even the scientific name "Hippocampus" comes from two words meaning "horse" and "sea monster."

"Come on, Sophie, we're going to be late. No telling what the traffic's going to be like on the way to the airport." Dad gulps the rest of his coffee and sets the cup in the sink.

"Yeah," Mom adds. "And no stopping for roadkill!"

She's referring to this thing I make my parents do when we see dead animals on the road. I like to move the poor critters to a grassy area with a shovel we keep in the back of the car. Dad helps me sometimes. Mom puts her foot down on anything bigger than a raccoon.

"Okay, okay. I'm *coming*."

I type out my final instructions to Dad on the care and feeding of Buddy. He insists he knows what he's doing, but I'm worried he'll forget something—like giving Buddy these teeny-tiny live shrimp (instead of the usual frozen kind) once a week to liven up his otherwise dull life. Hopefully, if everything goes according to plan, I'll be back home in less than a week before that even needs to happen. And no, my parents don't know that yet.

As I hit "Print" and the printer at the end of the counter cranks into gear, Dad helps Mom with her jacket. He's been acting like a gentleman with her lately, holding doors open, getting her cups of tea, which I know sounds nice and all, but if you knew my parents … well, let's just say Mom considers herself a liberated woman. But, *dang*. There she goes smiling at him again and squeezing his hand. If I didn't know any better, I'd say they really *are* looking forward to getting rid of me for a while.

The plane is packed and buzzing with the excitement of people on vacation. A bunch of passengers are wearing colorful Hawaiian shirts with plastic leis in neon pinks and greens. There's a man with a head of bushy white hair and a beard like Santa Claus, who keeps standing up and shouting, "A-lo-haaaaaa," after which about a third of the plane echoes it back to him.

"Tour group," Sandy, the flight attendant says, rolling her eyes. She's my official escort.

Sandy met me at the gate where my parents were struggling to relinquish their control over me. Turns out, they weren't so anxious to get rid of me after all, and I wasn't so anxious to leave. I'd been rethinking "Mission Buddy" at least a hundred times since I left home. As I watched my checked bag being swallowed up by a conveyor belt and sent down a tunnel, I nearly vaulted over the ticket desk to grab it back. Suddenly, this leap into a grand adventure wasn't sounding so grand.

I count the rows ahead of me to see where I'm going. It's just four rows down and to the left, a row with three seats which means my seat, 22b, is in the middle. *Great.* I'm already having a hard time getting enough air. I think about the empty lunch bag Dad handed me at the last minute. "In case you start to hyperventilate," he said. I look at the red exit sign by the row ahead of me and eye the handle.

In the row in front of mine, a tall, thin woman with flowing, stark-white hair settles into her seat. She's wearing one of those long, puffy-sleeved Hawaiian dresses my grandma likes to wear, a style that usually looks kind of frumpy but not on this woman. Her dress reminds me of one my father's paintings, with flaming red and yellow plumeria splashed all over it. She looks like one of those old queens out of the Hawaiian history books. I can't take my eyes off her.

But then, she lifts this small, rectangular piece of luggage up to her face and starts sweet-talking whatever's inside. I see a flash of white through black mesh and realize the woman's holding a pet carrier. So much for royalty. She's probably just somebody's tūtū on her way home to the islands. As Sandy and I pass her, she catches my eye and nods.

"*Aloha,*" she says.

"Aloha," I reply.

Her amber eyes latch onto mine for what seems like a full minute, yet it can't be more than a few seconds. Held in her gaze, my nerves no longer feel frazzled. I wouldn't say I feel more relaxed, but somehow more resolved—like I know what I'm supposed to do.

Mission Buddy. Right. Let's do this thing.

Sandy takes a few more steps and turns in the aisle. "Here you go, Sophie. And here's your new friend." She extends her arm out, like there's a prize at the end of it.

No prize. Just a skinny kid about my size wearing a gray hoodie and ripped jeans, slouched against the window. I can't tell if my new friend is a "he" or a "she," but the eyes looking out from under the hood are an icy blue.

"Hey." The sweatshirt pocket closest to me jiggles slightly. I guess that's an undercover wave.

"Hey." I slide into the middle seat.

Sandy looks around nervously. "I'm supposed to keep an eye on both of you and one other kid," she says, "at least, until the three of you are handed over to the Camp Koa folks at the Hilo airport." She tilts her head and frowns. "So, don't run off or anything, okay?"

"Don't worry, we won't," I say, even though just moments before that's exactly what I wanted to do.

"Good." Her voice is crisp and efficient, reminding me of my mother. "Meanwhile, the two of you can get to know each other until your other friend gets here." She looks toward the front of the cabin where a few stragglers are still boarding. "*If* he ever gets here," she adds. And with that, she slips down the aisle, shutting overhead bins right and left along the way.

"She's using that term pretty loosely, don't you think?" I shove my backpack under the seat in front of me. "*Friend*, I mean. I really hate it when adults think kids are going to be friends just because we're kids." I say this to try to get a rise out of the lump beside me.

It snorts.

Make that "she."

Her hood falls back, revealing a thick crop of unruly, copper-brown hair and black-studded earrings in the shape of skulls.

"Hi, I'm Sophie Bender." I extend my hand to shake hers, but when she doesn't take me up on it, I tuck a strand of hair behind my ear like that's where I was going all along.

"Leilani Wilkinson," she finally offers.

"That's a pretty name."

"I go by 'Wilks.'" She shrugs and turns back to the wall.

So much for "friend." Oh, well. I won't be staying around Camp Koa long enough to make any real friends anyway. My plan is to find a friend for Buddy, fake homesickness, and catch a plane back home as soon as I can.

I click open the cell phone my parents gave me as a going-away present. I've been clamoring for one for over a year, not because I have any friends to keep in touch with on social media or anything, but because it's convenient for looking things up—things I'm curious about. Mom and Dad made a big show of giving it to me this morning at breakfast, like they were proud of themselves for being so progressive.

"To stay in touch," Mom said.

"So you don't forget us," Dad said.

When I asked Dad how to upload a picture of Buddy onto my phone, he said, "What? Mom and I aren't good enough for your wallpaper?" They both laughed, but I still feel guilty about it.

I settle in with my new phone, tapping on photos. Mom said to look for the family album she downloaded to remind me of home. The first picture that comes up kills me. Not literally, of course, but close. It's Baby Girl and me, a few weeks before she died. How could Mom put it there?

The lump called Wilks shifts in her seat. I move my arm off the armrest to keep from bothering her. In the picture, Baby Girl and I are playing on my bed with my Wonder Woman doll. Her crib is beside us. Mom *knows* I don't like thinking about that crib.

The morning Baby Girl was found not-breathing, a few hours earlier I had heard her fussing. Usually that meant she was hungry or wet, and Mom or Dad would come in to take care of her. They kept a baby monitor on the wall between my bed and her crib. That night, I guess they didn't hear her and eventually she quieted down.

If only I had gotten up to check on her.

If only I had gone in to get Mom or Dad.

If only I hadn't covered my head with my pillow to shut out her crying.

"Is that your little sister?" I jump at the sound of Wilks' voice. Her eyes weirdly dart back and forth between the picture on the phone to somewhere over my left shoulder.

"Yeah…" I stop myself from saying *was* my sister." I look over my shoulder to see what else she's so interested in. Nothing, only the back of my seat.

"I thought so," she nods. "I can tell she likes hanging out with you."

Her comment is like having a bucket of ice dumped down my back. It seems innocent enough, but for some reason, her talking like my sister is still alive makes me mad.

My sister's dead, I want to shout, but then Sandy the attendant shows up again.

"Here's your new seatmate," she sighs.

Standing behind her is a boy. A really large boy. He attempts to swing his backpack into the overhead compartment, but it bounces back. "In-coming missile!" he laughs. Everybody around us lifts their heads in surprise. "Cancel that!" he announces, as he proceeds to stuff his bag into the compartment. "I didn't mean that *literally*, folks!"

Sandy just rolls her eyes. I bet she's wishing she'd taken a vacation day.

The boy seems nice enough—I mean, his smile is as big as his face—but when he looks down at the narrow seat he's about to occupy, I can tell he's wondering the same thing I am.

Will he fit?

6.

Living Large

*First classified as insects, seahorses were
misunderstood for centuries.*

With knees pressed into the seat in front of him and his stomach drooping over the armrest between us, the new boy fills up his seat and then some. I'd raise the armrest to make him feel more comfortable, but then I'd get more squished than I already am, and I don't think I can go there right now. I feel trapped enough as it is, belted in and vacuum packed.

Breathe, Sophie. Breathe.

Before Sandy stuffs the boy's backpack into an overhead compartment near us, she drops an extension belt into his hands. I feel sorry for him, but he seems to take the whole supersize thing in stride.

"Aloha, mates," he says, as he snaps his belt together. "I guess we're all going to the same place. My name's Keola, which means 'life' in Hawaiian. As you can see, I've got a lot of life to go around!" He pats his stomach and laughs.

Wilks reaches over me to shake his hand. "My name's Wilks, and this here's Sophie."

"Nice to meet you both," he says, smiling.

This is the most activity I've seen out of Wilks yet, and I think maybe we'll hear more from her, but no, she merely assumes her previous position. Meanwhile, someone's snoring loudly in the row just in front of us. The headrest is too high to see over, but I assume it's the old Hawaiian lady or maybe her pet. I reach overhead to turn up my air vent.

As Sandy starts speaking over the intercom about safety belts and flotation devices, Keola grabs the laminated instructions out of his front seat pocket and follows along. If I didn't know better, I'd say this boy is as nervous as I am. He's wearing a light blue, polo-style shirt and there are circles of sweat under his armpits.

He smells good, by the way … like lilies.

"First time?" I ask, after Sandy's speech is finished.

"Yeah, how can you tell?"

"Searching for the exits. Dead giveaway."

"Oh, man, of *course*. And I wanted you to think I was cool. Which, by the way, I am."

He turns his air vent all the way up like I did. "You see, it's all about attitude, Sophie. Yeah, I know I'm big, and Mom, God love her, is always trying to put me on a diet, but then Pops says I'm going for the Iz look, you know, that really big Hawaiian dude who sings *Somewhere Over the Rainbow*, island style? You should hear it. Maybe you have. Have you heard it?" I nod. "Who hasn't, right? Can't get on an elevator these days without hearing it. Anyway, you think I'm big? Wowser!"

"You know he's dead, right?" I hate to break it to him.

"Yeah, I know. Too bad, huh? I mean, just think about the music that guy would be making if only he had lived." Keola's shoulders slump. "Whenever Mom's trying to make a point about my weight, she brings up Iz and how being big like that shortened his life."

"Moms," I say.

"Yeah, moms."

The plane lurches forward. Keola grabs my arm. His hand is sweaty, and his dark brown eyes are as big as Frisbees.

"You know where your barf bag is, right?" I ask. "I put mine here." I tug at the edge of the bag I moved to the front of the seat pocket. "You know … just in case."

"Right. Good point," he says, scrambling to find his bag.

"Attendants, prepare the cabin for takeoff," the pilot's voice calmly announces over the intercom.

Keola pats my arm. "You're a sport, Sophie, really you are." At least, I think that's what he says, because the engines are now at high rev, and the plane is rolling down the runway.

Barely perceptible over the engine noise, Keola starts to hum. At first, it sounds like he's trying to remember the tune, but then he's singing with the deep, clear voice of an angel, as if it were coming straight from heaven—or at the very least, Hawaii—which according to Dad is the next best thing.

"Aloha 'oe e ku'u lei…" he chants with eyes squeezed shut. The effect would be mesmerizing if he didn't have a pincher-grip on my arm.

As if his incantation were working, a fuzzy-faced, white-haired dog pops his head out from under the seat in front of us and jumps up onto my lap. Without thinking, I put my hand on his back and sense, *Someone needs me! Must do something! Quick!* or doggy feelings to that effect.

"Right," I say out loud. "Here." And the pooch scrambles up Keola's mountain of a chest and starts licking his face.

"That tickles!" Keola giggles.

"I think it's supposed to."

"What do you mean?" He buries his face in the critter's silky fur.

I ignore the question. "He must belong to that old Hawaiian lady up front."

"What lady?"

"The one who's been snoring. Can't you hear her?"

"The only thing I hear are engines. Lift off! Here we go!" Keola whoops, cradling the little bundle of fluff in his arms.

Within seconds, we're sailing over Puget Sound, our bodies sinking back into our seats as the plane lifts us higher and higher. Even when the wheels crank up and close with a jolt, Keola keeps nuzzling that dog. It's as if he's flown a thousand times, he's that at ease, like how Iz once sang that rainbow song.

I glance over at Wilks to see if she's catching any of this. Her eyes are glued on Aloha Dog, and she's not looking so good, like she's seen a ghost or something. It's probably just the change in altitude.

Once the plane levels out, the little white pup settles across Keola's lap.

My work is done here, he sighs with a little doggy shudder.

Thank you, Aloha Dog.

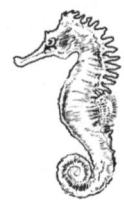

7.
Now You See Her, Now You Don't

As part of its camouflage, the seahorse allows algae and other organisms to grow on its body, making it almost invisible.

Thunk!

I wake with a start, gripping the armrest between me and Wilks. At first, I think a boulder has crashed beside me, the one that was chasing me down a mountain in my dream, but then I realize we just hit some turbulence and I remember where I am. I'm not riding a wave of red-hot lava down a crumbling cliff. I'm on a plane, and that *thunk* must have been someone's bag shifting in the luggage compartment above me.

Ironically, the once-terrified Keola is still sleeping beside me, as is Wilks on the other side. Aloha Dog is nowhere to be seen. He must have returned to his owner after we all fell asleep. Sun from the window pours across our laps, glinting off seat belts, making mine hot to the touch.

That dream. It felt so real. A woman with long, flowing white hair rode a stream of molten lava by my side, shifting her weight around tumbling boulders like a seasoned surfer as we plummeted toward the sea. She had just turned to stare at me with her amber eyes when I woke up.

Wait. It was the dog lady! I stretch to see if I can catch a glimpse of her white hair above the headrest, but there's no sign of her or her dog. Maybe she's slouched down in her seat sleeping, like my seatmates beside me. I stare out the window as the plane tips its wings toward Hawaii, small on the horizon, a velvety green splotch of land in a whole lot of blue.

The pilot comes on the intercom and tells us we'll be landing in about twenty minutes. I'm amazed that Keola and Wilks can sleep through the hustle and bustle of the cabin as passengers begin to gather their belongings and slap their tray-tables shut. I guess all that talking eventually wore us out.

It was Keola who got Wilks to open up first. Once Aloha Dog had eased his fears and we were thirty-two thousand feet above ground, Keola started asking questions in a way that made you want to tell him your life story and not just the facts but the underneath parts, too. He'd start out sharing something about himself but then he'd turn and say things like, "But what about you guys?" or "What's it like living with *your* parents?" And then he'd lean in and listen like our words were some kind of treasure.

So that's how we learned that we're all going into seventh

grade and that Wilks lives on a ranch east of Seattle where her family raises cattle. Ranching is in her blood, she says, through her Hawaiian-born mother who came to the mainland for college, met Wilks' dad, and never went back. Wilks says she looks like her dad, but she gets her "abilities" from her mom, which I took to mean riding horses and roping cattle. But then she muttered, "That's why I'm going to Camp Koa." Keola and I were waiting for more, but that's when she decided to pull her hood back up like a turtle escaping into its shell.

After Wilks checked out of the conversation, Keola talked about his own family, how his father grew up on the island of Hawaii just like mine did. His mother is from Molokai. His parents have insisted he learn traditional Hawaiian skills, which is why he belongs to a troop called a *hālau* in Seattle where he dances hula and chants. Even if his parents weren't making him, he says, he'd do it anyway. He loves it that much.

"I've even won some trophies," he said. "I'm kind of a big deal in the hula world." His brown-toned face pinked up, which is how I knew he wasn't bragging. "That's why I'm going to Camp Koa, to learn from my dad's former teacher, his *kumu hula*."

When he asked me why *I* was going, I shrugged. "Because my parents want me to?"

"Is that a question?" He laughed. "You mean, you're not sure?"

"Oh, I'm *sure*," I said, laughing, too. I'd only known the guy for about two hours, but there was something about his laugh that made me glad to be around him. "It's just that my parents and I have different reasons for my going."

Keola cocked his head and raised his eyebrows, like he *knew* I wanted to say more.

And I did ... want to say more. I don't know why, but I wanted to tell him *everything*.

So I told him about the incident in Sarasota and how Dad gave me Buddy, but how Buddy lost his mate and then his babies and how I was going to make it up to him by finding him a friend. The only thing I left out was the freaky telepathic thing, even though I was tempted to spill it along with everything else.

I cleared my throat. "Mission Buddy," I announced and handed Keola my "to do" list.

Arrive at Camp Koa.

Pretend I'm homesick if I'm not already.

Call parents and beg to come home.

Catch a ride to the seahorse farm.

Find the perfect friend for Buddy.

Figure out how to get to airport.

Arrive home with new seahorse.

Introduce Buddy to his new friend.

Keola looked up and flicked the list with his index finger. "Ya know, you can order a seahorse online, right?"

"Of course, but then how would I know it was the *right* one?"

"Hmmm, how are you going to know that *now?*"

"Well..."

My plan was to hold as many seahorses as possible—a feature of the Kai House seahorse tours—and zone in on their thoughts and feelings until I found a lonely seahorse with good memories and a gentle grip. I was just about to spill the beans about my particular brand of weird, when I thought better of it.

"I'll just *know*," I said with a sigh.

"Of course, you will," Keola replied. "When it's right, it's right. Right?" He held his fist in the air, and I bumped it. I think it was the first time I fist-bumped *anybody*.

"Right," I said, feeling hopeful.

Keola handed the rumpled list back to me. "Let me know if there's anything I can do to help, okay?"

"Really?"

"Really." No sooner had he flashed me a full-out aloha grin, his face darkened. "Sophie?"

"Yeah?"

"Maybe you could wait a few days, you know, after we get to Camp Koa before pretending to get homesick?"

"No worries, Keola. That's part of the plan," I said, already feeling guilty about leaving him. "I need to give it a few days, anyway. Got to make it believable, you know."

"Right. Like they say, timing is everything."

With that, he pulled a flat, crescent-shaped, inflatable pillow out of his backpack. He blew it up with three long breaths, wrapped it around the back of his neck, and was asleep in no time. Now, two hours later and with the plane preparing to land, he finally stirs.

"Ahhhhhhh…" Keola yawns and stretches his arms over his head, looking around. "Hey. Where'd our little *'īlio* go?" When he sees the puzzled look on my face, he translates, "You know, that little wiggle mop of a *dog?*"

"Oh, right." He obviously knows more Hawaiian than I do. I point to the row in front of us. "He disappeared."

"Well, that makes you right about one thing." Wilks throws her hood back and yawns. Keola leans over me and gives her a quizzical look. "Look," she says. "I know you guys thought that dog was real—and he was—just not in the way you think. Pretty cool trick, really."

"What in the worrrrrrrld are you talking about?" Keola asks.

"Yeah, what do you mean … *trick?*" I wonder what she knows about Aloha Dog. Can she read the minds of animals, too? The thought makes me uneasy.

"Ummm…" She winds the string of her hood tightly around her index finger. "Okay, I'm only telling you this because I think it might be useful later on." Keola and I must look at her like she's grown another head. "Okay." She takes a deep breath. "You two were playing with a spirit, one that for whatever reason is being seen on this plane only by us."

"Whoa," Keola says. "You mean that furry little rascal? But I was petting him. And he slobbered all over my face. That slobber was real!"

"Like I said ... pretty cool trick."

"Well, that just can't be," I say, feeling a little dizzy. "That dog belongs to the woman in front of us. I know because I saw them when I was finding my seat. She spoke to me."

"Okay," says Wilks, agreeably. "Then that makes *two* spirits. I could make a good guess as to who they are, but I don't want to freak you out."

"Like you're not doing that already." Keola leans back against his seat and laughs so hard his chest shakes.

Me? I'm getting chicken skin.

After we land and arrive at our gate, most of the people around us jump up to grab their carry-ons. Wilks rests her head on her backpack, while Keola and I stare at the row in front of us waiting for the woman and her dog to show themselves.

They don't.

Keola peers over the seat backs in front of us. "They must have changed seats while we were asleep," he says quietly and carefully slips his massive body into the aisle. "That happens sometimes, you know."

I nod and Wilks shrugs, but as the three of us lumber down the aisle to meet up with our escort, Sandy, I'm getting the sneaking feeling Wilks might have a psycho-telepathic-weirdness of her own. Maybe even weirder than mine.

It's not a relief.

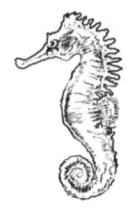

8.

Fish Out of Water

The seahorse may be classified as a fish, but it's an odd fish. It doesn't have scales, teeth, ribs or a true stomach…and it only has one fin.

At the Hilo airport, Sandy escorts us to baggage claim which isn't very far, and before we know it, our welcoming committee is standing right in front of us: a tall, older woman wearing a T-shirt and khaki shorts with a large, cotton satchel strapped over her shoulder, and a man—at least a couple inches shorter than the woman—with leathery skin and wavy, salt and pepper hair.

"That's my kumu hula!" Keola excitedly whispers as we approach, nodding toward the man whose face is all lit up. I guess that's his hula teacher. He's holding a hand-written sign that reads:

Aloha, Sophie Kai, Leilani and Keola! Camp Koa welcomes you!

He hands the sign to the woman and gathers us into a group hug. "Aloha, *keiki*—my children! It's so good to finally meet you! I'm Uncle Hanalei and this is Aunty Kuʻuipo, but you can call us Uncle and Aunty for short." We look up at the woman expectantly, but she's busy folding the welcome sign in half and then, in half again.

"Never mind her," Uncle whispers. "She's a little grumpy today." He looks over at Sandy. "*Mahalo* for bringing our *'ohana* home to us safely."

"No problem. Take care, you guys. Have a great time at camp!" Sandy gives us one final wave as she bustles away, wheeling her little black tote behind her.

Aunty? Uncle? Home? Family? Seems like Uncle is assuming a lot of aloha for having just met us. Keola's soaking it up of course. Meanwhile, Wilks has retreated into her hoodie as Uncle releases us from his all-encompassing hug. Me? My stomach is feeling a little queasy, and I'm already fretting about how Buddy's doing without me.

"I thought you said they'd give us *leis*," Wilks mumbles to Keola.

"Yeah, sorry about that." Uncle points a thumb at his partner. "She forgot 'em." Aunty shrugs like it's no big deal. "All she can think about is that scrawny little demon pet of hers."

Demon pet?

The three of us look over in Aunty's direction in time to see a rooster stick his bright red, wiggly head out of her satchel. His flimsy comb is cocked to one side and his feathers are all ruffled like he just woke up from a nap.

"Huh," Wilks says.

"Yeah, huh," Keola echoes.

All I can think about is how that rooster better not come near me.

Sometimes I'm drawn to an animal who wants to show me something—and I'm usually okay with that, as long as no one's around to see it—but other times, it feels like a reverse magnet pushing me away. This is one of those times and it's coming in waves. Maybe it has something to do with the company he keeps—I'm not jumping at the chance to know this aunty person, either—but I don't need to touch a feather on that bird to know he's trouble.

"Errr-er-er-er-errrrrrrrr-eeeeeech!" he screeches.

"Meet Moa," Uncle says, and for the first time since we met her, Aunty breaks into a grin as she runs her hand gently down the rooster's scrawny neck. "*Moa* means chicken in Hawaiian," Uncle adds, "but don't let that fool you. Moa will peck at your toes like a vulture if you come near him."

Like I said.

"Don't you listen to that mean old man," Aunty sweet-talks her pet and gazes into his beady little eyes. "Moa protects our camp from nosy tourists, don't you, little one?" And then she kisses him. On his beak. I *swear*.

Uncle throws back his head and laughs. "Yeah, a real watchdog, that one!"

❀ ❀ ❀

We're packed three across in the back seat of Uncle's open-air Jeep, our bags strapped onto this makeshift rack above the back bumper with bungee cords. Keola and I ignored Wilks' protests and insisted that she sit between us, which put the two of us hanging on for dear life as water in the streets splashed up into the cab on our way through Hilo. That's right. *Water in the streets.* Apparently, Uncle has taken a little detour to show us this phenomenon.

"King tide," he yells back at us as we ride along a shoreside road lined with banyan trees as wide as houses. "The highest tide this year, my friends. When a king tide joins higher-than-normal sea levels ... well ... this is what you get."

"Correction, Hanalei, this *is* normal." Aunty scoffs. "Get used to it."

"What Aunty is trying to say, as the planet warms, sea levels rise and—"

"—there's no turning back." Aunty slaps the dashboard. *Smack!* "And our children—our keiki—will be the ones who pay!"

"Hey, where's all this doom-and-gloom coming from?" Uncle leans his shoulder into hers while still watching the road, and I wonder if they're married. "The boys say fishing's crazy good right now. There's good news in everything, right? Even global warming."

She pushes him away. "Keep your eyes on the road, old man."

Yup. Definitely married.

I look over the side of the jeep and see a bright, yellow fish wiggling its way up the boulevard.

"Hey! It's a fish out of water!" Keola says brightly, as he points and laughs.

Wilks scowls. "Yeah, kind of like us."

You'd think that Hawaii being an island, everything would be close to everything else, but no, Uncle says it'll take us over an hour to drive to Camp Koa. At first after leaving Hilo, the landscape is really tropical—lots of lush green ferns, large colorful flowers, and coconut trees. I even see a humongous, poinsettia plant taking up a good portion of someone's front yard.

After we pass signs for Volcano National Park, the scene changes. Long bare hills of volcanic rock slope down to the ocean—some covered with dry grass and scrawny shrubs, while others have large patches of pure black stone. Some of that rock is smooth and swirly, some of it sharp and jagged.

"We'll be coming back to the park for a field trip in a couple of weeks," Uncle yells back to us. "You'll get to meet Madame Pele up close and personal."

"What do you mean, 'meet her?'" I laugh. "She's a myth." Dad sometimes paints scenes from ancient Hawaiian stories, and I recognize the name Pele as one of his subjects.

Wilks glares at me, her eyebrows knitted together. "You better be careful what you say about her, Sophie. She tends to take things personally." Wilks and Aunty exchange looks as if they share some special knowledge.

"Phhhht," I hiss, as Wilks flips her hood up. Well, good. I don't feel like chatting either.

Honestly, I've about had it with Wilks. Her comment back on the plane about my sister liking to hang out with me continues to bug me, even though I can't blame her for not knowing Baby Girl's dead. But now? She's acting like she has a personal relationship with this mythical goddess like she lives next door to her. Oh well. I take a few deep breaths and settle in for the rest of the ride. I'll be back home with Buddy's friend long before Camp Koa goes on that field trip anyway.

About half an hour later and several miles past a small town with only one stop sign, we turn onto a road where a sign points the way to Camp Koa. Wilks is brooding as usual and Keola's obviously excited, but all I can think about is Mission Buddy. The seahorse farm is just north of Kona. Google Earth made it look like an easy jaunt.

"How long does it take to get to Kona from here?" I ask. Now that we've slowed down, we can hear each other talk.

"Oh, about an hour and a half," Uncle says. "Depends on

traffic and what you're driving. When we take the camp bus up to CostSaver north of Kona, it takes a bit longer."

Dang. Mission Buddy just got more complicated. *Wait a minute.*

"You guys have a CostSaver?"

He nods.

Note to self: Better not tell Dad. He'll want to move us here for sure.

"There's an airport near Kona, right?" I ask. We're passing a golf course on our right where several black and white geese are hobbling around on the greens.

"Yeah, it's actually bigger than Hilo's."

Aunty shoots me a look over her shoulder. "What's with the questions? Plan on making a quick exit or something?"

"No ... of course not," I protest, but my heart sinks. One look at Keola confirms I've gone too far. His eyeballs are practically popping out of their sockets at me.

Aunty sniffs. "I sure hope not. Considering the three of you *mainlanders* (she says this like it's a dirty word) are here on scholarship." Keola, Wilks, and I exchange surprised looks. I'm guessing each of us thought we were the only one to receive one. "A scholarship's a privilege, you know." She sniffs again.

"Yes, ma'am," Keola chimes in. "It's a huge privilege to be here at Camp Koa, isn't it, Sophie?" He's nodding at me hard, like he's willing me to agree with him.

"Absolutely." I force a grin. I jab Wilks in the ribs. "Right,

Wilks?"

"Sure. Right." She glares at me, rubbing her side.

Uncle brakes hard and pulls off the side of the road. He twists in his seat to face the three of us. *Uh-oh*, I think. We haven't even gotten to camp and we're already in trouble.

"What Aunty means to say," he says slowly, shooting her a warning look, "is that previously, Camp Koa has only served island children. So, you see, *we* are the ones who are privileged to have the three of you here at Camp Koa. Right, Aunty?"

She shrugs like she's thinking about it, or maybe she's shrugging us off.

"No worries. She'll come around; she always does. After all, her name *Kuʻuipo* means 'sweetheart.'" He grins. "Her parents must have known she was going to need a little reminder from time to time." Uncle leans over to give his wife a kiss on the cheek, but Moa pops his head out of the sling and gives Uncle a peck on his arm instead.

Uncle winces. "Eh, Kuʻuipo! One of these days that demon rooster of yours is going to wind up missing ... or maybe *I* will." He sounds mad, but Aunty just pulls Moa closer. You wouldn't think you could snuggle with a rooster, but somehow, she makes it work.

"Oh, never mind." Uncle laughs and shoves the Jeep into gear. "I can tell I won't be winning that fight anytime soon."

A few minutes later, we round a corner, and a wooden sign

greets us in bright orange letters, "Aloha, Koa Campers!" The three of us look around expectantly, but there's really nothing much to see—just a few coconut trees, some scraggly shrubs, and what looks like a covered picnic area with no one in sight.

"Here we are, my fellow campers!" Uncle announces with a sweep of his arm. "Welcome home!"

Geez, I wish he'd stop calling it that.

I know he means well; I like Uncle, I do. But there's no way this place is ever going to feel like home. Besides the fact that it looks like we'll be living outdoors—a thought that totally creeps me out—I can never imagine any of these people feeling like family. Certainly not Uncle's ornery wife or demon pet. Wilks is a complete mess and even though Keola's been friendly enough, at the moment he won't even look at me. Honestly, it's kind of a relief. His cheerfulness was getting on my nerves.

No. This is *not* home.

Aloha

9.
Falling Up

Uncle and Aunty unload us just inside the compound, and then take off to find where everyone else went. "Back in a flash," Uncle shouts. "Feel free to look around!"

So much for aloha.

With our bags and backpacks slumped all around us, the three of us "mainlanders" begin squabbling like contestants on a survival show. Keola starts us off.

"Sophie, what were you thinking?! There are easier ways to get directions to the airport—like, say, with your *phone*—than to ask the very people who can stop you from going there!"

Before I can defend myself, Wilks jumps in. "Yeah, and what the heck was that jab in the gut back there? Like, I don't know how lucky I am to be here?" She puts the word "lucky" in air quotes. "I know you think you're hot stuff—what with talking to dogs that aren't really there—but it doesn't give you the right to be nasty."

"Well, at least I'm not checked out all the time. And oh-by-the-way, that dog was *there*."

"Wasn't!"

"Was!"

"Wasn't!"

"Girls!" Keola shouts, but I ignore him. Something's been bugging me ever since the plane, and it's time to get it off my chest.

"Hey, Wilks, what made you say my little sister 'likes to hang out with me,' anyway?" I choke on my next words. "Maybe you don't know, but … she's *dead*."

All the anger in Keola's face suddenly drains away. "Oh, Sophie, I had no idea."

"Well, I did…" Wilks says, somewhat defiantly, but then her voice softens. "That's what I've been trying to tell you."

"Tell me *what?*"

But before she can answer, something falls from the sky.

Thunk!

I look down in time to see a coconut coming to rest beside my foot.

"Aloha, newbies!" a voice calls from above. "Sorry! That one got away from me."

The three of us look up the trunk of a coconut tree and stare into its upper-most fronds where a dark-haired boy about our age is waving at us. We remain dumb-struck as the boy shimmies down the tree in about ten seconds flat. His arms and legs are all tan and muscle, and he's wearing a pair of long, cotton surfer shorts with turquoise swirls and a beige, Camp Koa T-shirt with a big orange turtle on the back. Several colorful leis hang loosely around his neck.

"Wow!" Keola says. "That was *cool*."

"What? Oh, that?" The boy laughs and his long, sleek hair shimmers in the late-afternoon sun. "That's nothin'. Been doing that for years." He starts to lean against the tree. "Oh, I almost forgot. I'm supposed to be your welcoming committee. *Here*." He gently lifts the leis from his neck and one by one, places them around our necks, ending with me.

"Aloha," he says, as he steps closer. His eyes are brown with little gold flecks, and they stare straight into mine as he places the lei around my neck. The intensity of his look makes me blush. *Ugh*. I turn my head away, hoping he doesn't see.

"My name's Nalu," he says. "That's my Hawaiian name. Everyone here at camp has one. How 'bout you guys?"

"Yes," Keola says, taking charge. "I'm Keola. Sophie Kai here," he says with a nod in my direction. "And this is Leilani." I expect her to tell him to call her Wilks, but she doesn't.

"Awesome, it's great to have you guys here, and like I said, I'm sorry. I stayed behind in case you came while everyone else went to the beach, but I got bored." He looks up the tree. "I was trying to break my record—we have climbing races here at camp—but then I got caught up in the view. You can see the ocean from up there. There are fishing boats offshore today. Looks like the fish are biting, too."

View? Beach? Ocean? I let my eyes run along the curved length of Nalu's tree, all the way up into the cluster of coconuts and feathery fronds at its top, inviting me into their shade. Suddenly, something inside urges me *up, up, up* and before I can think twice, I've kicked off my sandals and I'm climbing, finding toeholds on the ridges that circle the tree's trunk.

"Sophie Kai! What the heck are you doing?" Keola calls up to me.

"I'm *climbing!*"

I brace myself against the trunk with my arms as I push up with my legs and feet, all the while remembering how much I used to love doing this, back before Baby Girl died. Climbing gets me closer to the sun and the sky and oh-my-gosh, Nalu was right—the *view*—but I don't want to stop. Someone below sends out a long, low whistle, probably Nalu, but maybe it's Wilks, and before I know it, I'm at the top. *Hooray!* my heart sings.

Everything is so beautiful. The beach is as close as the beach is to our townhouse back home. And the sand is black. *Black!* There's a stone pavilion several hundred feet from the water's edge, and those fishing boats Nalu was talking about bob off the tip of a rocky peninsula. In the other direction, I can see how the whole camp is laid out. Five simple buildings with green, metal roofs line the back of the property—three large ones and two small ones, that are maybe bathrooms. There's a humongous open space with a fire pit at the center, and a covered area with picnic tables that looks like an outdoor kitchen.

With my legs wrapped tightly around the tree's trunk supporting my weight, I wave at the three faces looking up at me.

"Hey, everybody! How's it going down there?" I still can't believe I climbed all the way up.

"Oh, we're just g-g-great, S-s-sophie Kai." Keola sounds mad, or nervous, or both. "I sure do hope you know how to g-g-get down from there."

"A girl who climbs like *that?*" Nalu shakes his head and laughs. "No problem!"

Wilks points towards a footpath. "Whether she can or not, she's about to get an audience."

Sure enough, here comes what must be the rest of the campers, tromping barefoot single file through a thicket of tall grasses on either side of the path, their lively chatter floating up to meet me. Behind them, Aunty and another woman wearing a wide-brimmed hat follow at a slower pace with Moa the demon rooster tagging along like a little dog.

Great. And they'll be here any second.

Thing is … *down* isn't exactly my favorite direction.

As I gaze at the ground twenty feet below, my muscles seize up. My arms and legs are gripping the trunk so tight, I can't budge them even if I wanted to.

"Sophie Kai?" Keola's voice is trembling now. "What's going on?"

The palms of my hands are on fire and so are the inside of my thighs. I'm wearing jeans, so the burn comes from muscles that aren't used to clutching coconut trees or any other kind of tree for that matter for the last five years. Did I mention it's a long way down? Like two stories? Maybe three? What the heck did I think I was doing, anyway? And what if I fall? My parents will kill me for sure. That is, if I'm not already dead.

"Um … guys?" My voice sounds little-girl quiet and far away.

Keola starts to pace. "Oh no, oh no, oh no, I was afraid of this, oh no."

"I can't watch," Wilks says. She grabs her bags and heads for the compound.

Nalu, on the other hand, is all action. He leaps onto the base of the tree from a standing start and literally runs up the trunk. It's like he's got Velcro on the pads of his hands and feet. Before you know it, he's right below me, close enough to be staring at my butt, which I'm not too happy about, but golly, that kid is quick.

"Aloha, Sophie Kai." He grins up at me.

"Aloha. Uhhhh … I seem to have a problem."

"No worries." He gives me the *shaka* sign that Dad uses on me whenever I get up-tight—three middle fingers folded into the palm with the thumb and pinkie sticking out to the sides. "This happens all the time," he says.

"It does? Great. Any suggestions?"

"Yeah … jump!" He laughs.

"V-v-v-very f-f-f-funny…"

By now, the rest of the campers have gathered underneath us. And Keola? He's holding his hands over his head like he's preparing for a crash.

Yeah, *mine*.

"Hey, Nalu!" someone yells up. "You gonna cut down that coconut?!" A bubble of laughter rises up from the group.

"Hush! That's *enough*," says one of the elders. "Aloha, Sophie Kai! Tūtū Malia here!" I chance a quick look down. The light and breezy voice is coming from an older woman with a round face and short, gleaming white hair. She's holding her floppy hat in her hands. "We're so glad you and your friends managed to get here safely."

I almost lose my grip. "Aloha?" I squeak. Doesn't she realize I'm not exactly safe *now*?

"When you and Nalu get down from there, Sophie Kai, it'll be time to wash up for dinner." She says this in a steady, matter-of-fact voice. "Okay, everybody, let's go!" And with that, she shoos the rest of the campers away from the tree and back to the center of camp.

Wait! Aren't you going to call the fire department or something? I want to yell after her, but the words get stuck in my throat. Keola's worried face is the only one that keeps looking back.

"Okay, Sophie Kai," Nalu says in a commanding voice, as he scoots up closer helping to support my weight. "The fastest way down is *not* an option. Agreed?"

I nod. I know he's trying to make light of the situation, but it's not working.

Nalu pulls a looped scarf from his pocket and slips it around my ankles. "This band will keep your feet together as you scoot down the trunk." As he tightens the loop, gripping gets easier. "Here's another one for your hands."

One at a time, I shake out my hands to get the blood flowing again, and then he wraps the band around each wrist. Looped around the back of the trunk, the cloth is held taut by the backward pressure of my weight. I'm still gripping the tree, but my arms, rather than just my hands, are doing the work.

"Okay, Sophie Kai, the quicker we get down, the more muscle we have to work with. Let's go!" Nalu's head is right below my feet as I try to match his pace. Soon, we're shimmying down the tree in perfect sync—legs together, arms together—like inch worms moving half a foot at a time.

"Keep up with me now," he urges. "Don't stop. That's it! Gravity is your friend."

In what seems like no time at all, we're on solid ground, where I collapse into a heap.

"Good job, Sophie Kai." Nalu smiles. "I've got to admit, you had me scared there for a minute."

I gulp back a giggle. "Now you tell me."

"Oh, I don't mean up there." He waves his hand like he's shooing away a gnat. "I knew we'd get you down. No, it was when I saw you fly up that tree, I thought you'd break my record for sure.

But there's no chance of that now, is there, Sophie Kai? I mean, *down* is half the race."

Just a few seconds ago, I was ready to give this guy my National Geographic sticker collection for saving my life. But now? I scramble to my feet. "Is that a *dare*?"

"Nah..." He kicks a stranded coconut into the brush. "Statement of fact."

Every ounce of my being wants to say, "Oh yeah, we'll just have to see about that!" but then I remember Mission Buddy. "*Whatever*," I say instead, turning away to gather my bags.

I snatch the cellphone out of the front pocket of my backpack. Now that I know I'm not going to die, I feel an urge to text home.

"Best get that over with now," Nalu yells, walking backwards away from me. "No phones allowed at camp."

"Oh, that's just *great*," I say, trying to sound tough, when really, I feel kind of creeped out. No communicating with your loved ones, huh? Isn't that the first thing a cult does to take control of its victims?

> Hey dad how's Buddy?

> Hanging out on the same old seaweed. You?

> Weird

> Weird how?

> Creepy weird

Darn.

> Camp Koa might be a cult. This might be the last time you hear from me.

No worries Sophie Kai. You'll be fine. Love you, darlin girl!

> U2 daddy

10.

The Heartbeat of Aloha

The dining pavilion, as they call it, is mostly a concrete slab and a metal roof held up by six steel pillars, open to the Hawaiian breezes on all sides but one. What I guess you would call the kitchen is on the walled side, complete with a refrigerator, an industrial-size oven, and a large tub where I join a few other kids washing up for dinner. A six-burner grill stands just outside smoking up a storm, as Uncle plops fish fillets on every plate.

"Hey, it's da girl who thinks she's a coconut!" Some skinny-legged boy shouts as I step into the food line. Egged on by a few other kids chuckling at his joke, he adds, "She even looks like a nut!" Keola, who is already sitting at a table, glances up from his plate. We exchange a look that says: *Yup, it's starting already.*

Nalu joins in the laughter, I expect nothing less, but then he surprises me. "Shut up, Honi. She climbs like a gecko—not like some skinny little worm like you." Now everyone's laughing at the Honi kid. I look up at Nalu to silently thank him, but he's still on a roll. "Yeah, brah," Nalu continues, "you so slow, Moa's gonna think you're a snack!"

"That's enough, campers!" Uncle raps on the side of the grill with his barbecue tongs. "We speak aloha here, right?"

"Right," everyone mumbles back.

Dinner is tasty enough. All of us campers—twelve kids and three adults—sit on benches family style at two long picnic tables, woofing down fish and salad. Even though I'm a vegetarian, Mom insists that I eat fish for protein, and I've got to admit, everything tastes pretty good ... that is, except for the *poi*.

Let me just say, poi's a problem.

Poi is made from the taro root, a traditional Hawaiian dish, and one of Dad's favorite comfort foods. He says it reminds him of "home," which means Hawaii, of course, but my gag reflex simply won't let me eat it. It's altogether too gooey and gets caught at the back of my throat. If Dad were here, he'd say try it anyway, which usually annoys me, but now I kind of miss him saying it. I miss him a lot.

After dinner, every camper is assigned a cleanup chore. Aunty gives Wilks and me grill duty which means we're scraping charred fish skin off greasy iron grates in a tub of murky water. It's as yucky and stinky as it sounds, which only goes to prove one thing. Aunty has it in for us mainlanders for sure.

Wilks is attacking her section of the grill like she's trying to rub somebody's face off. Fortunately, our job takes not only muscle but concentration, so there's little reason to talk—not that either one of us has anything to say to the other. To take my mind off what I'm doing, I watch Uncle build a fire in the center of the talk story circle, as they call it, about thirty feet from the outdoor kitchen.

I've got to hand it to him; he's some kind of magician. Back home, Dad struggles to get a charcoal grill started with half a can of lighter fluid, while Uncle's turned a smoky little pile of sticks into a raging inferno. In cut-off jeans and a well-worn T-shirt, he dances around the edges, tossing in a handful of brush here, a log there, and then he seems to reach into the flames with his whole arm like he's fireproof or something. It's like he's sculpting fire. When Uncle dances over to the other side of the pit, he becomes a shimmering blur.

The rest of the kids have long since finished their chores. Tūtū Malia ambles up behind us on her way to the circle. "Come along, girls. Put those grates up on the rack to dry and come join us by the fire."

Trunks of coconut trees lie horizontally in a circle around the firepit. There's only one left open, so Wilks and I are forced to sit together, that is, until Keola comes over.

"Looks like you two could use a firewall," he chuckles, as he settles in between us.

Tūtū Malia walks—no, *floats*—to the center of the circle and raps her walking stick on the ground. Once. Twice. Three times. The chatter around the circle instantly stops. Everyone looks up with their eyes riveted on her, without her having to say a word. The fire crackles and hisses. Finally, she speaks.

"Every week, we will focus our *mana*—our sacred energy—on one powerful idea and put it into practice." She turns and faces Nalu. "That doesn't mean we stop practicing it at the end of the week, does it?" He shakes his head. "Of course not!" she laughs. "The ideas we learn here at Camp Koa will stay with us for our entire lives!"

She straightens her back. "Every summer, we begin the first week of camp focusing on the powerful idea of *aloha*." Tūtū turns to a shy, quiet girl who introduced herself at dinner as Luana. In a gentle voice, Tūtū asks, "But why? Why do we begin our time together with *aloha* do you think?"

"Because it means 'hello?'" says Luana timidly.

"Yes!" Tūtū raises her stick in triumph like it was the best answer she's ever heard.

"But aloha can also mean 'goodbye,'" the boy named Honi chimes in—the kid who teased me in the dinner line.

"Yes!" Tūtū turns to him and raises her stick again. "You're both right! And isn't it wonderful how a simple word like 'aloha' can hold both ends of our time together like that?" She looks at the ground and shakes her head in wonder.

"But *aloha* holds even bigger ideas than those simple greetings. Ideas like love. Affection. Peace. Kindness. Mercy. Compassion. All ideas—all *values*—wrapped up in that one, five-letter word. Isn't that amazing?"

Geesh. There must be as many meanings for *aloha* as there are names for rain in Seattle.

"But *aloha* is more than a word, my dear keiki." Tūtū pauses to look around the circle, stopping to make eye contact with each camper. No one looks away. When her eyes connect with mine, I'd swear time slows down. "*Aloha*," she continues, "is who we are."

Womp womp, chika chika womp, chika chika, WOMP! WOMP!

All eyes turn to Aunty, as she slaps the sides of a gourd-like instrument and bounces it on the ground. Womp womp, chika chika womp, chika chika, WOMP! WOMP!

"Aunty's gourd is called an '*ipu*.'" Tūtū Malia explains.

Keola whispers in my ear, "Aunty Kuʻuipo's ipu!" trying to hold back a giggle.

Just as I think I'm about to lose it—not so much at Keola's play-on-words, but at how the log we're sitting on is shaking with his barely contained laughter—Uncle's fire-building moves turn into a different kind of dance.

Uncle assumes a strong stance in front of the fire and points his long, muscular arms first left and then right—palms up, then down, his back ramrod straight—as the green ti-leaf lei he wears sways against his chest. Now he squats low to the ground—weight on toes—knees turn in, out, in, out—all in time with the ipu's beat.

Womp, womp, chika-womp, chika womp-womp.

This is not the flowy kind of hula you see on TV. No. It's a call to *war*, and Uncle is the general calling us to join him. No wonder he's Keola's kumu hula. His movements are so powerful. My heart pounds against the inside of my chest in time with the beat.

Chik, chik, chika, womp, chika womp, womp.

Suddenly, Keola flies off the log and lands by his kumu's side, squatting and turning, hips in-a-circle rocking, each dancer in perfect sync with the other. And as they squat, they kick one leg out straight to the side, first one and then the other. The weight has got to be *crushing*. Oh, my gosh ... Keola ... I got him all wrong. That's not fat; that's muscle, and he's *strong*.

When the beat stops, the two dancers resume a standing position and pause, heads bowed. No one says a word. No one applauds. The silence is louder than any cheer, and yet I swear I can hear my heart pounding out the rhythm of the dance in sync with every heart there.

As the two dancers quietly return to their seats, Tūtū finally speaks into the circle. "And that, my friends, is the heartbeat of *aloha*. The heartbeat of the Hawaiian people. Our hearts are *fierce*. If your heart was beating in rhythm with that dance, I don't care where you're from—the mainland or the island or the moon— you're one of *us*." The sky has taken on an orange glow and the silence in the circle is full and deep. Even the breeze seems to have settled down for the night to listen to Tūtū's voice.

"Mahalo, sister. Uncle. Keola." She looks from one to the next. "Mahalo for anchoring the spirit of aloha in our hearts." She pauses. "And now, it's time for talk story! 'Talk story' is when we

Hawaiians sit around and tell the stories of our lives, the stories of our ancestors. And since we're celebrating the safe arrival of three members of our ʻohana this evening—that's three of our *family*—I'm reminded of another traveler who came to our island way, way back after it was first formed, back before there were any people here." Tūtū extends her arm behind her and then circles it back. "Can anyone tell me who that first traveler might have been?"

I hear whispers around the circle. Beside me, Keola whispers, "Tūtū Pele," like she might appear before our very eyes.

"That's right. Tūtū Pele, the goddess of our volcano, the one who lives at the center of our island's fierce heart." Tūtū taps her chest. "We call her *Tūtū* Pele, out of respect.

"But here's what I want to think about, my dear campers: Tūtū Pele wasn't born here." Tūtū scans the circle of faces, settling on me, Keola, and Wilks on the log next to hers. "Just like some of us … weren't born here." The three of us take a collective gulp, knowing she means us. "No," she continues. "Tūtū Pele was called here by the higher gods."

Just then … CRACK! A flame shoots straight into the air and everyone jumps. If anyone around the circle hasn't been listening, they are now. Tūtū Malia pauses, looks around, perhaps waiting for the seriousness of her story to settle into our bones.

"Do you think Tūtū Pele had any idea where she was going or what waited for her here?" We all shake our heads, no. "That's right ... *no*. She just wanted an adventure. So, Tūtū Pele told her father, the royal king of their island, 'Father, I want an adventure. I want to explore other lands.' And because she was his favorite child, he granted her wish." Tūtū Malia raises her hand in the air and deepens her voice as if speaking like the king, "'However,' the king said, 'you must take your little sister with you.'

"Now, Tūtū Pele's little sister, Hi'iaka, was born in the form of an egg. Yes, that's right, an *egg*. So, Tūtū carefully placed her little sister under her armpit to keep her safe and warm, and off they went in a canoe navigated by one of Tūtū Pele's brothers, Kā-moho-ali'i, the king of sharks."

Tūtū Malia pantomimes rowing a boat with her walking cane. It feels like the story might end there until she stands her cane upright and leans on it. Tūtū slowly looks around our circle, gazing at each one of our faces, and then whispers, "It wasn't all smooth sailing."

"Uh-oh," Honi gasps.

"Yes, you see, Tūtū Pele had an older sister, Nā-maka-o-kaha'i. She was the goddess of the sea and water, and she was determined to stop Pele's voyage at all costs. Off she went, chasing after Pele's canoe with all the power of the ocean behind her."

Tūtū Malia nods at Uncle and he claps his hands.

"Okay, Koa campers!" he shouts. "*Moemoe* time!"

"Wait!" shouts Nalu. "We can't go to bed yet! What happens next?"

"Yeah, what happens to that egg sister?" Honi adds. "Does she crack?"

Everyone thinks that's funny, but I wonder how Tūtū Pele must have felt holding her sister, the egg, under her armpit the whole time in that topsy-turvy boat. Talk about scary. Reach for the side of the canoe to hold on for dear life and, oops, there goes your sister.

Things like that can happen, you know … without your wanting them to.

The orange fire at the center of the circle suddenly brightens. Sparks crack-crack-pop like someone threw a handful of firecrackers into the flames.

"Careful how you talk about our ancestors, Honi," Uncle nudges him. "They'll kick you in the butt if you offend them. Besides, Hi'iaka, that egg sister you're talking about? After she hatched, she danced hula. That's *my* sister you're talking about." Honi looks kind of sheepish until Uncle throws him playfully off the log and then pulls him back up again.

"But, Tūtū, what happens to Tūtū Pele?" the wispy girl, Luana, pleads.

"Another night, keiki." Tūtū Malia stands up and starts walking towards the sleeping huts. "I know this was a short talk-story tonight, but some of us have had a long day." She turns back to the circle and grins. "Meanwhile, let the story settle in you as you sleep. Who knows? An answer may come to you in your dreams."

Truth be told, I'm kind of mad about how Tūtū Malia ended tonight's talk story without actually ending it. I absolutely hate cliffhangers. But then I remind myself of what I'm really doing here.

"The only thing I'll be dreaming about is finding a friend for Buddy and heading for home," I whisper to Keola, as we get up from our log.

Wilks lets out a little snort, brushing past us. "That's the thing about dreams, seahorse girl. What you *want* to dream about, you won't. What you *need* to dream about, you will."

Yeah, like she knows everything.

11.
What's Not Amazing?

As luck would have it, I'm sharing a sleeping hut with the rest of the girls and Aunty, our assigned camp counselor, which means, of course, that we're also sleeping with Moa, the demon rooster.

"Lights out in five minutes, girls!" Aunty croons. "If you want to use the facilities, now's the time."

Let me just say, "facilities" is stretching it. We're talkin' a shack with a single toilet, a teeny-tiny sink, and a shower stall. Last time I used it after talk story, a bright green gecko wanted to share the seat with me. Thank goodness I looked before I sat down.

Who knows what might be creeping around there now that it's dark?

When we all get arranged in our separate cots—each with a two-inch mat and a sheet for a cover—Aunty nestles Moa down at her feet where he tucks his scrawny little legs up underneath his puffed-out body. His head and beak disappear under a scraggly wing, leaving his red comb sticking out conspicuously. It wobbles once or twice as he finds just the right position. I hope that's the last we hear from him for the rest of the night.

Once everyone has settled down, I try to go over the next day's plans in my head—I want to find the best way to get to the seahorse farm—but I'm so tired, my thoughts evaporate before I can string two thoughts together.

Next thing I know I'm camping with my family. We're asleep in our tent, and this obnoxious little girl is being a complete pest, tugging at my nightshirt, whining in my ears, trying to wake me up so I'll play with her.

"Up!" she keeps whining. "Up! Up! Up!"

I pull my pillow over my head, but she keeps bugging me. Now she's flicking my toes with her thumb and index finger. *Flick. Flick. Flick.*

"Get off me, you little brat!" I struggle to raise myself up so I can swat the little girl away—only it's not a little girl, it's a rooster, and he's pecking at my toes.

"Moa! What the heck?"

As soon as I call out his name, he stops and looks right at me with his beady little eyes. The sunlight flickers through the hut's screened-in windows. I squint to get a closer look at him, but it's no use. He scuttles out a flap in the door before I can focus my eyes.

I look around. Everyone's gone. I must have been so exhausted, I slept through the night and didn't even hear them leave. Our resident gecko is sunning himself on the window ledge that overlooks the compound. He raises his head in my direction and blinks. A faint smell of ham wafts through the warm morning air.

The only one in the kitchen is Tūtū Malia. She greets me pleasantly and hands me a stack of pancakes with a slab of ham and a glass of mango juice. "Everyone's down at the beach. You can join them when you're done," she says, as she finishes wiping down the counters. I think maybe she's mad at me, but then she says, "We decided to let you sleep."

"Thanks," I say.

A few minutes later, she sits down across from me as I finish the last pancake. "The only thing you missed this morning was the news of the day—basically we were looking ahead at the week and where we're going for our first field trip."

"Really? Where?" I'm thinking seahorse farm when she says it.

"There's a seahorse farm up north of Kona." She smiles. "We like to accommodate what our campers are interested in. Your essay showed us how much you care about seahorses."

I can't believe my luck. Not in a million years did I think Mission Buddy was going to be so easy. Nevertheless, I try to take the news in stride with the appropriate level of enthusiasm, so as not to tip my hand.

"Oh, wow. We're really going to see seahorses?"

"Yes. It's quite the enterprise up there. I think you'll find it interesting. They even let you touch them."

I try to act surprised. "So, when are we going?"

Tūtū pats the table as she lifts herself up with her cane. "Thursday, Sophie. Two days from now. Is that soon enough?" She levels me with her gaze, and I wonder if she sees straight through to my plan.

"Sure!" I say.

"Go on, Sophie," Tūtū says, nodding towards the ocean. "Throw on your swimsuit and go join your friends. They're waiting for you."

Like I believe *that*.

It's a free-for-all down at the beach. A few campers like Wilks and Luana are weaving baskets at a picnic table under a grove of coconut trees, but most of the kids are having a sword fight with weapons they've made from stripped down palm fronds, hard and sharp at the tips. Kicking up sand, Keola is whooping it up like a samurai warrior, maneuvering Nalu into a thicket until he spins away, leaving Keola lunging at air.

"You gotta move faster than that, brah, if you want to catch me!" Nalu plants his palm sword straight up in the sand and sprints to the water. One, two, three long strides and he's diving—arms stretched out, head down, shoulders rounded and flexed—into a sea-green wave.

"Hey, Sophie," Keola says, out of breath from the battle. "Did you hear the good news?"

"You mean about this week's field trip?"

"Yeah, pretty cool, huh? I figured you'd be over-the-moon about it."

"Shush, Keola. We've got to be careful what we say—or even *think*—around these people." I'm still fretting over how much Tūtū could read about my plans, and Aunty's staring at us from the water's edge.

"Geez, Sophie, why so paranoid? It's not like they're out to get us."

Aunty wades over to Uncle, and now they're both staring at us. Correction. He's staring. She's *scowling*.

"How do you know they're not out to get us?"

"I just know, okay?" He picks up a fallen palm frond and starts ripping off its leaves.

I'm about to ask Keola why he's getting so testy, when Uncle blows a whistle and waves us all over to shore.

"Listen up, campers. We're going to run a little swimming test this morning. Aunty and I will stand out from shore about a hundred feet apart and each of you will swim between us, starting and ending with Aunty. If you can only make it halfway, fine. Even if you can't swim a stroke, no worries. We just need to know your swimming level in order to keep you safe."

Keola catches my eye and smiles, as if to say, See? *They're not out to get us.*

I love to swim, so this test will be a piece of cake. After Baby Girl died, Mom and Dad enrolled me in swimming lessons at the local Y and wouldn't let me near the beach in front of our townhouse until I was officially certified as a Junior Swimmer.

I never understood why they made such a big deal of it. The water in Puget Sound is so cold, I usually can't stand to get my toes wet. Dad calls me a wimp, but I don't care. I like swimming where it's warm. Like here. Maybe Aunty will even smile at me when she sees how good I am. Not that I care, of course. I won't be around long enough for any of this to matter.

"We need to talk about what's *kapu* around here," Aunty says. "That is, what's not only 'sacred,' but 'forbidden.'" She points to a rocky promontory over to our left. "That's a *heiau*, an ancient site where many of our ancestors are buried. You are not to go there unless you're with one of us. It's sacred ground." Wilks is staring at that heiau like she's in a trance.

"Secondly," Aunty continues, "there's a strong current beyond the tip of that promontory that crosses east to west. Don't, I repeat, *don't* get caught in it. However, if you do get caught in it, don't fight it. You'll waste your energy, get tired, and die."

Uncle rolls his eyes, but Aunty glares at him. "Well, it's *true*."

The other campers and I look at each other nervously.

"As I was saying…" She glares at her husband for a second before continuing, "If you do get caught, you need to swim *with* the current and keep your eye on that outcropping of land." She indicates another promontory, this one further out and to our right. "If you're lucky, the current will deposit you there. Hopefully, someone from camp will have seen your problem and will meet you. However, do not try to swim back against the current. That would be stupid."

"Let me guess," Honi says, giggling nervously. "We might die."

"Well, yeah," Aunty says matter-of-factly. "And that would be stupid."

"Got it, campers?" Uncle asks.

"Got it," we mumble.

"My last warning is about our ʻaumakua, our sacred ancestors…" We all turn and follow her arm to a far corner of the beach away from the picnic tables. "The sea turtles, or *honu*."

My eyes scan the beach and for the life of me, I don't see any turtles, I mean, *honu*. Then, suddenly, like one of those magic pictures where objects lay hidden from plain sight, a honu appears, slowly, softly as if emerging out of the sand. Its green and brown mottled shell blends with its surroundings. And then, slowly, I notice another and then another—three in all—large heads curled to the side, eyes shut, napping. They look prehistoric. I wonder what they could tell me.

Uncle turns toward Aunty, but she's gotten quiet, as if she's too choked up to speak. So he takes over for her, speaking in a soft voice. "The honu is the protective spirit of this place, my friends, the bringer of wisdom and good luck. It is our *kuleana*—our responsibility—to protect the honu in return. That means we never pester them, and we always stay at least twelve feet away."

Just then, a sparkling white tour bus pulls into the lot by the park shelter, unloading dozens of tourists, many with smart phones recording everything around them. Half go in the direction of the restrooms while the other half come streaming toward the beach, gaping and pointing at the honu.

Suddenly, I have this impulse to wave my arms and shout, "Go back!" but I just stand there frozen, along with the rest of my Camp Koa buddies, staring at what we know is about to happen.

"Oh no, Uncle, Aunty! Don't they know the rules?" Luana pleads.

"The sign's right there at the entrance to the beach." Uncle nods. "Unfortunately, many tourists choose to ignore it."

"But can't we do something?" Luana begs.

Uncle and Aunty just shrug like they've seen it too many times before.

The tourists are closing in on the honu fast. Suddenly, Luana's arms spring out to the right and left of her like wings, and in an instant—like she's flashed this image into each camper's mind—we all know what to do. Hands taking hands, we move up the beach as one body, one Koa mind, with quiet Luana walking tall at the center of us all. Mere seconds before the tourists descend, we form a silent circle twelve feet or so back around the sleeping honu who seem oblivious to the drama taking place around them.

Suddenly, I have my doubts. Maybe these tourists were going to be respectful anyway. Maybe this is unnecessary. I glance at Keola who shakes his head, like he knows what I'm thinking and disagrees. As if to answer my wondering, a young woman with long black hair, a pink tank top and shorts, pokes at Luana, asking her to step back, so she can take a selfie with the closest honu. But we all know what that means—selfies call for being close—and we stand firm. Silent and firm.

Uncle and Aunty stand behind us, also silent, watching.

The honu closest to me on the ocean-side of the circle raises her head slightly and then sets it down again in the wet sand. I open my mind to her and immediately feel the cool, wet, pillow under her chin, the comfort of a much-needed rest, and the release of an inner sigh.

But *wait*. These are not my feelings; they're *hers*.

Wow. This has never happened before. I've always had to touch the animal to receive impressions from it. Maybe the island is amplifying my weirdness ... or maybe I'm getting power from the circle itself.

A few of the tourists begin to squabble with us.

"Hey, kids. Get out of our way!"

"What do you think? You own the beach?"

"Yeah! These turtles are here for us, too!"

I want to say: *Actually, these honu are here for themselves*, but who's going to listen to a kid? Besides, I'm sensing something happening among the three honu, something ... being discussed.

One of the honu's lids slowly opens, gliding over a dark, rounded globe of an eye. She sees shadowy figures, knows them as not-her-kind, senses danger in their voices, their tone, blinks away the dryness of the sandy breeze, senses something else, something reassuring; I want to believe it's our circle. Nevertheless, there's a shift happening in all three of them, like when something gets decided.

I nod at Luana who nods back.

Without talking—apparently, we don't need to—I let go of Keola's hand and we open the circle to the ocean. Still connected with the others, we maintain a protective line between the tourists and the honu they so desperately want to be close to.

Slowly, the honu stretch out their rubbery, flipper-feet, and with heavy-laden shells, pull themselves ever-so-slowly to the water's edge. It's as if the weight of the world is pressing down on them. When they slip into the ocean, however, I can feel their weightlessness, like I could kick off the ground and fly. And fly they do, into a world where water's like air. The only thing left of them on the beach are three wide, curving arrows of darkened sand tracks pointing toward the sea.

"Gee thanks for spoiling our fun, kids," a man with hula-dancers on his shirt says.

I think about saying something stupid like, "Don't mention it," or "Any time," but I'm proud to say we all stay silent. As we brush by the tourists and head back to the picnic tables to hear who's going first for their swim test, "Aloha" is the only word we speak.

"Sophie Kai!" Uncle says with his usual cheer. "You're up!"

Like nothing amazing just happened.

12.
Napping with Honu

Okay, so I passed the swim test, or at least I was good enough for Uncle to give me an "Atta-girl!" I'm not sure if he was referring to my speed or the fact that I accidentally rammed into Aunty with my final stroke forward. Come to think of it, he was laughing his head off.

But, boy oh boy—swimming in the ocean isn't nearly as easy as I thought. First of all, even a mere twenty feet out from shore, the water is cold—not Puget Sound cold—but still chilly. Second, there's this push and pull of the waves you're swimming against. They're not crashing over you like they do on shore, but they're still trying to roll you forward. And third, well, it's not the Y. Kind of a big duh, but it's not what I'm used to.

When I get back to the picnic tables, Tūtū Malia has joined the group waiting to be called for their swim test and is telling a story about this goddess, Kauila, who changed from a honu into a girl right here on this black-sand beach many, many moons ago.

"You mean, like she was a changeling?" Luana asks brightly.

Wilks perks up. "Yeah, like in those fantasy books?"

"Yes, girls. That sounds about right," Tūtū says. "Kauila originally hatched from a large brown egg right here on this beach. In fact, the nest her parents made to lay the egg was probably dug somewhere right under our feet." We all look under our tables like we half-expect to see it.

"Fortunately, back then," Tūtū continues, "these picnic tables weren't here. And neither were the coconut trees. You see, my friends, the park people meant well by providing us with a place to sit and eat our picnics while being shaded by the palms, but when they created this area, something very important to the honu was lost." A few campers are still finishing their baskets, but at the word "lost," everyone looks up. We all have a stake in these honu now, and Tūtū seems to know it.

Tūtū turns her gaze downward. "Their nesting ground was lost." She remains silent for a few seconds to let that sink in. "This part of the beach used to be soft and loose and as you can see, far enough from shore that the waves couldn't wash their nests away. It was the perfect place for the honu to dig and lay their eggs, up to a hundred fifty at a time. But when these trees were planted and more people started coming here, the sand got packed down hard. Roots dug in and spread out making it impossible for the mama honu to dig a hole big enough to lay their eggs."

My stomach starts to ache as I imagine their frustration. And confusion. *I used to be able to dig here. What's wrong?*

"But that's now. Back then, the sand was soft and easy to dig, and one summer day—much like the one we're enjoying now—sweet Kauila hatched and crawled out of her nest into the bright new world. Her mother nudged her over to that freshwater pond you see behind us and nurtured her there, waiting for Kauila to become old enough to swim out to sea and live on her own." Our eyes travel to the pond behind the coconut trees where ducks float lazily in the bright green algae.

"Kauila loved the island children, and they loved her. She loved them so much, she'd turn herself into a little girl so she could play with them freely, sometimes not turning herself back into a honu for days." Tūtū Malia looks over at Wilks and Luana who are now sitting together, quietly listening. She grins. "She really was a changeling, wasn't she?" The girls smile back.

"And that's how the honu became the 'aumakua of our beach. Kauila is still protecting us—all of us—but particularly our children." Tūtū scans our faces with that penetrating look of hers. "And that, of course, means you."

"If you ever get into trouble out there," she nods toward the ocean, "you can always call on the honu to come to your aid. You may think these stories are made up, but they don't come out of nothing. Like an egg, there is always something *inside* of the story—something living—that is very real."

Tūtū's words wash over me like waves rolling onto shore, and suddenly, I feel very sleepy. Uncle calls for Nalu to swim next, and although I'd like to stick around to see if he's as good as me, I'm desperate to get away from everybody so I can think. I feel like

I've lost my focus on finding a friend for Buddy and I need to get it back.

"Tūtū, would it be okay if I take a walk and do some exploring?" I ask, grabbing a beach towel from a stack. My plan is to find a nice, shady spot and take a nap. Maybe that will clear my foggy brain.

"Sure, Sophie Kai. But make sure you look behind you every now and then to take note of where you've been. You get out there among those tall grasses and sandy hills and everything starts looking the same. We'll ring a bell when it's time to head back to camp."

As I head west from the picnic tables, I check out where I've been once or twice, but honestly can't imagine having any problem finding my way back when I always know where the ocean is. Sure, sometimes it's hidden, but most of the time I catch hints of that sparkly gray-blue water and it always seems close. Besides, I can hear the voices of people back on the beach.

That is, until I can't.

One minute, I hear kids whooping it up and then next minute, nothing. Dead quiet. Only the rhythmic crash of ocean waves on the nearby shore. No worries, though. I haven't gone far and a tidal pool glistens a short distance ahead, inviting me to rest in the shade of a few sandy knolls.

When I draw near, I see something in the pool that breaks the surface. My heart beats faster when I realize what it is. A honu, half in, half out of the water, asleep.

"Well then," I whisper. "I guess it's nap time."

I quietly roll out my beach towel on a slant of sand a respectable distance away and lay down on my back. Gazing at my napping friend, I wonder if I can pick up on her thoughts like I did with those other honu on the beach. This new aspect of my telepathic weirdness is kind of cool. Being able to connect with an animal without touching it means my power is growing, not that I have a clue what to do with it. Heck, since no one is watching, I might as well play.

Emptying my mind of everything-that-isn't-honu, I open to all-that-*is*-honu. It's hard to explain what happens next. There's this slight tilt that happens in my brain, but then quickly drops to my chest, and I'm there *with* the honu, tuned in to what's happening beneath that humongous shell. As it turns out, it's not much. At least not while she's sleeping. Just a slow rise and fall of breath and this full-body stillness that makes me sleepier than one of my father's Hawaiian lullabies.

Next thing I know, a gull screeches overhead, and I wake with a start. I open my eyes and see a girl sleeping on a beach towel. At first, I think the honu has turned into that goddess-girl Kauila from Tūtū's story. But no, wait. That's *me*. I'm seeing myself through the honu's eyes.

Just as suddenly, my view flips back to normal and I'm seeing the honu raise her head, then set it down again. She feels a smooth, cool wetness underneath her, a gnawing hunger and an impulse for food. As she shifts her weight and begins to pull herself out of the tidal pool, there's a tight fullness in her belly that makes it hard to move. It's like what I felt from Buddy before his babies were born. *Could it be?* The honu is a *mama*.

I'm fully back to my Sophie self when I see something black and flimsy wrapped around the mama's left front leg close to its base. What *is* that? With horror, I realize it's a trash bag and imagine the enormous drag in the water when she swims. I must help her.

But as soon as I start to reach out, I remember I'm not supposed to touch the honu or even get close to them. It's not only a rule posted on a sign, but a sacred trust, according to Tūtū Malia. After all, just moments ago I had joined other campers in a circle of protection to keep people from doing exactly what I'm considering.

A familiar push-pull.

Help her, the impulse continues to nag, every cell in my body pushing me forward. I look around. Nobody's watching. And the mama honu is dragging that flipper like maybe it hurts.

Help her.

Okay, okay. If ever there were a time to break the rules, this is it.

Focusing again on everything-honu, I flash her a mind-picture of the bag on her flipper and of me touching her there. *May I?*

She stops her climb up the sandy bank and swings her head gently as if she's considering my offer. Meanwhile, I hold my question somewhere in the space between us and slow my breathing.

Breathing in ... honu.

Breathing out ... honu.

Breathing in ... honu.

Breathing out ... honu.

Moments pass. A light breeze rustles the leaves of a bush above the sandy hollow. And then, the honu settles her massive body down where she is and waits.

Oh my gosh. I'm *invited*.

I lift myself off the towel into a low crouch and crawl like a crab, feet and hands, to the honu's side. She keeps her eyes closed, lids tightly shut, perhaps to ease a fear coursing through her veins about this impossible choice she's making. But no, that fear must be mine because when I get close enough to smell the salty sea of her, a calm courses through me.

Still, I'm shocked to see how tightly the trash bag has secured itself. Somehow, her flipper found the way through a hole that was originally a handle, but then like a pretzel, wound its way around and around and somehow back through. In my mind's eye,

I see her flipper rotating wildly in the depths of the sea, trying to free itself, but making things much, much worse.

"Poor girl," I whisper as I lay my hand gently on her back, feeling the wet, rough ridges of her shell. *Not made for petting*, I think, but then quickly scold myself for having such a human, selfish thought.

The bag is slimy, black and wrinkled, making it impossible to tell where to start. I wish I knew my knots better. Heck, I wish I had my red and white Swiss Army knife—the one Dad gave me when I "flew up" from Brownies to Girl Scouts. Dad urged me to take the knife on this trip, but I knew I wasn't going to be at Camp Koa for long. "No worries, Dad." I told him. "I'd hate to lose it. Besides, it's not as if I'll be slashing my way through the jungle or anything."

Oh well, it's probably best; I wouldn't want to accidentally poke her. My hands are already shaking like crazy, and I've got to move fast. I don't know how long our bond's going to last.

I reach for the loose end of the bag, follow it up to the knot, finger the first place where the weave of the tangle has tightened and then pull, gently at first, to see if it budges. It does, but I need to get more aggressive.

"Okay, my friend. I'm going to get a little rough. Hang in there, okay?"

I send this idea to her in pictures, but I say the words because *I* need to hear them. Just then, she moves, stretching the other front flipper out in front of her. *Oh, no!* I remember this video of scuba divers cutting fishnets off a whale that went viral recently and send her that image linking it with the idea, *helping.* Apparently, she believes me or she's just getting comfortable, because she continues to lie very still as I tug and tug until finally, the bag breaks free.

"Hooray for honu!" I rest my hand on her flipper and feel a surge of relief—hers or mine—it doesn't matter.

Thankfully, it doesn't look like that stupid bag caused her any long-term harm. At least it won't hold her back from laying her eggs. I think of Buddy and his dead babies, and how no matter how much I tried to stay awake and help, it didn't work out. At least this psycho-telepathic-weirdness of mine has helped someone's life become less miserable. At least I don't have to play the "All My Fault" game. Hey. Maybe I could even play the "You Did Good" game. Wouldn't that be a relief? Dad would love that game.

Mama-honu turns and pulls herself in the direction of the water. I feel so happy. *I helped! I helped!* Then something catches my eye. A figure behind the thorny bush at the top of the knoll.

It's Aunty.

Frowning.

Not saying a word.

13.

Up a Tree

I'm up a tree.

I mean that both figuratively and literally.

People say "I'm up a tree" when they're feeling stuck, when they're in so much trouble, there's no way out. That's the figurative part and that sure is true for me. But I'm also up this coconut tree, the very same tree I climbed up yesterday when I got here.

Like yesterday, I don't know if I'll ever make it down.

Unlike yesterday, I don't care.

That's the literal part.

Nice view, though. The moon is waning, but still close to full. It tints the waves from shore to horizon, creating a shimmering road to who-knows-where. I wish I could go there. Anywhere but here.

So yeah, I'm up a tree, but it's the only place I could think of to get away from everything that's happening below. Problem is, it doesn't change a thing.

After Aunty yanked the trash bag out of my hand—the one that was dragging Mama Honu down—she gave me the silent treatment all the way back to camp. I was pretty sure I was in big trouble for touching that turtle, but I had no idea it was going to take away the very thing I came here to do.

"I'm sorry, Sophie Kai," Tūtū Malia said when she pulled me aside tonight after dinner and told me I'd lost my privilege to go to the seahorse farm. "I know you were just trying to help, but—"

"But I wasn't trying, Tūtū, I *did* help. I helped that honu get free of something that was hurting her." It felt like my head was going to explode with the injustice of it all. Adults have trashed this planet for eons, and when a young person tries to do something positive to clean up their royal mess, we get in trouble for it.

"I'd do it again, too," I snapped.

Tūtū pulled back in surprise. "But Sophie Kai, don't you see this isn't about the honu? This is about *you*. She might have bitten you. If a honu feels threatened, she'll protect herself. You could have lost a finger, maybe even your hand."

"But she wouldn't have hurt me," I said. "I asked her permission and she said 'yes.'"

My words came falling out of my stupid mouth before I realized I'd said too much.

"I mean, I felt like … we had a connection or something," I stuttered. But one look into Tūtū's eyes and I knew nothing I said from here on out was going to walk back my words.

She *knew*.

"It's okay, Sophie Kai," she finally said. "I wondered if you had inherited your great grandmother's gift, but it wasn't my place to pry. Now that you've shared this with me, well, it puts everything that happened today in a new light."

So, it's true, I thought, what Dad told me. Tūtū Malia knew my dad's grandma and I'm like her. Wow. My heart started pounding so hard right then, I thought it would thump right out of my chest. Now that Tūtū Malia knows I was just trying to help, I thought, she'll let me off the hook for sure and Mission Buddy will be back on track.

"I'm sorry, Sophie Kai," she said. "You're still grounded from the field trip. I know you had your heart set on it, but I'm afraid Aunty's right. We have rules here at Camp Koa and if we make an exception for one person ... well, you know how that goes."

She really did look sorry then, but all I felt was mad. So much for my telepathic weirdness putting things in a new light. If helping that honu didn't change anything, what difference did it make?

"This power you have, Sophie. It's a gift—one that I believe Tūtū Pele brought you here to explore." She said it like she just had tea with the goddess this morning and they'd been chatting about me. "Soon, we'll talk more about what this gift means to you and your life, but for now, Sophie, I believe you're here for a reason, and given how life works, probably more than one. It's not up to me to tell you what that is, however. It's up to *you* to find out."

Suddenly, I realize that my hands feel all prickly. Good thing this tree grew with enough slant, I can rest my weight against the uppermost part of its trunk and give my hands a rest. I shake them out as I think about what Tūtū said, about my being here for a reason. I wanted to tell her right then and there that finding a friend for Buddy *was* my reason, and that all I wanted was to do that and go home. I almost said it, too, but then, it was like she heard it anyway.

"You can leave anytime you want, Sophie Kai. No one's keeping you here. But you can never walk away from your gift. Your ability will grow whether you want it to or not, and then it will call and call until you answer."

"You mean, like I answered that call today?"

She nodded and smiled. "Yes. Like you did today."

"And this is what I get? I mean, *grounded?*"

"What you got, Sophie, was the joy of helping one of God's creatures live a better life. You might have even saved it. Isn't that enough?"

"But…"

"I know, I know. You paid a cost." She shrugged. "It happens."

Yeah, and you have the power to make that cost go away.

"Tell me, Sophie. Would you have made a different choice if you had known you'd lose your chance to go to the seahorse farm?"

After I freed Mama Honu's flipper from the trash bag, a feeling had rushed through me—a sense of relief mixed with gratitude so strong, there should be a separate word for it—and I knew that was coming from her. But then this other feeling washed over me, too, a humongous wave of humility. I knew I was in the presence of greatness, and I had helped that greatness, and all I ever wanted to do from here on out was help that greatness. It was like there was nothing left of me and all that mattered was the life of that mama honu and her eggs.

"No," I finally said. "I would still help."

"That's what I thought." She patted me on the shoulder before heading over to the fire circle. "If it's any consolation, I would have, too."

I felt good then—maybe even proud—for a few fleeting seconds, until I realized that Mission Buddy had just been dashed against the rocks. Why hadn't Tūtū made a choice to use her power to keep me from being grounded? Why wasn't she answering *that* call?

From where I now sit—make that, hang—I watch as Tūtū Malia walks around the fire circle, chatting it up with all the other campers, and all I want to do is slip down this trunk and run as far away from Camp Koa as I can get. But that's the thing about an island. You can only run so far. Which is, once again, why I'm up this tree.

Apparently, Keola had been watching the drama between me and Tūtū at the picnic table and came over to check on me after she left. He sat down on the picnic bench and leaned in. "What's up, Sophie girl?"

When I told him about being grounded, he said, "Oh man, that sucks," but then he got all business-like. He said stuff like,

"Mission Buddy is still on" and that this "bump in the road" only meant "it was time to pivot," like we were in a spy movie or something. He even offered to go to the seahorse farm and pick out Buddy's friend for me. "It's not the same I know, but I bet I can pick a good one," he said. His face was so open and hopeful.

That's when I started to lose it—not just because Mission Buddy was a bust—but because no one my age had ever been so kind to me before.

"Keola, I'm so sorry. The whole point of me coming to Camp Koa was to use this stupid weirdness of mine to find the *perfect* friend for Buddy. Not just some stand-in for the lifelong mate he lost because of me." The idea that it was *all my fault* hit me once again, and I started to cry.

Keola just sat there next to me, quiet and still. He looked all prism-like through my tears. "You have a weirdness, too?" he whispered.

I froze in mid-sob. Drat. I just gave my secret away *again* for the second time today, but then I thought, *wait*. "You have a weirdness?" I asked, wiping the snot off my nose with the back of my hand.

He nodded. "I pick up on things, mostly from people."

"What kind of things?"

He shrugged. "I guess you could say their intentions—like what they're hoping to do or what they think they want. I can tell if they want to be helpful or if they're up to no good. That's the one I hate. When I pick up on those no-good thoughts, it feels kind of yucky."

"Wow."

"Yeah, Mom says it's a gift." There's that word again. "But sometimes I wish I didn't have it. I mean, what am I supposed to do when I sense somebody's about to cause trouble? Call the police? I don't think so. I mean, I'm just some stupid kid."

Just then, Uncle had hollered for us to join the circle. I told Keola to go ahead without me, that I needed some time to be alone and think, which is how I ended up in this tree.

Yup. Just me and the coconuts.

I'm high enough to see out over the sandy knolls and high brush that cover the ground from here to the beach. A light breeze rattles the palm fronds overhead, like a loud whisper trying to get my attention, and I look towards the sea. My eye is immediately drawn to a shadowy movement, a disturbance in the glittery path of waves breaking on shore. I squint but it's impossible to make out what it is. That is, until I get slammed with a sonic blast of recognition that almost knocks me out of the tree. That blob of a shadow is someone I know. Mama Honu. Full and anxious. Longing for a dark place. A safe place. Longing to nest.

I watch her drag her body across the sand with a single destination in mind. She's headed for that knoll—*our* knoll—not for the pool but for the soft sand that surrounds it, easy for digging. I lose sight of her in some tall grass, but it doesn't matter; I can tell she's closing in fast, propelled by the heaviness of those big, rounded eggs ready to drop.

"Hey, Sophie Girl..." Breaking my connection, Keola's voice drifts up the tree.

"Hey," I answer softly, shaking my hands out one at a time to get the circulation going again. Clearly, it's way past time to climb down.

"Just thought I'd come by to see if you needed any help. Nalu thought you might be here. He wanted to come, but I said, 'No, let me.'" All I can see is the back of Keola's dark, round head, as he shuffles sand around with his feet.

"That's nice," I say, thinking how strange it is that not one, but two boys seem to be concerned about me.

Just then, I get a niggle to look out at the beach again. Two thin beams of light are swaying back and forth along the shoreline, connected to two shadowy figures moving toward the very spot Mama Honu is heading. They are a ways off, and it might just be two kids looking for shells, but...

"Keola. Spot me. I'm coming down."

"Oh my gosh, Sophie Kai. Be careful!"

Keola starts circling the tree with his arms open wide like he's prepared to catch me—a sight that would normally make me laugh if it weren't for this sense of urgency pushing me down the trunk—legs-arms-legs-arms, like a caterpillar speed-crawling backwards. When I land, Keola's all "way to go" and "oh my gosh" and "that was amazing" until I shush him.

"Keola," I tug at his arm. "We need to get down to the beach ... *fast*."

14.

'Aumakua

"How close do you need to be for that 'gift' of yours to work?" I whisper to Keola as we rush down the moonlit path.

Keola stops for a minute to catch his breath. "If you're asking, *Do I feel something out there?* the answer's 'yes' and it's not good. Which brings me to what the heck are we doing running *towards* it?"

"Sorry, Keola. I have no clue. It's just a feeling I have. Dad would call it a niggle. And…"

"And?"

"I'm pretty sure it has something to do with Mama Honu and some lights I saw on the beach while I was up the tree."

"Oh, geez, Sophie. Aren't you in enough trouble already?"

"Hey, you know what it's like to have a strong feeling about something, right?"

"Yeah, you mean, like the feeling I'm getting right now that we should head straight back to camp?" He shrugs and laughs. "Aw, come on. Clearly, your 'aumakua's calling and won't let you go."

"Auma… *what?*"

"'*Aumakua*. Ancestor spirit. A guide and protector, remember? Tūtū Malia talked about it earlier today. The honu seems to be yours."

Oh yeah, now I remember. I thought she was talking about stuff that happened in legends, not anything that matters to us now.

We climb a knoll that's high enough to see the ocean and outlying landscape. The shadowy figures with the flashlights are still near the shoreline and have come to a stop. "Hey, maybe they're digging for crabs," I say, hoping it's true.

"Yeah, maybe … but I don't think so." Keola rubs his arms like he's got a sudden chill. "Those guys are looking for something; I'm not sure what. They're not evil exactly, just … selfish." Keola leans his head in their direction, like he's adjusting an inner antenna.

"Uh-oh."

"Uh-oh, what?"

"Uh-oh, they're desperate. Never good. People do awful things when they're desperate, even if they're not awful people. We better get off this hill and out of sight … like *now*." He pushes me gently in front of him and back to the path.

A few minutes later, I see the pool up ahead, the place where I took a nap. At first, she's hard to spot, not only because it's dark, but because she's nestled into the sand, shell deep. I stick my arm out to keep Keola from stepping on her.

"Yikes," Keola yelps but then slaps a hand over his mouth. We listen for any tell-tale sounds of those creepy guys, but everything's quiet around us.

At first, I think Mama Honu is resting, but then my eyes adjust to the surrounding shadows, and I see she's hovering over a dark hole where she's laid a huge pile of glistening white eggs, each about the size of a ping pong ball.

"Oh my gosh," Keola gasps, "she's really doing it!"

I can barely nod. I'm so overwhelmed by seeing this thing that usually happens in secret and for some reason, I get to be here. Keola and I look at each other and smile. For a moment, we forget there's anything to worry about.

Mama Honu isn't worried either. Her eyes are glazed over like she's in a trance, not with pain like you might think, but with focus. It's taking everything's she's got to lay those eggs. *Plop ... plop, plop.* Three more join dozens of others and it seems like they're the last. Good thing, too, because she seems exhausted.

But then, just when I think she might nap—and I mean, who wouldn't?—she comes out of her zoned-out state and starts rocking her heavy-shelled body from side to side with a soft *thump-thump, thump-thump,* causing the surrounding sand to cascade into the hole beneath her. Back flippers get into the act, kicking and sweeping, and before you know it, those bright, shiny eggs have disappeared completely out of sight. Finally, she rests, and it's a good thing, too, because we can hear those men's voices coming closer.

"Sophie Kai," Keola whispers urgently. "I'm going to try to keep these guys away from us, but you've got to ask our friend to stay right where she is."

"Why? What's going on?"

"Not sure, but I'm afraid she might be the target." Keola shoots me a look and puts his index finger over his lips.

The creepy guys have already made it to the other side of the knoll. I can tell because I'm starting to make out what they're saying. For now, we're hidden by tall grasses and shrubs, but all they'd have to do is climb that hill and they'd be looking right down on us.

In between their chatter, I can hear them jabbing at the sand with sticks or maybe a shovel, like they're looking for something. My whole body goes into high alert, but I talk myself into remaining calm for Mama Honu's sake. I can tell she's starting to feel anxious to head back to sea. The call is so strong, I'm not sure I can stop her.

Staying about six feet away, I focus on her slow beating, worn-out heart, and try to sync up with it by making my own heart as quiet as possible, even though it wants to pound its way out of my chest. I send her thought-feelings:

Still.

Rest.

Stay.

"I told you already, we're too early for dis," one guy snaps at his buddy. "I could be shootin' pool over in Hilo right now."

"Aw, shut up. I for sure saw one crawlin' up here earlier. We should be able to see tracks."

Oh my gosh, they *are* after Mama Honu. I grab Keola's arm, but he ignores me.

"Yeah, yeah, brah, I get it. You want to catch 'em in da act," the one dude answers his buddy, "but you heard da Boss. He says wait 'til there's no more moon. Says da ancestors won't get huhū then."

"You stupid. He's just using that mumbo jumbo to keep you quiet."

"Oh yeah? My Tūtū's always telling us, no mess with ancestors. Says dis beach is full of 'em. She every time talk story about people who mess with 'em—like dey get thrown into hot lava, dat kinda thing."

I cringe, but Keola keeps his head down.

"You, wuss." The other laughs. "You gonna let some Tūtū scare you from some big money?"

"Eh, shut your mouth. No talk about my Tūtū like that." There's some scuffling as the tall grass around them bends and sways. "And no talk about the ancestors like dat. I swear you got 'em all huhū—you feel *dat*?! Brah, I getting chicken skin!"

They both go silent.

Meanwhile, Mama Honu lifts her head up and I hold my breath. She hangs there like she's trying to decide whether or not to bolt. That's not something honu are very good at, I remind her, but she senses the danger and wants to flee.

Yes, danger, I agree, meeting her where she's at, followed by, *Stay. Stay now.* I send her an image of the eggs she just laid and how we need to protect them.

Thankfully, she rests her head on the sand again, and I slowly let out the breath I've been holding. Keola hasn't moved a muscle.

Finally, the other guy says, "Yeah, okay ... I still no believe your mumbo-jumbo, but waiting another week can't hurt. We'll come back when da moon gets dark. We go, brah."

As their mumbling fades away, I let my body relax and gaze at Mama Honu in the faint moonlight. Her eyes are closed. Apparently, she's decided it's safe enough to nap.

I turn to Keola. "Did you do that?"

He shakes himself like he's waking from a bad dream. "Do what?"

"You know, freak those guys out and make them go away?"

He shrugs. "Who knows? Maybe? Mom taught me how to do this *thing*."

"Yeah, what *thing*? Come on, Keola, this is serious. Those guys were after Mama Honu, or maybe her eggs ... or both."

"Okay, okay." He rubs his eyes. "It's simple, really. First, you gather up the energy around you." He says this like he's talking about picking up a few books to stuff in his backpack. "You know … energy from the land, the ocean, the ancestors. Of course, you need to ask permission first."

"Of course." I haven't a clue what he's talking about.

"I would have grabbed your energy, too, but I figured you needed it for our friend here. Besides, I didn't think you'd give me permission."

"Darn right," I say, trying to make light of something that was kind of freaking me out. "Soooooo … then what do you do?"

"You send up a barrier. You kind of project that energy outward with your mind." He stretches his arms above his head. "But who knows? Maybe it was something else." He laughs and his whole belly shakes. "Hey, maybe it was Tūtū Pele. Heck, maybe it was the honu. Right now, all that matters is those dudes are *gone*."

"Yeah, right," I say, but I know what we're both thinking.

Not for long.

15.

Aloha ʻĀina

I want to believe we saved Mama Honu from something awful, but I can't shake the feeling that it's temporary. Those thugs were after something, and they seemed determined to come back. Last night—two nights after Mama Honu laid her eggs—the moon was a little less than quarter full. In another week, the moon will go dark—still there, of course, but without light. What will happen then? And what could I possibly do about it, even if I wanted to?

Feeling hopeless, I watched everybody squeeze into the "Camp Koa Express"—what Uncle likes to call this rickety old, passenger van—all excited about their field trip to the seahorse farm. Climbing into the seat by Uncle with the demon rooster Moa tucked under her arm, Aunty turned around and smiled at me. "Have a good day," she said.

As they pulled out of the driveway, Keola kept wiggling that shaka sign at me out the van's back window. "Everything has a way of working out, Sophie Kai," he'd told me earlier, gulping down his breakfast of scrambled eggs and rice. "You'll see."

Yeah, like things are really working out. I wipe a sweaty wad of hair from my forehead with the sleeve of my Camp Koa T-shirt. While everyone else is off to the seahorse races, I've been stuck skimming ooey-gooey green algae off the surface of a nearby pond and slopping it into buckets. Tūtū Malia works by my side—probably to make sure I don't run off and endanger the lives of other island species. She insists that it's our *privilege* to be doing this work. "We're expressing our *aloha 'aina*—our love for the land," she says. "Everything needs to breathe, Sophie Kai. It's our kuleana—our responsibility—to help keep the pond breathing."

Right about now, I wish I weren't. Breathing, that is. Up to my gloved elbows in bright green gunk, I smell like the inside of an abandoned fish tank.

It's still morning when we see a car pull onto the side road that leads to Camp Koa. Tūtū raises her head from her work. "We better go see who that is." We rinse our gloves in the pond and tug them off, as we walk quickly up the path to camp.

The last person on earth I expect to see getting out of the passenger side of the car is Wilks, and she looks absolutely *beat*—stooped over, head hanging. Her skin is sickly white. I say it before I can think it, "Gosh, Wilks, you look terrible. It's like you saw a ghost or something."

She glares at me before falling into Tūtū Malia's arms.

❀ ❀ ❀

Turns out I was right. Wilks *did* see a ghost. Make that, *many*.

And turns out the Camp Koa crew never got to go to the seahorse farm because a major water pipe broke down unexpectedly and the tour was postponed. I was thrilled to hear this, of course—Mission Buddy is now back on track and maybe I can get out of here soon—but my excitement didn't last long when I saw how royally messed up Wilks was.

According to Wilks, after they were told the tour was canceled, Uncle and Aunty decided to take the kids to an ancient battleground where hundreds of years ago two warring factions of islanders had fought to their deaths. Apparently, the ghosts of some of those warriors started clamoring for Wilks' attention, whereupon she freaked out, ran back to the bus, and threw up. Thinking she was sick, Uncle called Aloha Cab to take her back to camp while the rest continued their field trip. Wilks is rattling off this story at breakneck speed until I stop her.

"Wait! Ghosts? Are you *crazy?*"

Wilks turns to Tūtū Malia. "Do I have to explain this to her?"

"What's important right now," Tūtū says patiently, "is for you to tell us everything that's troubling you, Leilani." Tūtū guides the three of us to a picnic table.

"Nobody won," Wilks keeps muttering, shaking her head. "Nobody *won.*"

"I know, Leilani, I know," Tūtū says softly, "but, sweet girl, that battle is long over."

"But it's *not*!" Wilks sobs as she breaks from Tūtū's arms. "That's just it. Everyone from Camp Koa was climbing around this battlefield, joking around, while all these voices were slamming through my head about how angry they were—*still* are—at each other. Everyone wanted me to know their side of things. It was if they'd been waiting to tell somebody for hundreds of years.

"They wanted me to take sides, Tūtū, but when I refused, they turned their backs on me—not that they have backs to turn, but that's what it felt like—like they were cutting me off. You'd think that would be a good thing since I didn't want to hear them in the first place, but it hurt, Tūtū, like how it would feel if my own grandmother refused to see me. It hurt like that."

Wilks takes a big, gulping breath. "Those people who fought in that battle? It's not over for *them*. They're stuck in this horrible nightmare hundreds of years after they died, because they keep thinking they're going to win and that their anger is going to make a difference." She slams her hands against the picnic table punctuating her next words: "It. Makes. No. Sense."

All it takes is one look at Wilk's face to know she's not making this stuff up. If this is the kind of thing she picks up on, no wonder she spends so much time hiding under her hoodie. It's hard sometimes when I feel an animal's terror or pain, but what must it be like to feel the anger of people who are already dead?

I lean around Tūtū and touch Wilks on the arm. "Wilks ... I mean, Leilani. I'm sorry for what I said earlier. This thing that happened to you ... it sounds really *scary*."

"Yes," she sniffs. "It was ... and still *is*." She wipes her runny nose on her shirt sleeve and sends me a weak smile. "Keola and I were excited when we heard the tour got postponed. We knew you'd be happy about it."

I nod and smile. I can't believe she's thinking about *me* after the horror she's been through. Next to my psycho-telepathic-weirdness, hers is at least one-hundred times worse.

Later, we're finishing up lunch, when both Tūtū Malia and Wilks get this startled look on their faces. "You feel them, too?" Tūtū asks Wilks who nods. Tūtū turns to me. "The ancestors are calling us down to the beach."

Wilks holds her head in her hands. "More like *screaming*."

"Why?" I ask, like this kind of thing happens all the time. Actually, I'm hoping for some reassurance that we're not walking into an ambush of ghosts.

Tūtū shakes her head. "Don't know, Sophie Kai. But when the ancestors call, it's our kuleana to answer." There's that word again.

"Leilani," Tūtū whispers to Wilks who's still holding her head in her hands like it hurts. "Before we head down to the beach, you need to listen to me." She gently lifts Wilk's chin so she can look her straight in the eyes.

"You know how those ghosts wanted you to take sides? Well, when a spirit's communicating with you, what you always need to remember is what side *you're* on—the side of the living. If a spirit gets too demanding or too weird, you can always shut the door between the worlds. That's your choice and no one else's. We kūpuna call that having good boundaries.

"Most of the time, though, we can trust that the ancestors are calling us for something important—either for their protection, ours, or the land's. That's why it's good to listen *first*, before you decide whether to shut that door. If you take the time to really listen, Leilani, you can tell what kind of call it is. It just takes a little practice, and that's what you're here at Camp Koa to do." She turns to me. "That's what we're *all* here to do … *practice*."

Wilks shakes her head vigorously, as if she might shake all the voices out. Tūtū grabs her by the hand. "Come on now … shhhhh … stop blocking them for just a minute and listen. It's safe, I promise." Wilks takes a deep breath and closes her eyes. "There," Tūtū whispers, "can you hear them?"

Slowly, Wilks nods.

"Good. Now tell the ancestors respectfully but firmly through your thoughts, 'We hear you' and 'We're on our way.'"

Wilks nods again.

Tūtū lets go of her hand and leans back. "There, is that better?"

Wilks takes one more deep breath and stands up. "Yes, Tūtū, let's go."

"Alrighty then," I say, wondering if this day could get any weirder, but the two of them have already tossed their lunch plates into the sink and are heading down the path to the beach.

As I follow, I think about those thugs roaming the beach last night, and before that, those nosy tourists wanting to mess with the sea turtles, and before that, those fish flip-flopping their way up that flooded street in Hilo, and suddenly, I'm overwhelmed with dread. Forget those ancient battles. Seems like everywhere I look, the whole island is under siege.

And it's happening *now*.

16.

Hearing Voices

We hear it before we see it. The whirring grind of machinery, a sharp, pounding sound, and then something shatters. The noise all but drowns out the crash of waves on shore. Once we hit the beach and we see what's going on, the three of us break into a run, barefoot.

About a hundred yards off, a man is operating a bright yellow excavator, digging at the base of a long promontory. Once he grabs a full load of large, jagged rocks, he swings the machine around and steers it toward a pile in the dense brush. There are a handful of spectators standing on the beach watching, while others are up on the rock wall of the promontory looking down. A few of them are shouting. No one looks happy.

This *must* be what the ancestors are all up in arms about.

Tūtū Malia groans as we draw near. "Girls, stand behind me," she yells when we're just feet away from the digging. "Let me do the talking. You're supporting the ancestors just by being here." And then she does something incredibly brave—or colossally stupid, as my mom might say—and stands in the path of the machine, waving her arms above her head, shouting, "Hey, hey, hey! What you think you're doin'?!"

The guy looks like a brute. I'm pretty sure he could take on the whole crowd if he wanted, but he brings his machine to a stop six feet in front of Tūtū. He revs the engine at full throttle, a deafening sound that has Wilks and me shoving fingers in our ears while Tūtū just stands there, staring him down.

Taking off his sunglasses, he slowly pulls up the edge of his T-shirt to wipe the sweat off his face, like he has all day. Finally, to our great relief, he shuts off the engine.

"What's up, Tūtū?" he says into the resounding silence.

"You the one who needs to answer dat question, Haku." Tūtū's face looks determined.

Wilks and I exchange looks. *She knows the guy.* She's also slipped into talking pidgin—a way native Hawaiians often talk to each other. Even Dad talks like that sometimes, especially if he's mad.

"I no need answer nobody," the guy says. "I'm just putting in a dock for my boat to take tourists see the lava flow. The owners gave permission to do dis, Tūtū. They the ones who own the land."

"Not the heiau," she says pointing to the end of the promontory, the place Aunty told us about before our swim test. "And not these *pōhaku*, these rocks. This land belongs to the ancestors no matter who holds the deed." She pauses, then shakes her head. "They not happy 'bout what you doing." Some of the folks standing around watching the drama throw in an occasional, "Yeah!" or "You tell 'em!" But mostly, they let Tūtū do the talking.

"Those landowners, as you call them, are using you, Haku, you no see that? They use you to test us locals, to see how we act. They hope we sleeping. They hope our ancestors no longer matter to us, so they can come build their resorts and restaurants and spas and destroy this fragile beach forever. Your little dock? Here today, gone tomorrow, if you play into their hands."

For a moment, Tūtū lets her head fall to her chest, as if she's just used up every ounce of energy in her. But then, she raises her fierce gaze again to meet his eyes. "Those resort folks are hoping we asleep and stay asleep. Is dat what you like, Haku? Or you going hope for something more better ... for all of us?"

I think this guy must be getting mad about being told what to do by this short, bossy woman, but he just sits there on the machine, hanging his head. "Oh, Tūtū..." he finally moans. "What I supposed to do? I got no job 'cept fishing for feed my 'ohana. Where are the ancestors when I need *them*?"

"Where's your kuleana, Haku? Remember what I taught you all those years ago when you were still a boy?"

"Yeah, dat was when I believed in dat stuff. Before I had keiki who get hungry."

Tūtū doesn't say another word. She just stands there. Like a tree. Like a rock. Her thin brown feet sunk into the sand. Nobody else moves either. I have this strange impulse to link arms with

Wilks and so I do, and it doesn't feel funny at all. It feels right, standing together with our Tūtū, standing for our ancestors, and maybe for Haku and his family, too.

A moment, a breath, a wave or two against the shore later and something shifts, like the island itself has let out a sigh. Wilks breaks out smiling and I wonder if she's hearing voices again.

Haku lets out a little laugh. "You always knew how to get to me, Tūtū. Take care da land and da land take care you, you used to say."

"I still say it, Haku. And you still know it."

As he starts up the excavator and swings the shovel away from the rocks, Haku shakes his head like he can't believe he's giving up on his plan. When I think about his hungry kids, I wonder how much courage it must take for him to do the right thing and quit.

Tūtū yells above the engine's rumble, "No worry, Haku! Everything going to work out for you and your 'ohana, you'll see," an echo of what Keola said to me this morning.

With his back to the crowd, Haku gives a half-hearted wave before he heads towards the entrance road.

"Girls?" Tūtū puts a hand on each of our shoulders. "Before we head back to camp, we need to pay a visit to the ancestors to thank them for this opportunity to answer their call."

A terrified look passes over Wilks' face.

"Not to worry," Tūtū adds quickly. "We're catching them on a good day."

She guides us to the end of the promontory to the ancient burial place where presumably the ancestors are hanging out. Wilks and I sit on a rock, while a few feet away, Tūtū faces out to sea, chanting. Her strong voice blends with the waves pounding against the shore, as if they accompany each other.

"Are you okay?" I finally whisper to Wilks after the chanting comes to a quiet end. "This day's been kind of intense, huh?"

"Ha! No kidding. But yeah, I'm good."

"Any voices?"

"Strangely, no. Just this feeling of … calm."

Tūtū's face is radiant as she joins us on the rock. "Yes, my 'ohana, that's *it*. Breathe in that calm." She closes her eyes and takes a deep breath. "Can you feel it? The ancestors are so grateful!"

Sometimes, I struggle to feel something when I know other people want me to feel it, but this time, it's different. I don't have to close my eyes or even take a deep breath to know what Tūtū's talking about. It's like every cell in my body is expanding to receive this really big hug.

"That's aloha, my friends. The ancestors are opening their arms to you." Tūtū takes our hands and looks lovingly into our faces. "They're saying … you *belong*."

kuleana

17.
Sibling Rivalry

Tonight's dinner was fish again with rice and fried, purple, sweet potatoes. I've never eaten a purple-anything, but this veggie was crisp, tender, and a tiny bit sweet—even better than the sweet potato fries back home. Even Wilks ate them, and I haven't seen her eat much of anything since we arrived.

It's weird, but Wilks and I have been kind of hanging out all afternoon since the ancestor thing—even after all the Koa kids came back from their battlefield adventure. I think it's because we shared this experience that no one else at camp knows about yet. We haven't even told Keola. Getting called by the ancestors isn't something you go around bragging about, I guess. It just wouldn't feel right.

Anyway, Wilks and I are among the first to arrive at the fire circle tonight so we can grab our favorite log—the one directly across from where Tūtū usually sits to talk story. When Keola ambles over a few minutes later, I guess he sees us whispering and giggling, and takes a leap backwards, making a show of rubbing his eyes hard. "Whaaaaat?! I can't believe my eyes! You two look like you're 'ohana or something!" And then he ever-so-gently sits his weighty-self down, making a show of giving us plenty of room.

"Okay, Koa campers," Tūtū taps her walking stick. "Where did we leave Tūtū Pele when we talked story last time?"

"She was being chased across the ocean by her evil stepsister!" Honi blurts out.

"Well, yes and no, Honi. This is not a Cinderella story." Tūtū smiles. "Tūtū Pele was being chased by her elder sister, Nā-maka-o-kahaʻi, who was jealous of how their father had favored Pele, but that didn't make her evil." Tūtū pauses. "How many of you have a sibling?" Lots of hands go up.

I never know how to answer this question. I keep my hand down by my side.

"Has anyone ever heard of sibling rivalry? That's when kids who are related are always fighting to get the upper hand, to prove they're faster or smarter or stronger or more deserving of their parents' love. Sibling rivalry happens in a lot of families," Tūtū adds matter-of-factly.

My face flashes hot at this, and it's not from the campfire. I think about Baby Girl and how jealous I was when Mom and Dad brought her home from the hospital. I threw a hissy fit when they told me I had to share my room with her. They said it was going to be fun being a big sister, that I'd get to show Baby Girl how to climb trees and build sandcastles and stuff, but I still didn't buy it. Give it time, they said. "She'll grow on you, Sophie Kai. You'll see," Dad said.

It's hard to admit, but there were times when Baby Girl first came home, I wished she hadn't been born. And then she died. Did my wishing make it happen? I've wondered that a lot.

Just when I feel like running and climbing a tree again, Wilks grabs my hand. A feeling of calm moves through me from head to toe, not unlike what we felt earlier today at the heiau.

Stay, her firm but comforting grip seems to say.

"So yes, Honi," Tūtū continues, "Tūtū Pele's sister chased her across the ocean, kicking up storms all along the way, until they came to the northern most Hawaiian island, Kauai. Believe me, no one was ever happier to see land than Tūtū Pele that day. She thought she had found her new home.

"But, no sooner does Tūtū Pele dig a deep pit for her sacred fire, than her sea sister conjures up this humongous wave and drowns it out." Tūtū Malia's arms suddenly fly up over her head as she shouts, "WHOOSH!"

"Well, Tūtū Pele grabs up her digging stick and with her egg sister, Hi'iaka, still tucked safely under her arm, she heads south to the island of Oahu. And there, she starts digging again. At first, she thinks she's done it; she's found the place her sister cannot reach. But *then*, what do you suppose happens?"

"WHOOSH!" Honi shouts as he stands up, arms raised.

"Yes!" Tūtū exclaims.

"WHOOSH!" Honi shouts again, this time with two of his buddies.

"*WHOOSH!*" Uncle jumps up joining them, arms over head, followed by Keola, Luana, Nalu and all the rest.

"*WHOOSH!*" Wilks and I join in because, well, it looks like *fun*—kind of like doing the wave at a Mariner's baseball game.

"Well!" Tūtū slaps her knee. "Do you think this stops our Tūtū Pele from searching for home? No! She picks up her digging stick one more time—and with her egg sister in tow—off she goes to the island of Maui where, of course, she starts digging another pit for her fire."

"And then what happens, Tūtū?" Honi shouts across the circle.

"What do you think?" Tūtū asks with a twinkle in her eye.

"*WHOOSH!*" everyone shouts, leaping up off their logs, arms flying up and down all around the circle like one big crashing wave.

"Yes, that's right…" Tūtū pauses for a few seconds with a somber look on her face, waiting for us to settle down. "Only this time, it ends very differently. It's a fight to the death, I'm afraid."

"But Tūtū Pele can't *die*," Luana whispers.

"Oh, but she does." Tūtū pauses, letting us take that in. "Except … death isn't the end of her. With the death of her mortal self, Pele's spirit could now be free. Even though she was an ancestral spirit before the fight, her death turned her into a goddess with eternal life. Pretty cool, huh?"

Honi's nodding like a bobblehead doll. Me? I can't believe Tūtū has forgotten to tell us what happened to Hi'iaka.

"What happened to Pele's *other* sister?" I blurt out, startled at the sound of my own voice. "You know, her sister, the egg? What with all that fighting, she could have been smashed to pieces." My face feels like it's on fire.

"Never fear, Sophie Kai." Tūtū rises to her feet and takes a step in my direction. "Hiʻiaka must have had a thick shell because she's still alive. And now that Tūtū Pele's been transformed into a goddess, she scoops up her little egg sister and escapes to the last island on their difficult journey. And what island do you suppose that is, my dear ʻohana?"

"This one!" Nalu shouts.

"That's right, this one! Our beloved Hawaiʻi. This is where Tūtū Pele finds *home*."

Tūtū's so close to me now, I can see the fire's flames reflected in her eyes. "Pele climbs up, up, up to the top of Mauna Loa," she continues, "way higher than her sea sister can possibly reach. Once there, she digs the deepest crater she's ever made with her mighty stick. And *that's* where Pele's sacred fire resides to this day. Sometimes that fire rises up as red, hot lava. Sometimes it flows down the mountain, and sometimes, it even flows out to the sea where the forces of Tūtū Pele, the fire goddess, and Nā-maka-o-kahaʻi, the sea goddess, clash again."

Honi and his buddies make more wooshing sounds, but I don't participate. Neither does Wilks. I think she senses my anxiety about Tūtū Pele's little sister. When the boys finally settle down, Wilks asks Tūtū, "What happened to Hi'iaka?"

"She *hatched*," Tūtū says brightly, "which makes her the only god or goddess native to Hawai'i by birth, although we consider Tūtū Pele native, too, since she *became* a goddess here."

"So, they lived happily ever after, right, Tūtū?" Keola stifles a yawn.

"Well ... not *exactly*."

"Oh, noooooo!" Honi smacks his forehead with the flat of his hand.

"Sorry, friends." Tūtū leans on her stick. "Now that Hi'iaka is hatched, well, let's just say things were easier between her and Tūtū Pele when she was an egg."

Geez. Just this once, I'd like to hear a happy ending between sisters.

Like the happy ending I never got to have.

This last thought starts a downhill slide into a confusing mishmash of mad and sad—much like how I felt the whole year after Baby Girl died. Mad and sad that I never got to know her. Mad and sad that I'm here and not home. Mad and sad at Mom and Dad. I miss them, but why in the heck were they so anxious for me to go?

"Go on, now, my keiki." Tūtū stands up. "Time for bed. We'll pick up where we left off tomorrow night."

"There she goes again, leaving us hanging." Wilks laughs as she rises from the log, offering me a hand up.

"Sounds like more of the same to me." My words come out snippy, but I can't seem to help it. "One sister has something the other sister wants. They fight. Someone gets hurt, and they never speak to each other again. Where's the suspense in that?"

"Whoa, sounds like you've got something against sisters," Wilks says quietly as we walk towards our sleeping hut.

"How would I know?"

"You're a sister," she whispers.

"Past tense. I *was* a sister."

18.

My Sister, the Egg

I can't sleep.

I'm feeling guilty about being so snippy at Wilks. And then there are those stories about Tūtū Pele and her sisters. They've got me all churned up. Every time I'm about to drift off, I feel like I'm falling off a cliff, and I startle myself awake before I land.

This last time, though, I fall all the way down and land in the middle of a dream with that annoying little girl again. This time, she's pulling out my hair one strand at a time, chanting, *Wake up, sleepyhead! Wake up!* There's something vaguely familiar about her, particularly how irritating she is. *Who are you?!* I snap. I'm on the verge of recognition when my eyes pop open.

It's pitch dark in our hut, but the shadow in front of me is unmistakable. It's Moa, his beady little eyes staring straight into mine.

"Go away, you little demon," I whisper under my breath, but he just keeps staring. Okay, that's *it*. I throw back the sheets, pull on some shorts with my T-shirt, and slip out of the hut before I strangle a rooster and wake everyone up.

There's a hammock strung between two coconut trees down by the freshwater pond, but when I get there, someone's already in it. Tonight's quarter moon is behind a cloud so I can't make out who it is. I'm about to turn back when the shadow speaks.

"It's okay, Sophie, it's me." Wilks flips herself to a sitting position.

"Hey," I say quietly as I slip into the hammock beside her.

The slope of the netting on both sides causes us to lean into each other, no matter how much I try to keep some space between us. It's futile of course—it's a freakin' hammock—so I give up and shuffle my bare feet in step with hers, three steps forward, three steps back. Leaves rattle in the breeze above us, a loud sort of whispering, as if the palms are telling secrets. As always, there's a flowery scent in the air, so thick you'd swear you were wearing it.

"Sorry about earlier," I tell her. "I don't know what came over me."

"I do," she says quietly. "It's…"

She pauses, and in that pause, I know who the girl in my dreams is. I also know what Wilks is about to say.

It's like what some kids must feel right before their parents tell them they're getting a divorce, or like that awful morning Mom and Dad came back from the hospital, when I heard the front door open and close, but before they walked into my room. *That* moment. The one before everything changes.

"It's Baby Girl, isn't it?" I say it before she can. "She's … *here*."

I suddenly realize how crazy that sounds and I want to take it all back. But Wilks has seen and heard crazier things, and she simply nods.

Suddenly, everything falls together—like how Wilks kept looking over my left shoulder on the plane, and how she said she could tell my sister liked hanging out with me, and how mad I felt at her use of the present tense, because I thought, *That's not possible*, even though I wished it were. And now, these dreams I've been having about that pesky little girl always trying to get my attention. They make me feel like I did that night Baby Girl cried, and I tried to ignore her—how irritated I was. The memory still burns.

As the awareness continues to settle in, a gazillion questions rise: *Oh-my-gosh-she's alive … or is she? Why isn't she in heaven? Why has she decided to show up now? What does she want?* I'm having trouble catching my breath.

"Oh my gosh, Wilks. Am I *possessed*?"

"Steady now." Wilks pats my arm. "You are *not* possessed … at least I don't think so."

"Oooo-kaaay…"

Wilks shifts in the hammock. The moon now casts enough light for me to see her face. "Look, from what I can tell, your sister's spirit has kind of *attached* itself to you. I don't know why; she's not talking. But I do know that she can't make you do anything you don't want to do, and I'm pretty sure this isn't forever. Tūtū says spirits usually attach themselves to a person for a reason. Once that reason is met, they move on."

"Then … why? Why *now*?"

The question hangs in the thick night air. And then it hits me like one of those ocean waves that sends you tumbling. "She's mad at me," I say. "That's it. She's mad that I didn't get my parents when I heard her crying. For being such a terrible sister. For letting her … *die*."

There. I said it. Tears fill my eyes as I think about that night, how I held the pillow over my head so I wouldn't hear her crying. A few hot tears fall, but I swipe them away. "She's been pestering me in my dreams because she wants me to know it's all my fault. And you know what? It *is*. I deserve to be haunted."

Wilks plants her feet on the ground, and we rock to a stop.

"Okay, that's enough, Sophie Kai. You stop right there with this 'aren't I awful' crap. I don't know much about this ridiculous gift I have, but I do know that if Baby Girl was mad, I'd know it. Besides, you don't need anyone else haunting you. You're doing just fine by yourself."

I hook my fingers into the netting. "Then … *why*? It's been over four years since she died. Why in the world did she attach herself to me *now*?"

Wilks shrugs herself out of the hammock. "Maybe she wanted a Hawaiian vacation?"

"This isn't funny."

"I wasn't trying to be."

19.
Getting what I want

Maybe it's this idea that my dead sister is hanging out with me that's got me in a funk. I mean, I'm glad to know Baby Girl is still with us—that life goes on and all that—but what am I supposed to do with this information anyway? It's not as if we can go build sandcastles together or have a sisterly chat about our secrets. And if Baby Girl's hanging out with me for the thrill of it, then I must be a huge disappointment.

I've done absolutely nothing exciting over the last few days unless you count crawling through lava tubes, which I don't. All I got were skinned knees. And certainly, shimmying up coconut trees must be getting old, since I do it every night to keep watch over Mama Honu's nest. Those thugs said they'd come back when the moon goes dark—to do *what* is still unclear. And so, I climb and watch and wait.

Even my lessons with Aunty are boring, especially since she insists on my practicing my long-distance telepathic skills on geckos—or *moʻo* as they are called here in Hawaii. Don't get me wrong—moʻo are ʻaumakua, ancestral spirits, to many on the island and deserve our respect—it's just that I don't receive much from them in the way of communication. Their attention is mostly focused on the present moment and the sensations they experience as they scurry from one surface to the next—*warm, slick, bright, crunch.* Yesterday, we found a moʻo basking in the sun and even though I was about twenty feet away, I could feel the wet warmth it felt soaking up the sun's rays. That felt good, but I wouldn't call it thrilling.

All of us Koa campers have been sitting at the picnic tables down by the beach for our daily lesson in the traditional Hawaiian arts, this one supervised by Uncle Hanalei. He keeps looking at me over his reading glasses with the saddest look in his eyes. It's like he can see into my heart. Most of my fellow campers are on their second and third leis.

Meanwhile, the ti-leaf braid I've been trying to form over the last half hour suddenly snaps, and I throw the whole thing to the ground. "This is *impossible*," I blurt and suddenly, the whole situation with Baby Girl, Mama Honu and her eggs, and my plans for finding a friend for Buddy all come crashing down around me. Isn't there anything I'm good at? Apparently not.

Worse, I'm a terrible sister. Was then. Am now. Always will be. So, Baby Girl—if you're listening—you'd be better off haunting somebody else.

Keola leans into me after my outburst. "Chill, Sophie Kai. It's okay. Maybe lei-making isn't your thing."

"Then what *is*, Keola? I feel like an absolute failure. I've blown Mission Buddy. What am I even doing here?"

"Ummm, how about having *fun?*"

"Yeah? What's that?"

Keola gently places the lei he just finished over my head. "Everything's going to work out, Sophie Kai, you'll see."

"You keep saying that." I force a smile, but don't feel it.

"This time I mean it." He laughs. The sharp tips of the ti leaves poke into my skin as Keola leans into me for one of his big-armed hugs.

"Mahalo," I say, swallowing back tears. Just then, Luana plops down beside me.

"Sophie Kai? Tūtū and Aunty want to see you back at camp. They say it's urgent."

"Now what?" I groan as I toss my ruined lei into a nearby bucket. One thing's for sure, if Aunty's involved, it can't be good.

Tūtū Malia's hut is about twice the size of our sleeping hut. There's a roomy living space with straw mats and wicker chairs and sleeping quarters behind a bamboo screen. I peek inside the door and stare at a basket of cell phones resting on a table by the only electrical outlet I've seen at camp besides in the kitchen. I wonder if the phone with a power cord plugged into it is mine.

What I wouldn't give for Facetime with my dad right now.

The sisters are sitting at a side table peeling mangos, having a good laugh over something and I wonder if it's me. Yeah, like, "That girl doesn't even know how to braid ti leaves without breaking them all to pieces," or "When she says something in Hawaiian, she sounds like she has a mouthful of poi."

"There she is!" Tūtū Malia's face brightens when she sees me. "Come on in, Baby Girl."

Even though I know that name's a common Hawaiian term of endearment, I flinch.

"Don't worry, Sophie Kai," Tūtū says softly, misinterpreting my reaction. She holds out her hand to take mine and gently pulls me into a chair next to theirs. "You're not in trouble. We've been worried about you." I try not to look at Aunty's face, but I can't help but notice it has softened a bit which to tell you the truth, scares me even more than her Grim Reaper look.

"Aunty tells me you're making great progress in your work with moʻo," Tūtū says. I roll my eyes and Tūtū laughs. "I know! They seem like such simple creatures, don't they? But don't let them fool you." Tūtū sets the mango she's been peeling into a bowl. "I remember when your great-grandmother first taught Sis and me to communicate with a moʻo who lived in our shower."

Aunty nods, smiling, "Ahhh, right, *Gibby*," she says. "We thought he was our pet ... until we discovered that's what he thought of *us*!" The two sisters laugh.

Tūtū turns back to me, this time with a look of concern. "Sophie Kai, we really love having you here at Camp Koa, don't we, sister?" When Aunty hesitates, Tūtū kicks her sister's leg under the table which inspires a begrudging nod.

"We think you have a very special gift to offer the world," Tūtū continues. "I'm sure by now you know that's why we invited you here to Camp Koa, why we invited all your friends here. We believe the planet needs all of you using your gifts to their fullest potential, *now*."

Aunty clears her throat. "My sister is using the word 'we' pretty loosely. I agree that you have an extraordinary gift, but unlike my sister, I believe children are meant to be children and not saints or saviors. They are meant to play and get into trouble and do stupid things. That's why I've been so tough on you, Sophie Kai. It makes me mad that we've dragged you all the way out here to our island, when you belong back with your family doing ... well ... *kid* stuff."

Wow. Even now, she talks about "our island" like I'm not a part of it. I know she means well, but even saying I should be doing "kid stuff" feels like a slam. Why couldn't I save the world? Or at least try if I wanted to?

Tūtū reaches out and grabs her sister by the arm, as if to stop her before she digs herself into a bigger hole. "Here's the deal, Sophie Kai. What Aunty wants or what I want doesn't matter one bit. It's what *you* want that matters, and we've been wrong not to let you have your say in that." She leans in real close and holds my gaze and for the life of me, I cannot look away. "I told you a while ago when you first got here that no one was keeping you here. You've seemed so down lately, like your heart's not with us, and we're wondering if you're homesick."

Tears well up at the corners of my eyes and I know that if I let it all go, I'll blubber myself into a puddle.

"We've talked to your parents about our concerns, and they said to leave it up to you." She takes my hand in both of hers. "Sophie Kai, Daughter of the Sea, would you like to go home?"

Home.

It's like the gates of my heart fly open at the sound of it. And behind those gates, a flood. But behind that flood, something else, something hidden.

I want to say: Yes, I want to go home, but ... what about Baby Girl?

I want to say: Yes, but ... what about Keola, Wilks, and Nalu?

I want to say: Yes, but ... what about Mama Honu and her eggs?

I want to say, yes, but ... what about Buddy? About finding him a friend? Breaking that promise feels unbearable.

I look up at Tūtū Malia who is looking at me—*through* me is more like it. "We know you wanted to go to the seahorse farm, Sophie Kai and you can ... tomorrow, if you like. It's within a few miles of the Kona airport. We can all go to the seahorse farm and then give you a proper sendoff on the way back to camp. Is that what you want, Sophie Kai?"

Of course, that's what I want. That's what I came here for … Mission Buddy, right?

I should be gushing with gratitude right now, but my answer comes out flat.

"Yes, Tūtū. That sounds good."

20.

Watching the Moon Go Dark

After I make my decision, Tūtū lets me have my cell phone to call my parents and firm up the arrangements. I walk out to the public pavilion where there's cellphone service and try Mom first—I'm not sure why—maybe I'm hoping she'll say she wants me to come home and that she misses me. Oh well. She must be in a meeting because the call goes to voicemail.

Dad, on the other hand, answers his cell on the first ring. "Hey, Sophie. What's up?" He's trying to sound casual, but I know he's been staring at his phone waiting for me to call. "Tūtū Malia says you seem kind of down." We're on Facetime, so I can see he's wearing a white linen shirt with a design of palm fronds stretched across the front of it.

"I'm coming home, Daddy." I want to jump right through the screen and into his broad, strong arms. He lets out a big exhale and his shoulders slump with it.

"We should never have pushed you into this, sweetheart. It's all my fault."

"Hey, now look who's playing our favorite game," I tease, gulping back tears. "It's okay, Dad. I've met some really cool kids." *And then there's Baby Girl*, I wish I had the guts to say. "I guess I just got homesick."

After their conversation with Tūtū Malia, my parents figured I'd probably want to come home, so they placed a hold on a ticket from Kona to Seattle for the following afternoon. The hold is good for twenty-four hours before the ticket becomes non-refundable. "In case you change your mind, Sophie girl, and want to stay," Dad says before we hang up.

"No chance of that," I reply.

Rumors spread like wildfire around Camp Koa, and I know I have to tell Keola first before somebody else beats me to it. I pull him aside after Uncle's lei-making workshop.

"Oh, man, Sophie Kai! I can't believe you're leaving us *now*, just when all the cool stuff is about to happen." Keola acts like he's pulling his hair out by the roots. "There's a field trip to the volcano, Tūtū's stories around the campfire, jumping off cliffs … well, okay, so I won't be doing that … but *you* could. And, of course, there's protecting Mama Honu's eggs. How can I do any of this without you?"

His reaction takes me completely off guard. I don't think I've ever had anybody plead for me to stick around. *Ever.* "Hey, what about Mission Buddy?" he continues. "You can't just let that go."

"Hold on, Keola." I tell him about Tūtū's plan to visit the seahorse farm tomorrow before going to the airport. "See? I'll be able to pick out a friend for Buddy and bring her home myself. You're always telling me how things are going to work out and see, now they are."

"Well, that's cool." He shrugs. "But I wouldn't exactly call that 'working out,' not for me anyway. Besides, who's going to climb up a coconut tree to watch for the bad guys? That's certainly not going to be *me*." I imagine Keola lifting his bulk up a tree and laugh. "See?" He shakes his head. "Not my skill set."

"Maybe Nalu will do it," I say. "Besides, even if I were to see those thugs, I don't know how we'd stop them. We're just kids."

"Yeah, but we're not just *any* kids. We have gifts. That's what the kūpuna say."

"Look, Keola. I know they mean well, but tell me how a kid who reads intentions and a kid who communicates with animals are going to take on two grown men who are up to no-good? And speaking of skill sets ... sure, I can communicate with honu and moʻo, big deal. Last time I checked, just about anyone can outrun a honu, and what's a moʻo going to do to stop a thief? Nibble them to death?"

"I see what you mean. We kind of lack a plan."

"You think?" The idea of Mama Honu's nest getting destroyed and me not being able to do anything to stop it threatens to kick the All My Fault game into high gear. For once, however, I decide to buck up and ignore the guilt gnawing a hole in my heart.

"Right now, Keola, I need to stick to Plan A. Find a friend for Buddy and go *home*."

One look at his face and I know I've broken his heart.

Tonight's moon is one sliver shy of dark. If those thugs are still up to no good, they should be coming back to the beach any night now when, according to them, the ancestors won't be so active. I shimmy up my coconut tree one last time to watch over Mama Honu's nest. I know it's pointless, but I still need to do what I can, while I can.

Up here in the palm fronds, there's a wisp of a breeze, giving way to the sound of waves lap-lap-lapping along the shore. I scan the shadows of the beach for any sign of intruders. Nothing, not even a campfire, so I settle in. I wrap a long, broad scarf around my backside and tie the ends tight around the trunk of the tree to hold my weight, just like Nalu showed me a few nights ago. The effect is like sitting in a hammock. "You can even take a nap if you want," he told me.

He was one of the campers who seemed the most surprised when Tūtū Malia told everyone at the end of talk story tonight that I'd be leaving early. I was shocked by how all the kids gathered around me, giving me hugs and telling me how much they'd miss me—all except for Nalu who turned away from the group early without saying a word. Wilks didn't say much either, but she probably figures she'll catch up with me back at the hut.

I told everyone, "I'll miss you, too," which at the time felt like the right thing to say. Only now, as I sit up here in my tree, am I feeling that it's actually true.

I *will* miss them. All of them.

I'm no stranger to missing. I've been missing my parents, especially Dad, ever since I got here to Camp Koa. And then there's Baby Girl. Missing is a way of life around my house. You'd think the feeling would have disappeared by now, but it's kind of like the air we breathe.

"Baby Girl," I whisper. "Are you there? I mean ... *here?*"

As usual, nothing.

"I wish you'd talk to me. Even though you can be kind of annoying in my dreams, I want you to know that I really haven't minded your enjoying Hawaii through me ... if that's what you've been doing. And I'm sorry that I've got to go."

Still nothing.

"Anyway, you're a good sister, Baby Girl. I wish I could be the same for you."

I feel a stirring over my left shoulder, and I think maybe I'll catch a glimpse of her, but all I see are the pointy ends of palm fronds curving around me, whispering *shhhhh, shhhhh*. I scan the horizon one more time for honu or flashlights or thugs. My eyelids are getting heavy. I think maybe I'll rest my eyes for just a second when I feel something like an inside hug.

Is that you, Baby Girl?

I want like heck to believe it is.

21.
Something's Going Down

That annoying little girl is poking me again, only this time it turns into a tickling match, and the girl turns into my sister. She tickles me under the arms; I tickle her behind her chubby knees. We've turned into one big, giggly-girl mess when the next poke doesn't tickle; it *hurts*.

"Ow!"

"Sophie Kai, wake up!" It's Nalu. "You've been asleep all night in our tree."

Our tree? His face is inches away from mine.

"Uncle says we get to go to the bakery this morning—you, me, Keola and Wilks—kind of a going-away treat, I guess. We're leaving in ten minutes."

Going away? I shake my head.

Oh, right. I'm going home.

As soon as we pull into the bakery's parking lot in Uncle's open-air Jeep, the sugary aroma of baked goods fresh out of the oven just about knocks us over. "Oh man," Keola says, taking a dramatic, deep breath in. "I think I've gained a pound already!"

The bakery is hopping even though it's only seven in the morning and the line is long. After Uncle puts in his order for the camp, he invites each of us to pick something out to eat while we wait. Wilks and I choose a spongey, sugar-coated pastry called a *malasada* and head for a picnic table behind the bakery to eat them.

The boys are joking around with the owners' son, a friend of Nalu, so it's just me and Wilks at the table. We're surrounded by lush, flowering plants filling the morning air with their scent as we savor our pink, guava-flavored pastries. The only other people in the garden are two guys sipping coffee along a stone wall near the parking lot.

Neither of us have said anything about my leaving. The silence between us would feel awkward if it weren't for the malasadas, which are warm, soft and just the right amount of sweet—better than any donut I've ever eaten. Wilks tears off a small piece at a time, but my malasada is gone in less than a minute.

"Hey, Wilks…" The feeling of this morning's dream washes over me suddenly, and I break our silence. "Do you suppose my sister could be contacting me through my dreams?" I'm pretty sure of the answer, but I figure it doesn't hurt to ask.

Wilks looks at me as if I'm as dense as this picnic table we're sitting at. "What do *you* think?"

Three small, gray, orange-beaked birds are hopping around the table, cocking their heads. I shake the crumbs off my paper napkin, and they gobble them up. "I don't know what to think," I say.

She snorts. "Right."

"Hey! Why are you mad at me? I didn't do anything to you … lately."

She brushes her sticky hands off on her shorts. "Because I think you're a coward, Sophie *Kai*." She says the last part of my name like it's all wrong, like maybe I don't deserve to have a Hawaiian name. "Because I think you're running away."

"From *what*?"

"From *her*." She looks over my left shoulder, like she's looking right at my sister, but then she drops her head. "From … *us*."

"Hey, girls! What's up?" Keola plops himself down on my side of the table. The bench lifts a little with his weight. "Uncle says we'll be ready to go in a few minutes."

Nalu strolls up and starts playing with a hacky sack. He bounces it off his knees, and then flips around, kicking it way up in the air with the sole of his foot. Keola laughs, shaking his head. "Is there anything you can't do?"

Just then, one of the guys who has been sitting on the wall near the parking lot stands up and starts shouting at his friend. Keola looks over at them and says, "Uh-oh" under his breath.

"Uh-oh, what?" I ask.

"I think those are our guys," he says, and I know he means the thugs on the beach.

Keola turns to Nalu and Wilks and quietly fills them in on what little we know—that these guys are after Mama Honu's nest and they're waiting for a moonless night.

"Oh, they're after those eggs, for sure," Nalu says. "Turtle eggs sell on the black market for a lot of money. They sell them in bars in other countries as a 'delicacy.' It didn't used to be a problem here, but the money looks pretty good for folks who are desperate." Keola whistles quietly. Nalu nods. "Yeah, and my guess is Mama Honu's nest isn't the only one they're after."

"*Dang*. It would be good to know exactly *when* they plan on doing it," Keola says. "If only we were closer, we might overhear something."

"Leave it to me." Nalu turns to go.

"Wait, Nalu," I say. "Those guys might be dangerous."

"No worries, Sophie Kai." He flashes that big grin of his and gives me the shaka sign. "I'm a behind-the-scenes kind of guy. You might even say it's my super-power."

And with that, he bounces the hacky sack into the air—off his knee, his foot, his elbow—as he angles himself ever-so-closer to the subjects at hand. Whatever the two men were arguing about apparently has been settled, because they're heading for a rusty old van in the parking lot, paying no attention to Nalu's acrobatics whatsoever.

With one final kick high into the air, Nalu lands the hacky

sack within feet of the wall, and then pretends he's lost it in a tangle of vines. Honestly, I think he could stare right at those guys, and they wouldn't see him. Anyway, the thugs open the back of the van, but the door blocks our view.

"Hey, campers," Uncle shouts at us from the sidewalk. We barely glance at him, we're so riveted on Nalu. "Come on, let's go!" He waves at us impatiently. The men look over at Uncle and quickly slam the van doors shut.

The thugs have taken off by the time Nalu joins us at the Jeep. "Did you see anything?" Keola asks him anxiously.

"Yeah. At least a half-dozen Styrofoam coolers, a couple of long-handled picks, and a shovel. Something's definitely going down."

"Did they say *when*?" Keola asks.

"One said something about the moon going dark and 'Boss says tonight.'"

Keola slaps Nalu on the back. "Good work, brah."

At the Jeep, Wilks hops in back with the boys, leaving me riding shotgun with Uncle. "It's like we're a spy ring or something," she says, and I feel a surge of excitement like I'm part of something important—as Nalu said, "something going down." But then it hits me.

I'll be boarding a plane in just a few hours and their spy ring will happen without me.

I hear the three of them joking around in back.

It's like I'm already gone.

22.

Heads and Tails

Back at camp, Uncle Hanalei sets the large, white bag of goodies down on a picnic table, and like a school of piranha, Koa campers come from all directions to attack what's inside. I'm about to head for the girls' sleeping hut to pack up my stuff, when Uncle dares to interrupt the feeding frenzy by reaching into the bag.

"Back off, you crazy kids, back!" he shouts with a wide, toothy grin. "One for the road, Sophie Kai?" he says, tossing me a malasada.

"Mahalo, Uncle!" I smile back. I hold it up to my nose before taking a bite. It smells like mangos. For some reason, this makes me want to cry.

Stop it, I tell myself. This is what you wanted, remember? Plan A: Find a friend for Buddy and go home.

At our hut, I check my wallet to make sure I still have the cash for the seahorse farm. Sixty bucks. Yup, that ought to do it—at least according to the Kai House website. I stick the wallet into the front pocket of my backpack and then reach for my swimsuit. I guess I won't be around to see who's the fastest swimmer, or the fastest climber for that matter. I really wanted to leave Nalu in the dust on that one—or rather, in the sand. Oh well. I guess we'll never know who's the fastest. Of course, *I* know. But still. I'd give anything to prove it.

Well, almost anything. Finding a friend for Buddy is the most important thing.

"Hey." Wilks slips into the hut as I'm stuffing my swimsuit into my bag.

"Hey."

Silence.

Our resident moʻo—who we've named Slitherin—stares at us from the window ledge, his bright green and red-dotted head pumping up and down. The little guy's an easy read: He wants us out of here so he can take a nap. He likes getting out of the sun before the heat of the day, and this promises to be a hot one.

"Look," Wilks finally says, sitting on the edge of her cot. "I'm sorry about what I said earlier at the bakery. You're not running away. You're accomplishing a goal. I admire that."

"Thanks, Wilks."

"You're welcome." Her next words tumble out fast. "I guess maybe I was mad because I'll miss you." She ducks her head, then looks up shyly to check for my reaction.

"Aw, that's okay. I'll miss you too. Life won't be nearly as interesting without you and your noisy ghosts." She snorts. By now, we're both blushing, as I throw the rest of my things into my pack.

"Ummm, there is one more thing … about Baby Girl," Wilks adds.

"Yeah?"

"I don't think you have to worry about her haunting you when you're back home or anything. I mean, I think she'll always be with you in some way, like in your dreams, but spirits usually come and go as they please. Unless—"

"Unless?"

"—unless they're stuck, you know, like those spirits from the battlefield."

I zip up my backpack and stare at her. "Your point?"

"Oh, probably nothing," she says a little too brightly. "You two aren't fighting about anything, right?"

I hesitate. There's this nagging guilt I feel around my sister's death, I guess, and sometimes it feels like there's a battle going on inside of me, but Baby Girl and I are not the ones fighting.

"Right," I say.

"Girls!" Aunty opens the flap to the hut. "Come on! Let's go! The bus is waiting. Oh, and here's your phone, Sophie. Tūtū wanted to make sure you got it back." And off she goes, her demon rooster tucked snuggly under her arm.

"Gosh, she seems almost happy this morning," Wilks says.

"Figures," I mumble. Figures that she'd be happy to get rid of me. Figures that she already dropped the *Kai* from my name, like it never really belonged.

"What's wrong?" Wilks says.

"Never mind," I say. "We better get going." I stuff my phone into the same pocket as my wallet and give the sleeping hut one last look. "Aloha," I whisper.

Slitherin tilts his reptilian head in my direction. I try to connect with him to say goodbye.

I get *nothing*.

On the way to the seahorse farm on the Camp Koa Express, Keola, Wilks and Nalu can't stop talking about "what's goin' down" tonight and their Big Plans to save Mama Honu's nest of eggs. This, despite Uncle's warning to "let it go" when he overheard them talking about the two thugs on the way home from the bakery.

"Dang, Sophie Kai," Keola leans into me, during an awkward pause in their conversation. I guess he realized I was still here. "I'd feel better if you were with us."

I feel a sudden wave of sadness and swallow hard. "I'd be there with you," I finally say, "if I could be in two places at once."

"Of course, you would," Keola says quietly.

We sit like that for a few minutes until Nalu and Wilks lean back into their seat and stare at the passing scenery. In true Keola fashion, he flips an internal switch and he's suddenly all hyped up about my "getting to go home"—as excited for me as he was sad for himself just minutes before. He starts with a string of questions.

"What's the first thing you'll do when you get home?"

"Give Buddy his friend."

"Besides that, what are you most looking forward to?"

"Sleeping in my own bed with no geckos or demon roosters to bother me."

"Will you miss me?"

"Of course, I'll miss you."

"What will you miss about me?"

"Your pesky questions!"

Keola smiles at this last answer, pauses, and then asks, "How will you know when you find the *right* friend for Buddy?" Unlike the other questions, this one has me stumped.

I thought I'd feel more certain about this part of Mission Buddy. I never once thought about *how* I'd choose; I just figured I'd know. But suddenly, the responsibility for finding the right friend for Buddy starts weighing me down. What if I pick the wrong one? What if I pick a seahorse that's boring or just wants to be alone or one that nags or is just plain mean? Worse yet, what if they like each other and Buddy gets pregnant, losing more babies all over again?

"I don't know," I finally say.

"Hey, if you need help figuring it out, I'm your guy." Keola pulls a quarter out of his pocket. "We can always flip a coin. Heads or tails?" He flicks the quarter up in the air, where it spins and lands smack-dab in the crack of the seat between us, round edge up.

"See?" He breaks out laughing.

"Yeah, Keola. Real helpful."

I don't know what I was expecting but this wasn't it.

After we get checked in through the Kai House gift shop and wash our hands at a special sink, we file around to the back of the building where we see several long rows of round concrete tanks, each one about the size of a large, above-ground kids' pool painted aquamarine. Our guide, Trish, tells us about the network of narrow pipes we see, and how they're part of a filtration system that maintains a constant flow of natural seawater that keeps the tanks clean. As we walk up and down the aisles, we see that each tank holds a special type and color of seahorse—from dark brown and black ones to bright orange ones, flaming red ones, and canary yellow ones.

"Geez," says Keola, "you guys have every seahorse under the sun in here! Where are the rainbow ones?"

Trish laughs. "Hey, if one of these ponies were to park next to a rainbow, you might just see it—they're that good at camouflage."

Keola, Wilks and I step onto a narrow ledge to take a closer look into one of the tanks, only to discover that it looks nothing like Buddy's aquarium back home. There are no green, feathery plants waving gently in the current. No pink rocks, no multi-colored gravel, no cute plastic crabs or treasure chests with lids that open and close. We have no trouble spotting where the seahorses hang out, though. A large, white, plastic grid hangs at the center of the tank where in this case, a cluster of mostly brown and green seahorses hang out.

Trish must see the puzzled looks on our faces, because she reminds us that this is a seahorse *farm*, not a zoo or a public aquarium and we are here—not as tourists—but as special guests. "We're raising seahorses in captivity to try to decrease the pet trade's demand for seahorses in the wild. Over a million are caught annually but barely a thousand survive beyond six weeks. That's not sustainable." I had read all about this for my school report, and it's making me mad all over again. At least these people are trying to help.

"These tanks are designed for breeding, growing, and keeping seahorses healthy until we can find them their 'forever homes,'" she continues.

Well, that makes sense. But I can't help but think it must get pretty boring with nothing to look at except the curved walls of your tank and, of course, each other. I flash back to that time in Sarasota when I held that seahorse skeleton and next thing I knew, I had thrown the entire box of skeletons into the sea. I grip the edge of the tank to steady myself.

Please, God, I silently pray, do not let me do anything like that here.

Keola nudges me gently. "At least they've got a lot of room to roam," he says. "You've got to give them that."

"Not that they're interested in using it," I say. Even though the tank is wide and deep—about two dozen of these prehistoric-looking creatures are smushed together at the center of the tank, their curving heads and curlicue tails all linked around the white plastic grid or each other.

"Yeah, it's hard to tell one from the other, isn't it?" he replies. "It's a mish-mash of heads and tails. Hey! Heads and tails! Get it? Who needs a coin when you can flip a seahorse?"

I laugh, but then give him the evil eye.

"Just kidding!"

Just then, Wilks sidles up to us and leans in. "Anyone speaking to you, Sophie Girl?"

I gaze at the blob at the center of the tank and shake my head.

"Hey, Koa campers!" Tricia yells from a tank closer to the gift shop. "Anyone interested in holding a seahorse?"

A chorus of voices chime in: "Yeah!" "Cool!" "Me, me, me!"

"Come on, Sophie Kai, let's go. I've got a good feeling about this," Keola says, and with that, he, Wilks, and I head for the next tank together.

When we get there, all the other kids are already listening intently to Tricia as she explains what will happen next. "Actually, you don't really *hold* a seahorse," she says. "It's more like the seahorse holds onto you, a decision the seahorse itself will make. Here at Kai House, we don't force a seahorse to do anything it doesn't want to do, okay?"

"How do you know what they want? Do they tell you?" Honi elbows his buddies, but everyone else seems to be looking at me. Oh great. I guess the news of my special weirdness for chatting with animals has gotten around camp. Fortunately, Tricia is quick to answer Honi's question.

"Well, no, they don't talk … but they do communicate in other ways. Take that one over there, for instance." She points at a lone seahorse at the edge of the plastic grid. "You can tell by where she's positioned herself that she prefers to be alone. She'll probably not approach any of you. In fact, it usually takes a while before these seahorses warm up to our guests at all, but that's okay, right?"

"Right," everyone echoes.

As soon as everyone, besides me, dips their hands into the water, seahorses start peeling off from the outer edges of their post, dorsal fins all a blur, looking for a place to land. Swimming upright as they do, they look like those little motorized segues tourists ride on the sidewalks of Seattle.

"Wow, it's a stampede!" Honi shouts as dozens of seahorses vie for a hitching post on someone's finger. I figure it's always like this, but then Tricia appears to be in shock. Her long, blond ponytail swishes back and forth as she shakes her head in wonder.

Huh. Maybe there's something special about us after all.

I'm lost in thought when Keola nudges me. "What are you waiting for, Sophie Kai? This is your chance. Mission Buddy and all that."

I look up into Keola's face and am bowled over by what I see. Mom says she can read a witness's face "like a book," and now I see what she means, except Keola's face reads like his heart. Excited, hopeful, and yes, loving—but not the goofy-romantic kind. It's an aloha kind of love. A totally accepting, wanting-the-best-for-you kind of love. It's all there. On his wide-open face. He wants me to find a friend for Buddy, because that's what *I* want, even if it means I'll be leaving. And that's when it hits me.

I've got a friend.

"Sophie?" Keola's looking worried now, like maybe I've lost my mind.

I put a hand on his arm. "Wait a sec," I say, because a memory wants to come.

I stare down into the crystal-clear water of the pool in front of me and remember what Buddy told me the night he lost his babies:

Go. Find friend.

Dang. I could have sworn he meant a friend for *him*.

But now I wonder—make that, *know*—he meant it for me, too.

I scan the perimeter of the tank and see all the faces of my Koa friends lit up with wonder as seahorse after seahorse finds a finger to curl its tail around. Behind the tank, over by the gift shop are our kūpuna, all three smiling. And then I turn my attention to inside the tank, alert for a sign that any of these seahorses now buzzing around might be a friend for Buddy.

The right friend. The perfect friend.

Out of the corner of my eye, I see the seahorse Tricia talked about at the edge of the tank—a girl and a loner. She can't be the one. I begin to look elsewhere, even as this niggle starts to tickle me at the back of my brain.

No. Really. She can't be the one.

Keola pulls a quarter out of his pocket. He's still looking hopeful, if not a wee bit desperate. He makes me smile—not because he looks silly or anything—but because looking at him makes me *happy*.

"Look, Sophie Kai, pick a seahorse, any seahorse. We'll flip a coin. It will be perfect. You'll see."

I smile and nod, ready to stick my hand into the water.

But then, that lone seahorse hanging tight to the edge of the plastic grid, shudders, and all I can see is her. One of her eyes—the one closest to me—swivels in its socket, keeping tabs on the activity around her, but then it latches onto my gaze, and we both become eerily still.

There. We've made contact.

Good. Answer me this: Are you a loner? Or are you lonely?

Her answer comes fast and clear.

Oh my gosh, you're just like I am—or rather, *was*.

Still holding the connection, I'm about to stick my hand in the water, when something—maybe it's that niggle—makes me hesitate.

"Go on…" Keola whispers. "You know it'll work. You've got the touch."

He's right, of course. If I lower my hand into the water, Mission Buddy is as good as done. But his voice … it's so full of trust for *me*, just like the trust I felt from Mama Honu that first day I saved her from the trash bag and again, on the night we watched her lay her eggs. It's a trust that makes me want to do the right thing. But what is that?

Perhaps the lonely seahorse across the way hears the question and weighs in, or perhaps the answer has been in my heart all along. Nevertheless, I know what I must do. I also know what must wait—a decision I communicate to her before I break our gaze.

"Ya know, Keola…" I say, stepping back from the pool. "I'm just not feeling it."

"What do you mean?" He's still holding his hand out with the quarter.

I look over at Wilks who's been silently observing a seahorse that has curled its tail around her pinky. I can tell she's been listening to every word and she's smiling, like she doesn't just read the spirits of the dead.

"Really, Sophie Kai," Keola is pleading with me now. "You're worrying me. What do you mean 'you're not feelin' it'?!"

I gently take the quarter from his up-turned hand and put it in my pocket.

"I mean, Keola—heads *and* tails—I'm staying."

23.

Change of Plans

While us Koa kids wait in the bus with Tūtū, Uncle and Aunty run into CostSaver for some supplies, and I call my parents about my change in plans. This time, I start with Dad.

"Good thing that ticket's refundable," I begin shyly, and then tell him about my change of heart.

"Oh, sweet girl, I'm glad you've decided to stay. What changed your mind?"

Not wanting to "unleash the floodgates" as Mom likes to say—Dad cries at the drop of a hat—I don't tell him about the friends I've made or the nest of honu eggs we have to save or that a lonely seahorse is waiting for me to swoop her up at a time yet to be determined. I especially don't tell him about the sister I thought was dead. Well, *is* dead ... but ... *you know*.

"I guess this place finally got to me," I say instead.

"Oh, Sophie Kai," he says softly, "our ancestors have called you. I can feel it."

I'm pretty sure the ancestors have other things to do than convince a twelve-year-old girl to stay at summer camp, but I don't want to argue. Upon Dad's urging, I call Mom next. Her reaction is a bit different.

"Well, that's unexpected," she says. "What made you change your mind?"

"Something Buddy told me," I say coyly, hoping she'll ask what I mean. But all she says is, "That's nice, sweetie," and "I'm glad you've chosen to tough it out," which of course has nothing to do with it.

Anyway.

Now that we aren't dropping me off at the airport—all the Koa kids cheered when Tūtū made the announcement—the next stop for the Koa Express is a place called Southpoint Beach. It's the southernmost location of the non-continental United States they tell us, that is, if you count Hawaii as a state, which is a sore point for some islanders. According to Aunty, some Hawaiians aren't too crazy about being a state; they'd rather be their own country. There's a lot of history involved which she seemed too grumpy to go into, but I've made a mental note to write a school report on it someday. Besides, I'm curious. Why would someone not want to be a part of our country?

Anyway.

We're here at Southpoint to "exercise our kuleana," Tūtū says, meaning, "our responsibility." The last time I exercised my kuleana, I was knee-deep in pond scum. This time, we're here to clean up the beach.

"I bet you're having second thoughts about staying," Aunty snips, handing me a rake and a bucket from the back of the bus.

"Nah, I'm good," I reply, smiling.

Uncle has parked the bus in a parking lot by the side of a cliff where a bunch of local kids are hanging out in swimsuits. They call Nalu and Honi to come join them.

"Can we go jumping, Tūtū? *Please?*" Honi begs.

"Not today, boys," Tūtū says. "We'll be back to jump the point on our last day of camp. Right now, we've got work to do."

Jump the point? I scan the cliff's edge and decide that it's at least as far down as my mom's fourth floor office in downtown Seattle. Not so bad when you're riding an elevator, but jumping from there? *Yikes.* I watch as a young girl about my age backs up to the end of a diving platform, runs full tilt, leaps off the edge, hangs in mid-air for one oh-my-gosh moment, and then drops to the sea below. My stomach plummets with her.

"You've *got* to be kidding me," I mutter to Keola.

He laughs and says, "I know I won't be doing that. I'd make too big a splash, you know. Might cause a tidal wave or something." This is his way of saying he's perfectly comfortable being a coward. Me? I'll be obsessing about it—Will I jump? Won't I jump?—for the rest of the week.

There are only enough rakes for four people at a time, and a couple of shovels, so we're working in three shifts. Nalu, Wilks, Keola and I ask to be on the first shift, so afterwards we can talk about our plan to guard Mama Honu's nest later tonight. As we head down the path, we pass a sign that says, "Danger! No jumping! Could cause death." Under this last line, someone has written in black magic marker "...or worse."

"What could be worse than dying?" I mumble, as we trudge to the beach.

"Oh, that's island code for getting chicken skin and not jumping at all." Nalu grins. "No worries, Sophie Kai. That sign's for tourists, not islanders like us."

When we get to the beach, we see a three-foot-wide swath of what looks like multi-colored sequins shimmering in the sun all along the shoreline. There are bits of blues and greens and yellows, oranges and reds. *Swishhhh, swishhhh.* The waves gently lift the edge of the glittery blanket then set it down again. The word "beautiful" almost leaves my mouth, but something stops it. What are we seeing? Shell fragments? Beach glass?

"Plastic," Uncle grunts. "Tiny bits of plastic broken-down from God-knows-what—bottles, toys, packaging. Every day, it washes up onto shore and every day, ocean life like honu, seals, fish, and seabirds swallow it as they eat other things. Eventually, it builds up in their bodies and sometimes they die."

"You mean to tell me all of this will be back tomorrow?" Honi whines. "Why start?"

"Because this is where our work is." Uncle seems grim but determined.

"Actually, none of *this* will be back tomorrow, because we're going to clean *this* up," Tūtū adds cheerfully. "If we do nothing, then nothing will ever get better. We take care of our island, because we love her, and we know she loves us back. That is the way of kuleana. Even cleaning up this little bit of plastic means something to our island. We do what we can."

Tūtū hands out a pair of rubber gloves to each of our team members on the first shift—Keola, Wilks, Nalu, and me—and we begin to rake and load up our buckets, while the other kids chase each other around the beach. We dump the sandy muck from our buckets into large garbage bags which Uncle says he'll take to a central recycling center in Hilo the next day. I'm flabbergasted at how many buckets we fill.

After half an hour of sweaty work, Aunty announces it's time for the next team. You'd think I'd be glad to be done with the nasty job, but the more I rake, the madder I get, and the more I want to do.

The three others, however, are anxious to fill me in on "Mission Honu"—their plan to save Mama Honu's eggs—so after we hand off our tools, we follow Nalu to a small clearing where we sit cross-legged on a large, flat rock overlooking the ocean. The heat of the stone burns my skin, so I hug my knees, making sure my shorts and the soles of my flipflops are the only things touching it.

Wilks begins. "We're thinking nothing will happen until later tonight when everyone at camp has gone to bed. That's when you,

Keola, and I will sneak out of our sleeping huts, grab some pots and pans from the kitchen, and head down to the beach. Do you think you can lead us to Mama Honu's nest?"

"You bet." I give her a thumbs up. "Hey, where's Nalu going to be?"

Nalu smiles, but it's Keola who answers. "We'll guard Mama Honu's nest, while Nalu is up your coconut tree keeping an eye out for the bad guys. When he sees them far off, he'll hoot like an owl to alert us."

"Hooooo, hooooo, hoot, hoot!" Nalu demonstrates.

"Two long hoots, followed by two short ones," Keola explains.

"The three of you will wait quietly until you hear my *second* call," Nalu jumps in. "That means the thugs are close and it's time to mobilize your forces." When he sees the clueless look on my face, he adds, "Sorry, I mean, bang on your pots and pans like there's no tomorrow. Got it?"

"Got it," I say, swallowing hard. I think it's the phrase "like there's no tomorrow" that makes me realize how serious this is. *Dead* serious, as Mom would say.

Nobody says anything for a while.

"What if they don't scare off?" Keola finally asks.

More silence.

Nalu suddenly brightens. "Hey, Wilks. Maybe you could ask the ancestors to spook those guys ... for real?"

"Hmmm ... iffy." She shrugs. "So far, the ancestors are the only ones giving the orders."

"Okay, so what about you, Sophie Kai?" He nudges me gently. "How 'bout you call a shark for help? Uncle says they're out there."

"If only sharks could walk on land," I say sarcastically. "I'm sorry, Nalu. I want to help, but so far, my gift is limited to moʻo, honu, and an occasional seahorse."

"Hey, I could try to talk them out of stealing the eggs," Keola offers. "I'm pretty good at that." We all nod, having witnessed Keola's power of persuasion. He hesitates. "Thing is, I'm not sure it works with guys who really want to do bad things." His eyes scan the ocean, as if he might find an answer there, but soon he looks as glum as the rest of us.

Keola drops his head in his hands. "We're sunk."

I never thought I'd see the day when Keola lost heart. I frantically search my friends' faces for a glimmer of hope.

"Guys!" I shout. "This can't be happening!" They look up at me, dazed. "Look, I didn't decide to stay here at Camp Koa to fail. Come on, *buck up*. Let's think about this a little harder." I peer into Nalu's eyes, Mr. Self-Confidence himself. If anyone can get us out of this funk, he can. "We haven't heard from you yet, Nalu. What can *you* do to help?"

"Well…" He rubs his chin like he's scratching a beard that isn't there. "I'm a behind-the-scenes kind of guy, so I won't know until everything's going down, of course … but I'll be working the edges. No worries." He gives us the shaka sign. "I know this land like the back of my hand. Hey, that rhymes!"

Wilks snorts. "From now on, we should call you 'Poet Boy.'"

Nalu laughs but I can tell he likes the idea.

"Hey, *yeah*." Keola brightens. "We should give each other code names. Poet Boy's perfect for Nalu, and Wilks, you could be … how about … Spirit Girl?"

She shrugs, but she seems okay with it, too. "What should we call you, Keola?" she asks. "I know. How about Mr. Rogers? You know … because you're always so good."

Keola chuckles. "Okay, sure. Mom used to let me watch Mr. Rogers re-runs when I was a kid. I *loved* that guy."

Now we're talkin'.

"I guess that leaves me." I say shyly. I've never been part of a spy ring before, or even a club or a team for that matter. Everyone gets quiet for a few seconds, thinking hard.

"Hey, I know!" Nalu raises his hand like we're in school. "How about…" He hesitates, like he doesn't want to get it wrong. "How about … *Dr. Doolittle* … you know, like that dude in the movie, the one who talks to animals?"

"Yeah, Sophie Kai," Keola chimes in. "We could call you 'Doc' for short."

I have to say, it's got a ring to it. When I was a little girl, I used to play vet with Baby Girl's stuffed animals. The memory makes me smile.

"'Doc' sounds good," I say. Who cares that we don't have a fool-proof plan when we have code names?

Nalu—I mean, Poet Boy—invites us all to stand up, put our hands together, and give a cheer like you see teams do before a big game.

"On the count of three!" he shouts. "One, two, three..."

"Mission Honu!" we shout.

"We're going on an adventure!" Keola—aka Mr. Rogers—proclaims as we head back to the bus. And for once in my life, I feel a part of something.

Something *good*.

24.

That Old Kahuna Trick

Before I came to Camp Koa, I used to think that Hawaii was all sun, sun, sun—like people think of Seattle as all rain, rain, rain. Once you live in a place, I guess, you see things differently. Even though the island does get a lot of sun, it never gets too hot. There's usually a breeze, and they say there are even summer thunderstorms that come ripping through now and then, although I have yet to see one. And yes, it *does* rain a lot in Seattle, but the summer is so dry that everyone winds up praying for rain.

People are funny.

It also gets dark earlier here in Hawaii. And when it gets dark, it gets really, really dark. No street lights. No shop lights. No lights on balconies or porches. Just *dark*. That's why there are telescopes from at least eleven different countries on top of Mauna Kea, the tallest mountain on the island. No light pollution. Not that the locals are crazy about all those telescopes. Aunty says the mountain is sacred and nobody asked the locals if it was okay to put their observatories up there.

Here at Camp Koa, the dark usually doesn't bother me so much. Uncle starts stoking the fire as soon as the sun goes down, and Tūtū's talk-story is one of my favorite times at Camp Koa. But tonight feels different. Tonight, for every degree the sun fades over the horizon, the heavier the night feels around me. Soon, the moon will be as dark as it gets, and Mission Honu will begin.

Aunty taps her gourd, laying down the beat for Uncle's hula. Keola, Wilks, and I are slumped on our log. A few kids jump up and dance with Uncle now that hula lessons have kicked into high gear and nobody's afraid of looking silly. Uncle's good at keeping things loose.

"Hey, Keola." I nudge him gently. "Why aren't you up there?"

"I'm just not feelin' it," he says, teasing me with the same words I used on him earlier today, but I'm guessing he's just as nervous as I am about tonight.

"Oh great. Now I know we're in trouble." My mouth is so dry, I can barely get my words out. "Come on, Keola, I really need to hear you say that thing."

"What thing? Oh, you mean, how everything's going to work out?"

"Yeah, that thing. Please, tell me you still believe it."

He waves his hand in front of his face. "Of course, I believe it. When you do things for good, good always wins in the end."

"In the end? What happens in the meantime?"

Keola shrugs, but Wilks leans in like she's telling us a secret. "All hell breaks loose."

Aunty rattles her gourd super loud to get everyone's attention.

"Mahalo, sister." Tūtū nods, then scans the circle. "I can't tell you how much it means to me to see *all* of your shining faces." She rests her gaze on me for a moment and smiles. "The aloha is strong in our circle tonight. I have seen how we continue to welcome each other, to help each other know that we all belong. Uncle, Aunty and I couldn't be prouder of who you are and what you are becoming. Here at Camp Koa, aloha is the very air we breathe; kuleana is the fire—the fire in our bellies that moves us to act, to say the right thing, to do what is ours to do."

When she says these last words, the fire in the circle flares up and makes a resounding CRACK! We all jump an inch or two off our logs, laughing nervously.

Ignoring the dramatic effects, Tūtū continues, "Tonight, we have a special treat! A number of you have been asking if Tūtū Pele ever shows up on the island in modern day. Those of you who live on the island might have heard an aunty or uncle talk story about a time when they saw an old lady with white hair show up on a dark night—maybe near the volcano, or maybe along the side of the road walking her little white dog."

Keola and I exchange quick glances. I know we're thinking about the lady on the plane.

"Well, there's a popular story about Tūtū Pele that started making the rounds back when we kūpuna were kids about your age. Well, our very own Uncle Hanalei was there, at the very spot where this story happened, and I thought maybe you'd like to hear it from him." Everyone nods and sits up a little straighter.

Uncle stands up and pokes at the fire with a long stick, staring into the coals and making us wait. For once, Honi keeps his mouth shut, which is a good thing because none of us want any interruptions that might delay the story.

"It was almost fifty years ago to the day, my friends," Uncle finally begins. "My mama was nagging at my brother and me to stop pestering each other, something we did a *lot* in those days." He shakes his head and laughs. "She wanted us to go with her to see this artist who was painting a mural near this fancy restaurant and historical center down the road from us." Uncle waves a hand in the direction of the pond where Tūtū and I skimmed algae. "As most of you know, the remains of those buildings are still here today."

All the island kids nudge each other. They clearly know what Uncle is talking about. This would usually make me feel like an outsider, but not tonight.

"Things were a little different back then," Uncle continues. "Developers were getting a toehold in the area and had built this fancy restaurant to attract tourists with plans for a big resort. Mama was always sayin' that Tūtū Pele wasn't happy about any of it, but it always seemed to us kids that the adults were the ones who were mad." Uncle was working his way around the fire as he talked, gesturing with his hands as if conjuring the story from thin air.

"Anyway, Mom was all worked up about us seeing a 'genius at work.' She said we'd never have another opportunity like that—you know, the kind of thing adults say when they want you to do something? And so, she dragged us down to the restaurant late that afternoon and, sure enough, there was the artist. His name was Herb Kawainui Kāne. He'd later be named an 'Hawaiian national treasure,' that's how much people came to think of him, but at that point he was just a cool-looking dude—you know, like yours-truly." Uncle turns in place like a fashion model, which makes us all laugh.

"Well, right away, my brother and I were absolutely transfixed by what this artist was painting. It took up an entire wall—around twenty-five feet long and maybe eight to ten feet high—a mural of our black-sand beach here in ancient times. There were huts made of thatched grass, women making tapa—a cloth made from bark—men repairing fishing nets, a village chief wearing a long, red and yellow headdress and other men with spears kneeling around him. There were outrigger canoes on shore and out at sea. It was eerie standing there. You could almost hear the villagers talking, it felt that real.

"Mom, my brother, and I stuck around with a few other spectators for almost an hour, all of us quietly watching the artist work. It felt … *holy* … like we were in church.

"Suddenly, I felt something move in the vegetation behind me. I elbowed my brother and he saw her, too. An old lady with flowing, white hair, wearing a red-flowered mumu, standing quietly watching the scene. Her amber eyes fell upon us, and it was like we were frozen in place. She held a finger up to her lips, warning us to be quiet, and we quickly looked away. When we looked back, she was gone.

"My brother and I couldn't wait to tell our mother when we got to the car, but she shushed us, saying we were seeing things."

"Years later, I read an interview with the artist in which he told a story about working on that mural—maybe it even happened the very day we saw him. He was painting late one night when he noticed an old lady, one who fit the description of the lady we saw, standing behind him watching him paint. She even asked him for a cigarette, which he gladly gave her. But when Kane turned around to say something to the woman, she was gone. Later, he asked a security guard if he'd seen the woman on her way out, but the guard hadn't seen anybody that night come or go.

"A year or so later, a tsunami up to fifty feet high came crashing up our beach destroying everything in its path. If Camp Koa had been here at that time, it would have been destroyed, too. The gigantic wave pushed out most of the walls and windows of the restaurant and the unfinished historical center, demolishing furnishings, artwork, cabinetry, artifacts—everything inside. Everything, that is, except one wall."

Uncle stands absolutely still, his head tilted, listening, waiting for all the murmuring around him to stop, as we all come to the same conclusion.

"That's right, my friends. The only wall left standing completely intact was the one with Kane's artwork on it. There was a three-to-four-foot-high mudline that stopped right at the bottom edge. The mural, itself, was completely untouched."

"Whoa," Honi gasps.

"Now…" Uncle whispers into the darkening night, "…why do you think that was so?"

"Tūtū Pele," the answer escapes from every camper's mouth including mine.

Uncle shrugs. "Maybe."

"Maybe?!" Honi shouts. "It's got to be Tūtū Pele who protected that mural!"

"Does it?" Uncle turns to face Honi. "Tūtū Pele rules the volcano, but it's her sister that rules the waves, and her egg sister as you call her could have had a hand in it too, working a spell with her dance. And then there's Tūtū Pele's shark brother we don't hear much about—you know how it is when you live in a family full of sisters—but believe me when I tell you, he also has the power to bend the ocean to his will." Uncle pokes the fire with his stick, sending sparks into the air. "Who knows? Maybe it wasn't just one of them. Maybe it took all the siblings to carry out a plan.

"Or maybe, my friends, it was just a coincidence that a fifty-foot wave destroyed everything but the painting. And maybe that old lady my brother and I saw was just … an old lady. But there *is* one thing I know is true. That development everyone said Tūtū Pele was so mad about? It never happened. At least, not yet."

"Wait, not *yet?*" Luana speaks up in her strong, soft voice. "It could still happen?"

"Oh yes, dear girl. That resort is still someone's dream. But I've said enough. Aunty and Tūtū are giving me the cut-off sign. And when two powerful sisters tell you to stop, what *must* you do?"

"Stop!" we shout in unison.

As much as I love the sound of Uncle's voice, I'm terrified that we've sat by the fire too long and that the thugs are on their way. We need everybody to go to their sleeping huts *now*. I look across the fire searching for Nalu, but he must have slipped away. *Good.* Hopefully, he's taken up his post in our tree.

Thankfully, Uncle has no intention of carrying on, because he starts throwing sand on the fire to dampen it down for the night. When Tūtū stands, everyone becomes quiet.

"Uncle has given us a lot to think about, hasn't he? But hey, I know we're tired, so let me leave you with this." She does one of those full-circle scans to make sure she's got everyone's attention. "Whether we think it's God or gods or luck or coincidence, never underestimate the resources that are available all around us to do what is ours to do. You never know who will come when you need them. The world is full of helpers. We are never alone."

While the rest of our friends head for their huts, Keola, Wilks, and I sit on our log, staring into the fire's embers. I don't know about the other two, but Tūtū just gave me a super-duper case of the chicken skin.

Keola finally breaks the silence. "What Tūtū said just now ... you don't suppose she knows what we're planning? I mean, what she said could pertain to anybody, right?"

Wilks snorts. "*Exactly*. What she did there? It's the oldest kahuna trick in the books. Speak the truth and it applies to everybody, but you think it was meant only for you."

"Right," Keola says. "That makes sense."

"Right," I say.

So why does my skin still prickle?

25.

All Hell Breaks Loose

Everything starts out smoothly enough.

Once everyone makes it back to their sleeping huts, it doesn't take long before Aunty is snoring, and Wilks—I mean, Spirit Girl—and I are able to sneak out. We meet up with Keola, also known as Mr. Rogers, at the camp kitchen where we snag a few pots and pans, wave up at Nalu—aka Poet Boy—in his watch tower—aka our coconut tree—and head down to the beach to stake out our position by Mama Honu's nest.

The kūpuna have forgotten to ask for my cell phone back, so I use the flashlight to show us the way down the path in the dark. Hopefully, the battery will hold out until we scare off the thugs and get safely back to camp. Unfortunately, there's no cell service out here, so calling 911 is out of the question. We couldn't even order a pizza if we wanted to, not that there's a pizza place within fifty miles.

Once we find the nest, we settle around it, listening for Poet Boy's call. You'd think staying quiet would be the easy part, but Mr. Rogers keeps on wanting to share his feelings. "Man, I've got the creeps," he whispers and then seconds later, "…but I'm sure we're safe. We've got each other, right?" Spirit Girl and I keep shushing him, but he's getting on our nerves.

I keep checking my phone for the time. An hour goes by and then another. We take turns napping. There's a distant rumbling of thunder and the wind is picking up. Great. We must be about to get that rare summer thunderstorm. Just our luck.

Soon, it's two in the morning. Spirit Girl is sound asleep while Mr. Rogers can barely keep his head propped up on his hand. I'm beginning to think those thugs aren't coming, when I hear Poet Boy's call: *Hooooo-hooooo. Hoot! Hoot!* By now, the wind and the *BOOM-CRASH-SHUSH* of the waves is so loud, I can barely hear it.

CRACK!

Lightning zigzags across the sky.

Electricity crackles through the air.

CRACK!

"What the heck?" Wilks jerks awake.

Keola shakes himself and peers over the knoll.

"Get down, Keola!" I whisper-shout, tugging at his T-shirt. I'm so freaked out, using code names no longer seems important. "I heard Nalu's first call. Get your pans ready."

CRACK-BOOM!

RRR-RUMBLE-RUMBLE,

RRR-RUMBLE-RUMBLE!

It's like an entire squadron of Hells Angels motorcycles are tearing through the clouds coming straight for us, but still, no rain.

"How are we going to hear Nalu's second call when I can barely hear *you?*" Keola shouts in my ear. Good point, I'm about to say, when something grabs me from behind.

I hear the *thunk* of what I see is a shovel dropping to the ground in my peripheral vision, as a hairy arm wraps itself around my neck. "No try anything stupid, fat boy," a man's voice growls at Keola, "or I'll squeeze your girlfriend's neck like I'm one boa constrictor." I can feel the warmth of the man's breath on my skin, and I can smell it too. Fish, tobacco, and what could be stale beer.

His tone with Keola sends a surge of anger straight through me. I kick and squirm, but the jerk's chokehold only tightens, and I'm afraid he might break my neck.

Keola makes a move to pick up a pan, but the thug stops him cold. "Don't even think about it." Meanwhile, his buddy is trying to get a similar hold on Wilks who is apparently landing a few sharp kicks in some choice places.

"Yyyyy-owwwwww!" the guy screams, but the struggle finally ends with him jerking her arms behind her back and pinning them there.

She goes limp and lands in the sand sideways. For a breathtaking minute I think she's passed out, but then she twists around and spits in his face. She's a fighter, that one. But then he yanks a rope out of his shoulder pack and ties her hands behind her back, pressing her face into the sand. Just when I think he might suffocate her, my own vision goes gray, and I feel weak in the knees.

"I can't breathe," I croak.

Where are all those helpers Tūtū was talking about? Come to think of it, why hasn't Wilks called the ancestors? And why hasn't Keola tried to talk these guys out of what they're doing? And where the hell is Nalu anyway? We must have missed his second call. Or maybe we missed his first.

The evil one nods to his partner who grabs a flashlight from his shoulder bag and shines the cold, white light on the sand where the nest is.

"Okay, geniuses, dis how it's goin' down." He loosens his grip on my neck as he speaks. "You, brah! Grab da shovel." He kicks it over to Keola who picks it up reluctantly. "Now, dig."

All three of us gasp. Poor Keola looks like he's about to throw up. "I said, dig!"

Trembling, Keola starts to dig around the edges of the nest, working his way to the center, lifting a slim layer of sand at a time. As he uncovers the eggs, they glisten in the beam of the flashlight. According to Aunty, in six weeks or maybe a little more, these honu babies would have cracked their way into the world.

My captor drags me backwards about three steps, reaches down and tosses a Styrofoam cooler in Keola's direction. "Here. Put 'em in dis."

Tears fall from my eyes onto the bad man's hairy arm. He's so intent on Keola's work, he doesn't seem to notice. I've never felt so helpless in all my life, except when...

Oh, Baby Girl, I hope you're not around for this.

"Mahalo, friends, for showing us dis nest!" The bad guy laughs. "If it wasn't for you, we never would have found it."

Well, isn't that just great? I'd like to chomp down on his arm right about now, if only it wasn't choking me.

"Yeah, we found plenty da last few nights, yeah, brah?" He looks over at his partner who grunts. "But dis one been hard to find. After we saw da honu crawl on top da beach that night a week ago, something kept making us go off track." He shakes his head. "Anyway, here we are. When we saw your friend's shiny head there peaking over the hill, we figure we struck paydirt. Didn't know what a handful you delinquents would be." He laughs again. The laugh of someone who thinks he's won.

Meanwhile, Keola is lifting the eggs one by one and carefully placing them in the container, and I think, if God were choosing someone to do this part, there'd be no better choice. I also know what he's up to. On the drive back to camp from the bakery, Nalu filled us in on what he knew about honu and their eggs. Sometimes the conservancy people on the island need to move a nest to a safer place, he told us, and the key is to return the eggs to the nest in the order in which they were laid. That's what Keola's doing. He's thinking ahead. Unfortunately, our chances for saving these eggs don't look so good.

I was furious when Nalu told us how eggs like these were probably headed overseas where patrons at fancy bars pay dearly for them. How can people do that? Maybe they don't even think about it. They just lay their money down on the bar and the bartender hands 'em a big ol' egg out of a big ol' glass jar and they just pop it into their mouths and let it slide right down their greedy little throats.

I hope they choke on them.

Meanwhile, Keola continues to transfer Mama Honu's eggs first along the bottom of the cooler, and then in one loving layer after another on top of that.

"Come on, Picasso!" our captor rages. "This no work of art."

Just then, Mother Nature delivers another resounding *Crack-BOOM* and unleashes a drenching sheet of rain—like one of those tilting barrels at a splash park. It's the moment I've been waiting for. Swiping the rain from his eyes, my captor loosens his grip for a split-second, and I stomp on his foot, breaking free.

"Get her!" he screams at his partner and the chase is on.

I scramble over the knoll and sprint for the beach, hoping to gain some distance from my pursuer before I turn towards camp for help, but he's onto me, driving me down to the shore. I take out my cell phone for some light, but it slips from my hand, and I don't dare stop to pick it up. The man is gaining fast.

In ten more steps or so, I'll be at the water's edge and the only place to go will be "in," but that's *nuts*. I scramble to think of an alternative, but it's a moonless night in the middle of a thunderstorm and there's no other way.

I kick off my sandals and dive headfirst into an oncoming wave, hoping the big guy behind me isn't strong or stupid enough to follow. And I'm right. He just stands there on the beach, shining his flashlight into my eyes, as I rise and fall with the waves.

"Nice night for a swim," he yells, following me along the beach. Now and then, a wave breaks over me as I pull further away from shore.

The water is colder than I expected. To make it out of this alive, I need to figure out where I'm heading, preferably where that creep can't get me—but where? Maybe if I can make it a few hundred yards to the west, I can find a path to the nearby golf course and then follow the road back to camp and get help.

Out past the breakers, I begin a slow, steady breaststroke in that direction. Rain is coming down in needles now, pin-pricking my arms and shoulders as I swim. Soon, I can't even see the dude's flashlight. No doubt he thinks he's taken care of me, which seems to be the case. He's probably on his way back to join his buddy who's doing who-knows-what to my friends—a terrifying thought, but I can't let it stop me. The only way I can help them is to survive this myself.

I *must* keep swimming.

I must find land.

Where are those helpers Tūtū told us about anyway?

Suddenly, I feel this pull. It's like an underwater serpent has curled its tentacles around my torso and is dragging me away from shore. What the—? I try to free myself from the monster by swimming faster and harder, but it's like I'm swimming in place.

CRASH-BOOM! A zig-zaggedy bolt of lightning shows me how far away from shore I really am. Each wave lifts me skyward, then drops me like dead weight, leaving my stomach behind in its wake. Meanwhile, Aunty's voice hammers away in my brain, warning me about something. What is it? My thinking is as frozen as my limbs.

Wait, a *current*. That's it. I'm caught in a current. *Fight it and you'll die*, she says.

But I have to fight. Keola and Wilks need me. Those thugs mean business. Who knows what they'll do to my friends? It may already be too late.

I swim harder.

But Aunty is just as stubborn as ever, pushing her way into my brain. "The current will take you where you need to go," she pleads. And then I remember—the other promontory—like the one where Wilks and I met the ancestors only further west. If Aunty is right, the current will drop me there.

It takes everything I have left in me to stop fighting, but I do. This is my only hope of survival and, therefore, my only hope for saving my friends. If only I can keep myself above water. A big "if."

Whether it's my weakening limbs or the deepening cold, I can barely raise one arm and then the other over my head and yet I do, stroke after stroke. Half the time, I forget to kick. My legs are so frozen, they're dragging behind me. Dead weight.

Call the honu.

Wait. Where'd that come from? Baby Girl? Tūtū Malia?

No, I think numbly. Just a thought.

Call the honu.

Right. I can do that.

I focus on Mama Honu and cast my thought out to sea: *Come, please, come.*

As if taunting me, a super big wave shoots me up and then slams me down, tumbling me underneath the water like a helpless ragdoll. It takes every ounce of energy I have left to push myself up to the surface once I figure out where "up" is.

Help, please help, I call again. Never have I wanted my psycho-telepathic weirdness to work more than I do now.

But then, a feeling of hopelessness overwhelms me, as big as the next wave and the next. Too late, too late, too late, they seem to be saying, and suddenly I don't even care. I'm cold and I'm tired and my arms feel like jelly and I want to give up.

So, give up.

We've got you.

As I lift my arm over my head for one last stroke, I feel something soft brush against my leg. When I look toward my left, I notice the head of a honu bobbing out of the water as it swims, its flipper grazing me softly.

Is that you, Mama Honu?

Feelings and pictures flip through my mind: *a girl napping on a knoll, a trash bag, a gentle touch, relief, eggs dropping, hope, a fearful stillness, waiting, a feeling of safe.*

Oh, Mama Honu, it *is* you!

As I broadcast this thought, I feel another flipper brush against my other leg. How can that be? A rounded shell breaks the surface. It's another honu swimming—no, *flying*—in the current with me and there are others too, maybe a dozen more, lifting me buoyantly on the draft of their wings.

Okay, Mama Honu, okay.

I give up.

26.

Not Dead Yet

Shushhh-shushhh ... shushhh-shushhh ... shushhhhh ... shushhhh.

Now that the storm has passed, the waves have gotten quieter and are lulling me to sleep. Baby Girl and I are all stretched out on a blanket at our home on Alki Beach. She's been whispering secrets that sound like waves. *Shushhh ... shushhh.*

"Sophie?" she whispers so close to my ear I can feel her breath.

Hmmm?

"Will you always be my sister?"

Uh-huhhhh.

"But what if one of us goes far, far away ... like to Mars? Would we still be sisters?"

Why does this question feel so hard? I try to form a "yes," but the word turns cold on my lips. My lips are cold. I'm cold.

Please, Baby Girl, let me sleep.

"Sophie Kai, wake up! I didn't see you dying. Please wake up."

Words? Why am I hearing words? *Go away, I'm sleeping.*

But then, gray fades to light, and I'm rising up out of a cold, dark place. And someone is pinching my nose. And, *yuck!* They're trying to kiss me!

"Stop!" My eyes are crusty and hard to open. A shadow hovers over me.

"Oh, thank God, Sophie Kai! You're *alive*." Oh, it's Nalu … and he keeps repeating, "I didn't see you dying" like it's a confession or something.

Dying? Who's dying?

It isn't until I hear the *shushhh, shushhh* of waves below me, that I remember what brought me here. That sound must have lulled me to sleep after Mama Honu and her friends guided me safely to shore.

Safely, yes, but sharp pricks of pain remind me that the last leg of my late-night swim wasn't much fun. Close to the promontory, the current dragged me across a bed of crusty old sea urchins and pointy rocks until I found my footing. The red welts all over my body tell the story.

But wait. Where are the honu?

I sit up, ignoring Nalu's pleas to reassure him I'm okay. The sun has yet to rise—it must be around four in the morning—but the pre-dawn sky is beginning to lighten. Several feet below the rock's ledge I'm on, my honu friends are sleeping, nestled into the black, pebbly sand.

"Mahalo," I whisper.

"Sophie Kai?" Nalu's still trying to get my attention.

One look into his face and the night's events prior to my swim come rushing back to me. I grab his arm. "Keola? Wilks? Where are they? How long have I been out?"

"They're okay, Sophie Kai, but they're a little tied up at the moment, and they need our help." Nalu's voice cuts through the fog in my brain. "Close as I can tell, you've been out for about half an hour. Do you think you're okay to walk?"

"Yes. We need to go!" I jump up only to collapse onto my butt. The jolt to my spine makes my head hurt.

"Careful, Doc!" Nalu chuckles.

"No worries." I rub my calves. "Just a little cramping, that's all."

"Here, drink some water." He hands me a bottle that was strapped around his shoulder. "I think you swallowed half the ocean during that heroic swim," he says. "That's why I thought you might need some, you know … resuscitation," he adds shyly, as I gulp the cool drink.

"Oh," I say, remembering what I thought was a kiss. "Right…"

The water must be working, because I'm feeling more energized, or maybe it's the fire I feel in my veins at the idea of Keola and Wilks in the grip of those bad guys. I force myself to stand. This time, my legs hold, and I will myself to ignore the stinging red welts all over my body.

"Come on, let's go." I pull at Nalu's arm. "Every second counts."

"Wait, you'll probably need these." He hands me my sandals

and lets me lean on him as I strap them on. "Oh, and I've got your phone, too, although I think I better hang onto it since you're still pretty wet."

"Wait a minute." I stare at him as he puts the phone in a side pocket of his khakis. "Where did you find it ... and my shoes? Come to think of it, how did you know where to find *me*? And while you're at it, where the heck have you been?!"

"*Whoa*, there she is!" he says. Even in the shadowy dark, I can see him smile. "You can thank me later for saving your life."

"You didn't save it," I scoff. "I called the honu and *they* saved me."

Nalu tilts his head slightly like he's tuning into a radio frequency. "No time to argue, Sophie Kai. Our friends are calling." He grabs my hand and guides me over the rocks toward the base of the promontory. "I'll explain as we go."

Beside the fact that it's still so dark and I can barely see the back of Nalu's head, there are multiple paths winding this way and that through prickly bushes and knobby trees all sticking their roots out trying to trip us. It's a maze, but Nalu seems to know the way.

Turns out, that's his gift, or rather his superpower, if you're into that kind of thing.

"Tūtū Malia calls it being 'prescient' ... seeing what lies ahead," he explains as we wind our way down a sandy path with tall, thick grasses on either side. "She's been working with me to extend my sight. At the moment, I can read what's going to happen about half an hour ahead, which is pretty good, considering you can figure out a lot by noticing the general direction things are going. It has its limits, of course. It takes a lot of focus, and I can only do it with people, but it's why I'm good at working behind the scenes."

"So, like, you 'read' that I would get caught in that current, for instance?"

"Exactly. Careful here," he taps his foot on a branch blocking the path and helps me step over it. "A flash of lightning showed me where you and that egg thief were headed. Once you dove into the water, I knew you'd get caught in that current and where it would take you. I know you're a strong swimmer, Sophie Kai, so your ending up on that promontory was a no-brainer."

We've been speed-walking along the path, so I stop to catch my breath. "You have a lot more faith in me than I do."

"Hey, I knew you'd have helpers. I also figured that shark wouldn't bother you," he adds off-handedly.

"Shark?"

"Yeah, that was a guess. Him not bothering you, I mean. Sometimes I can see only so much, and I have to fill in the gaps."

"Okaaay ... *great* ... so if you 'didn't see me dying' like you kept on repeating over my not-dead body, then why did you try to 'resuscitate' me?" I eye him suspiciously.

"What can I say?" He grins. "You looked dead. You were very convincing." He tilts his head again, doing that future-frequency-wave thing. "Keola's about to lose his grip. We've got about ten minutes to get there. Run!"

❁ ❁ ❁

After sprinting over the golf course and down the road past camp, Nalu and I slow down a bit when we come to the pond where Tūtū Malia and I skimmed algae, a chore that feels like years ago. As we edge ourselves around the pond in the still-dark morning, the surrounding vegetation seems to block us at every step. I could swear the trees—what Uncle calls "false *kamani*" trees—are calling in the breeze, *turn back, turn back.*

Not on your life, I whisper.

I'm anxious that it's taking us so long to get to our friends. I put out a call to any critters who might hear my thoughts: *Tell our friends we're coming! Show us the way!* I don't have a lot of hope for that landing in anyone's brain, but who knows? Nalu signals me to stop at a long, rickety old bridge that crosses over the east side of the pond—something I hadn't noticed the other day when I was helping Tūtū closer to camp.

"Our friends are close," he whispers, barely loud enough for me to hear.

I see the flash of a low-lying creature zip by me, and because I've spent the last week mind-melding with them, I'm pretty sure it's a gecko. But wait. It's not just any gecko. It's our resident moʻo, Slitherin.

Hi there. You heard me, I think-say, trying to hide my disappointment. Unfortunately, "just a moʻo" comes barreling through my brain.

Slitherin stops in the middle of the bridge. She flips around and stares at me, and boy is she miffed. It's like she's saying, *I'm not just any moʻo, girl-they-call-Sophie Kai. I've got skills.* But before I can ask for forgiveness, Nalu interrupts.

"Change of plan, Sophie Kai."

And no, I do not like the sound of that at all.

27.
The Power of Little Things

Turns out, Nalu's getting a message that he's needed elsewhere. "Go ahead and cross that bridge," he says, meaning, like, on my own.

"Right," I say. "What if I fall in?" But when I turn around, he's already headed for the access road that leads to the highway in one direction and in the other, the heiau—the sacred place where Tūtū Malia, Wilks, and I gave thanks to the ancestors.

About thirty feet in length and six feet above pond level, the bridge has lost a lot of its planks, and the ones that remain have seen better days. There appears to be a thick wall of tangled brush at the other end of it with no path in sight. How can this possibly be a good idea? And yet, Nalu seems to think this will lead me to our friends; never mind that he's left me alone to find them.

I could swear that I hear an "*ahem*" coming from the direction of the bridge. Can a mo'o clear its throat? Slitherin's tail swishes back and forth. Nothing much phases geckos, so her annoyance with me is clear.

Alone? she glares.

Okay, okay, I glare back. *Not alone.*

I step gingerly onto the first plank expecting it to give way at any second, but it holds firm, so I step with all my weight onto the next. *Crack!* The weathered board under my foot splinters, and my leg slips halfway through, pitching me forward. It takes all my resolve to stifle a scream. Blood trickles down my leg where the splintered wood has pierced my skin just below the knee.

Dang, I'm a mess, but the throbbing wound is the least of my worries as I lean my ear into the darkness. Did anybody hear me? I listen for the sound of voices or anything that might indicate alarm, but the only thing I hear is the hoarse, high-pitched croaking of frogs below and the rustle of palms overhead. Meanwhile, Slitherin is waiting for me to get my act together.

I gently set my right knee on what appears to be the next solid board and test my weight. It holds, so I lift myself up, trying to pull my leg through the broken plank without inflicting any more cuts or bruises. Regaining my balance, I inch forward, stepping ever so gingerly over the dark voids between planks. Midway across, I find secure footing and stop, checking to see if Slitherin is still with me. Sure enough, there she is hanging out at the end of the bridge, scratching behind her ear—or cheek—or head—or whatever you call that part of the mo'o behind its slitty little mouth.

Some help you are. I shoot this thought into her lizard-brain, hoping to get her attention but she just keeps scratching. I let out a sigh. *Okay, then, here I come,* and I pick the rest of my way across—feeling every bruise and cut and sore on my body—until I'm standing again on sandy ground.

Even though the sun has begun to throw its light over the horizon, it's still plenty dark in the midst of all this tropical foliage. As for Slitherin, just when I think I've lost her, I see her long, skinny tail slip through a curtain of leaves. Syncing up with her, I bend low like a moʻo, moving more like a fluid than the solid human I am.

Wait for me now, I signal her. *Take me to my friends.*

Minutes later, I peer up through a big-leafed fern and see the shadow of a building with a hut-shaped roof ahead. The building's rough exterior has chunks out of it, like it's been bombed, or rather … a tsunami crashed over it. Could this be the former restaurant that Uncle told us about? He said it was close to camp. That would also explain the bridge to nowhere—a bridge that used to go from the restaurant to the beach. One section of the complex is still fairly intact with square, empty spaces where windows used to be. Through one of them, there's a dull light and moving shadows. Two men are arguing. I'd recognize those voices anywhere.

I creep closer, hoping at any minute to hear the voices of my friends, too—anything to indicate they're still alive. Despite what Nalu said about them being okay, he also said that Keola was losing his grip, and for sure, it's taken longer than expected to get here.

I flatten myself against the outer wall near the window frame, as Slitherin leaps onto the window ledge. I silently gasp. *What are you doing? They'll see you!*

She shrugs. *I'm a mo'o. So what if they see me?*

Weirdly, as I enter Slitherin's awareness, my eyesight flips from staring at her on the ledge to a shimmery prism of shadow and light that seems to see into the room. Could this be how she sees? In one segment of the prism, I see Keola sitting on the floor, his hands tied behind his back, facing toward the window. At another angle, I see Wilks tied up below the windowsill. Unfortunately, I can't see the details of their faces or any other clues that might tell me what they're feeling or thinking—something I desperately want to know.

It feels like the Earth has tilted on its axis and I'm about to fall off, when that terrible man—the one who came close to strangling me—suddenly rams his fist through the wall right next to the other guy. *Crrrrack!* Plaster goes flying.

I jump. Slitherin jumps. And I'm cast back into my own way of seeing.

The evil man spews a string of swearwords only half of which I recognize. "Our tires are flat!" he growls. "I think it's dat stupid girl. I like choke her neck!"

"I told you I took care of her," the other thug shot back. "No way she survived."

Just then, I hear a loud moan. It's probably Keola. He sounds like a wounded animal, one that's given up hope. Oh my gosh, he probably thinks I'm dead. If only he knew I was here.

Slitherin. I blast a thought in her direction, followed by a picture of what I'd like her to do. Not even a split second later, she starts running in circles, chasing her tail like a dog—certainly not like a mo'o. Look up, Keola, I want to scream. Please, look up.

And then, I hear his voice. His sweet, awesome, aloha voice.

"Ummm ... guys? I know you're planning to leave soon—to call for a ride or something—but I was wondering if you could untie us before you leave? I mean, we're okay and everything (he practically shouts), but I'm kind of losing the feeling in my hands over here and I might need a *doc* or something."

My codename! He used my codename, *Doc*. It worked! He knows I'm here.

"Shut up!" the evil one swears. "You think we're idiots?"

From the other side of the window above me comes a snort—a *loud* snort—and then something smashing against the wall, a near miss with Wilks the intended target. The shadowy figure of the bad guy fills the window frame and I duck, but his focus is all on Wilks. My friend. A fist raised over her head.

What should I do? Jump through the window? I'm about to scream when the other thug shouts, "Brah! Chill! She just one girl."

"More like a *devil*!" his partner snarls, but he lowers his fist and moves away from the window. I draw in a deep breath to calm my racing heart. "I'm gonna walk up da road and call da Boss. He's not gonna to be happy about all dis."

"I know, brah," the other answers, "but we gotta get out of here with these eggs before someone comes looking for these kids."

"You think I don't know dat!" And then I hear rustling around the corner from where I'm hiding. I duck behind a bush, but apparently the creep's going the other way like he said, up to the road. That will take at least five minutes, I guess, maybe ten. My chances of saving my friends are a lot better with just one bad guy to deal with.

I take a chance and raise my head up ever-so-slowly to peer into the room. This time I can see more detail than I did through Slitherin's eyes. What a mess. In the dim light of an over-sized flashlight standing on end, I see the shadowy figures of old, broken-down cabinets, upended bar stools, and dozens of cracked tiles strewn across the dirty floor of what must have been the restaurant's lounge. The white Styrofoam cooler holding Mama Honu's eggs rests off to the side near the doorway where the remaining thug sits on a stack of wooden pallets, his head in his hands. Thankfully, he doesn't know I'm here, or even that I made it out of the ocean alive.

Keola raises his chin ever so slightly and sends me a quick smile. Then he turns to the thug. "Man, you brudahs got yourself into a real jam."

"No need tell me dat," the thug mumbles.

"Yeah, I mean, stealing eggs from a protected species is one thing. Kidnapping is a whole other thing, right? Not to mention what you did to our friend." Keola makes his voice crack a little, like he's all choked up about me maybe being dead.

The thug doesn't respond at first, but then he says, "Ah, she probably okay. She look like one strong swimmer." He shakes his head like he's trying to convince himself he's not a murderer. "*Man*, I never like hurt nobody."

"Hey, I get it, brah," Keola continues with that silky-smooth, aloha voice of his. "I'm sure you got a reason for all this—like maybe a family to feed? Man, this has gotta be a hard way to make a living." Just when I think Keola has the dude where he wants him, Wilks' voice chimes in.

"You think the Boss's gonna be mad about all this? Wait 'til you hear from the ancestors. I'm getting the chicken skin just thinking about it."

"How you know about ancestors?" the thug shouts, glaring in her direction and mine.

"They're talkin' to me," she says quietly in the eerie light.

"Sure, they are," he says, but he sits up straighter.

Out of the corner of my eye, I see Slitherin crawling across the wall, stopping now and then to look around the room. What on earth is she up to now?

Suddenly, the other guy storms back into the building, grabs the cooler with Mama Honu's eggs, and starts shouting orders.

"Boss coming in his boat. Too risky on da road. He gonna moor off the heiau and we gonna wade out to meet him. Says drag da kids with us." He looks between Keola and Wilks. "What you think he gonna do wid you guys?" And then he laughs like a madman.

Even in the dim light, I can see Keola is terrified.

"Stay here and wait for my whistle," the evil one shouts to his buddy. "No sense take chance with those kids until we ready to take them on board." Seconds later, he tears by me mere feet from where I crouch, carrying the cooler of turtle eggs.

Dang. I really thought my friends' special powers would get that other guy to leave. What should I do now? Run for help? By the time I do that, those thugs will have been here and gone—my friends and the eggs with them. I peer into the room. In the absence of his partner, the other guy is doubled over like he's about to be sick. Keola's arms are folded tight to his chest. Wilks is sitting there, muttering to herself. And who the heck knows where Nalu is?

No! I want to shout. This can't be happening. Somebody *do* something!

Calling all helpers!

Seconds later, a flash of white comes bounding out of the brush. What's this? A dog? A *white* dog? And he's bouncing all over me, licking my wounds, and now my face. Talk about chicken skin!

"Aloha Dog, it's you!" I whisper into his fur.

And then I get an idea. *The boy is here, too!* I think-tell him. *In there!*

Oh boy, oh boy, oh boy! he yips and leaps through the window, lickety-split.

Certain that Aloha Dog has everyone's attention, I peer over the ledge. He's dancing in circles at Keola's feet, yapping his head off, and then he leaps into Keola's lap. His stubby tail wags his whole body, making Keola break into deep, belly laughs. All that puppy-love is irresistible, of course. Wilks scoots on her butt, her arms still tied behind her back, over to the middle of the room to join them, all the while stealing glances toward the door. The thug in the corner just sits there on his stack of pallets, gaping, clearly at a loss as to what to do.

Just then, out of the corner of my eye, I notice a tall, thin figure standing in the doorway. At the sight of her, I freeze—not in fear, but in *awe*. Oh my gosh, Wilks must have called the ancestors and look who showed up! The lady looks just like she did on the plane: white hair, piercing amber eyes, and a long, flowing muumuu covered in flashes of red and gold.

"Young man, have you seen my dog?" she demands.

The poor thug springs to attention, sending pallets flying.

"Oh, there you are," she says, patting her leg.

Aloha Dog gives Keola's face one final lick before he runs and leaps into her arms.

The lady starts to leave, but then turns back. "These your keiki?" she demands.

Shockingly, the thug nods yes.

"Thought so." She jabs a long, pointy finger in his direction. "Take care of them, see?"

He nods again, and then, *poof*, she's gone.

Obviously, our thug has heard all about Tūtū Pele, probably from his Tūtū just like we have, and he's starting to connect the dots. I can tell he wants to run—from the building, from us, from all the trouble he's gotten himself into—but for some reason, he's not budging. Maybe he thinks Tūtū Pele is still out there. Or maybe all he needs is a little push.

I look hopefully at Keola and Wilks—aka Mr. Rogers and Spirit Girl—thinking surely, they'll step up and do something, but they're staring at the floor, not moving a muscle. Could they possibly be thinking it's *my* turn? But what can *I* do? Storm the building? Push that barrel-chested thief out the door with eighty pounds of super girl muscle? I don't think so.

But then I remember something Tūtū Malia said: "There's power in little things." Out of the corner of my eye, I see Slitherin skitter across the wall.

Ah, yes, just the little thing we need.

I send her an image of what I want, and she slides across a beam until she's right over the guy's head. *Steady now.*

The man's eyes are already bugging out of their sockets from the recent Pele visit, and then, as if on cue, comes a call from the wild. *Whoooo, whoooo, hoot, hoot!* And you can tell the dude is now thoroughly spooked. Keola and Wilks look up, grinning.

Perfect timing, Poet Boy. Now it's my turn.

Jump! I think in mo'o and Slitherin leaps into the air, her skinny little limbs sprawled wide. For a few suspended seconds, she seems to fall in slow motion until she lands squarely on top of the man's bushy-haired head.

"Yaaaaaaaaaahhhh!" he screams, shaking Slitherin off. "I give up, Tūtū Pele! I done with dis business—for *good*. Have mercy on me!"

And with that, he staggers out the door.

28.
My Turn

"Doc! I thought you were dead!" Keola shouts, as I scramble over busted-up pallets to free my friends. "But when that moʻo of yours showed me those moves, man-oh-man, I knew you were out there. I've never been happier to see a moʻo in all my life!"

I tug at the rope around his wrists, making him wince. "Talk about moves, Mr. Rogers. You didn't just change that poor thug's mind, you changed his heart. You and Spirit Girl were brilliant. Speaking of which…" Now that Keola's freed, I shift to Wilks. "That was some powerful conjuring you did there." Her rope is tighter than Keola's was.

"I had no idea who I'd be getting," she shakes her head in disbelief, "but I'm guessing Aloha Dog was all your doing."

"Who knows?" I shrug. "I'm just glad we're on the same team … and that Tūtū Pele's with *us*." I toss the rope aside, revealing raw, angry burns around Wilks' wrists. "It was good to hear Poet Boy out there a minute ago. Who knows what he's been up to?"

"Letting air out of those thug's tires, would be my guess," Keola says, chuckling.

"Yeah, and saving me from certain death," I add.

"*Really?*"

"Nah, but *he* thinks he did." I grin. Keola staggers to stand. "Hey, you okay to walk?"

"Yeah, I'm good. Just need to get my circulation going again." He shakes out his arms and legs. "Should we go for help?"

"Yeah, maybe we should?" Wilks says, turning to me, both waiting for an answer.

Just then, a shrill whistle cuts through the air—the bad guy signaling for his partner, the one who ran.

"No time!" The words burst from my mouth. "Mama Honu's eggs. We've got to get them back." I stop to let Slitherin hop onto my shoulder on our way out the door.

Although the sun isn't up yet, the sky's a deep turquoise and purple with a streak of pink along the horizon. I lead my friends through the thick brush and over the bridge as quickly as we dare. As we near the beach, we hear the putt-putt of a boat's motor and men shouting. The thief stands at the shore's edge with the Styrofoam cooler at his feet.

"Where is that idiot?!" The deep-throated growl of Boss Man comes barreling over the water. "And where those kids?!"

If I thought the dude with the cooler was bad, this one seems like the devil himself. It's too dark and he's too far away for me to see the features of his face, but he's a hulking big shadow with enormous shoulders. The lit tip of what must be a cigar floats near his mouth, glowing eerily. Nalu says these black-market guys would just as soon kill you as look at you, and I believe it.

"I don't know, Boss. He was right here," his buddy calls, but his voice sounds tense. He whistles again, looking back over his shoulder toward the access road, as if he'll see his partner dragging two kids behind him at any minute.

No such luck, sucker.

"Leave him," Boss Man shouts with a snarl. "We've got to get out of here ... *now*."

The Boss Man's boat—a good twenty-five feet in length with a ginormous outboard motor—is anchored right off the tip of the promontory. His partner starts wading out to the boat, holding the cooler in front of him like it's a chest of precious jewels.

Something's got to happen fast, but I'm all out of secret powers. Apparently, so are Keola and Wilks because they suddenly take off after the guy, screaming like banshees.

"Guys! Wait!" I charge after them.

Boss Man looks up and sees us. "Hey, keiki! You're making this way too easy." He reaches for a dark object hanging from his belt. Is that what I think it is?

Look *out!* Slitherin think-yells in my ear.

"Get down!" I scream, catching up to my friends,

Pe-shew! Pe-shew! Shots ring out over our heads, as we fall flat to the ground.

"You better believe I'm a better aim than that," Boss Man thunders. "Stay back if you know what's good for you."

The three of us are one trembling mess. I raise my head to see what's happening. The thief is almost halfway to the boat. Waves break against his waist, as Mama Honu's eggs draw closer and closer to the point of no return.

Again, Slitherin screams in my brain: *Look! Out there!*

I look, and several hundred yards offshore is what looks like a triangular piece of steel gliding back and forth, back and forth, lit up by the first sharp rays of the sun.

Shark!

No sooner do I name it, than the humongous being underneath that fin grabs ahold of me with its thoughts and the biggest, darkest, void-sucking hunger no human has ever felt. I swear, I could eat my arm right off, if I had the teeth for it.

"Sophie Kai?" Keola shakes me gently, breaking my trance. He looks worried, but I know what I have to do. Mama Honu's eggs are hanging in the balance.

I raise myself up on my elbows, careful not to draw Boss Man's attention. "Friends." I look each one in the eye. "I've got this."

No sooner do I say that, however, than a chill of doubt runs through me. I'm about to try to summon a thousand-pound eating machine, when my last successful mind-meld was with a six-inch gecko. *Sorry, Slitherin, but you know it's true.*

Wilks pats me on the back. "Go on, you can do it, Sophie Kai. Do your thing."

"Right," I say, "but would you mind putting in a good word for me with Tūtū Pele's brother, the Shark King?"

Wilks grins and gives me a thumbs-up.

"Yeah, Sophie Kai, go for it ... whatever *it* is!" Keola chimes in.

Buoyed by their encouragement, I plunge back into that small but ferocious shark-mind and shoot him an image of the guy with the cooler. My plan is to get him to move in that direction—not out of hunger, but curiosity—just close enough to scare the guy. Once I've made contact, however, everything moves fast, and the shark rears out of the water as it turns with only one thought in mind: *Food!*

Noooooo! I try to stop the him, but it's too late. I've lost our connection.

"Shark!" I scream at the thug in the water, frantically pointing at the fin speeding his way.

"Shark! Shark!" my friends join in.

At first, the guy waves us off, but then he sees it.

"Aaaaaaaiiiiiii!" he screams.

"Swim to the boat!" Boss Man yells, but the dude turns toward shore instead. Maybe he thinks he'll have better luck getting away in shallower water, but the shark is gaining fast.

I've got to get back into that shark and stop this attack. But how?

Suddenly, the guy drops the cooler midway and Keola, Wilks, and I gasp. It wobbles on its side, but then rights itself, bobbing up and down with the waves. Think, Sophie, think. What do I know about sharks? That's when it comes to me. Something I saw on *Shark Nation*.

I set aside my terror and plunge back into shark mind, desperately searching for what he sees. There it is. A vague, blurry shape moving through the water. He imagines *fish* or *seal*, so I've got to break it to him fast. He's only a body length away from the man's legs, kicking furiously in the surf.

Human! Yuck! I shout into his shark-mind with all the disgust I can manage.

The guy lets out a blood-curdling scream. Oh no, I'm too late!

But wait! The shark veers away from him at the last nanosecond, grazing the guy's legs with his tail. Meanwhile, Boss Man is having a hissy fit, screaming at his partner to "get the hell back here with those eggs!" when I send the shark one last thought.

WHAM!

The shark slams against Boss Man's boat and sends it rocking before he heads out to sea. I'm thrown out of shark-mind with a jolt. Meanwhile, Boss Man is spitting out a string of curses, as he scrambles up the boat's ladder after being knocked overboard.

Keola and Wilks stare at me in shock.

"What in the world?" Keola stutters.

But there's no time for explanations. Those eggs are still out there and who knows what these thugs are going to do next.

"Quick, Keola. How likely is that guy going to shoot me?"

"Oh, maaaan, Sophie Kai," he says, his face wrung with worry, "maybe ... fifty-fifty?"

"Okay, guys, gotta go." I hand Slitherin over to Wilks and sprint to the water.

"Wait!" Keola yells.

Ignoring him, I dive headfirst into the surf.

I swim a wide berth around the thug struggling through the breakwater. He still thinks the shark is after him. Unfortunately, the tide must be on its way out because the cooler is floating closer to the boat with every wave. I've got to swim *fast*.

I'm a stroke away from the cooler, when I hear Boss Man shout, "Not on your life!" He's managed to pull himself back into the boat. He drops the propeller and tugs at something with all his might.

RRRRRRRRROAR! The engine storms to life. One look in his eyes tells me he's ready to mow me down. I hear shouts from shore, as Boss Man engages the engine, ramming the throttle forward. I throw my arms around the cooler and squeeze my eyes shut, thinking, *I'm dead, I'm dead, I'm dead,* when this ear-splitting, grind-screeching, metal-bending, clunk-clanking sound splits the air all around me. I duck ... but nothing strikes.

When I dare to open my eyes again, the boat's still right there—not an inch closer to me or the eggs—with billowy, black clouds of smoke pouring out its rear end. My ears are ringing.

A metallic smell hangs so thick in the air, I can taste it. I frantically search for Boss Man, but he's nowhere to be seen. I hear muffled shouts from shore.

Still clinging to the cooler in shoulder-deep water, I look around, confused. Standing along the shore are my friends, Keola and Wilks, and next to them, two cops putting handcuffs on one of the bad guys while another cop wades out to help me.

"Come on in, Miss," he says when he gets close enough for me to hear him. It's like I have cotton in my ears. "Here, let me help you with that." He reaches for the cooler, but I shake my head, no, clinging to it with all my might.

"Okay, then," he says, taking my arm and guiding me shoreward. "This is over now."

"But what about…?" I turn back toward the boat to warn him about Boss Man, when I see another cop already on the boat, yanking the devil to his feet.

Where did all these cops come from?

As if reading my mind, the cop helping me says, "Some old lady flagged us down on the main road a while ago, said there was something bad going down here at the beach. I didn't believe her, but my partner got the chicken skin and called for back-up. Good thing, too."

"Let me guess," I rasp. "She had white hair and a little white dog."

"How'd you know?"

I shrug and silently thank our ancestor, when a large wave breaks over our backs and nearly knocks us over. We're close enough to the water's edge, that I can hear Keola and Wilks laughing, I guess out of relief that I'm okay. No other sound could make me happier.

When the cop and I regain our footing, we notice the cop's buddy dragging Boss Man, now handcuffed, toward the beach. "Man, oh man," he says. "If that's who I think it is, that's one bad dude. We've been trying to catch him in the act for years. You keiki are lucky to be alive."

"Not luck," I whisper, when I notice someone dancing along the rocks of the promontory. I've been expecting him. "Poet Boy!" I shout, finding my voice. Keola and Wilks wave and shout, too. Beaming, Nalu raises this mangled-looking steel rod high over his head like it's some kind of trophy.

Minutes later, the police are loading the thieves into the back of their cars while the four of us gather into a group hug. Slitherin has hopped back onto my shoulder. The cooler with Mama Honu's eggs rests safely on the sand. Meanwhile, after we begged him to tell us, Nalu fills us in on what he was doing behind-the-scenes. Of course, he *was* the one who let the air out of the bad guys' tires—no surprise there. But his next feat?

"Those idiots left their van doors wide open," he begins, "so I snuck in and grabbed that rod-iron pick they use—or rather *used*—for poking around looking for nests." We stare at the mangled piece of metal lying at his feet. "Turns out it also stops propellers and burns out engines. Cool tool!"

The rest of us look at each other and burst out laughing.

Nalu looks puzzled, but then his face brightens. "Hey, that rhymes!"

"Hurray for Poet Boy!" Keola shouts, still catching his breath from laughing so hard.

"A behind-the-scenes kind of guy!" adds Wilks.

They all turn, waiting for me to add something. When I don't, everyone gets quiet, their eyes fixed on the cooler of eggs. I gulp back the tears pouring down my throat.

"Hey, Poet Boy … *Nalu*." He meets my gaze across the circle. "I hate to say this, but you really did save my life … *this* time." I sniff back a laugh. "Heck, you saved the *day!*"

He shakes his head, and oh my gosh, Mr. Confidence himself is blushing. "No way, Sophie Kai." He looks at Keola, then Wilks, and finally, back to me. "We *all* saved the day."

"…with a lot of help," I say, nodding toward Slitherin hanging out on my shoulder, and silently thanking our ancestors in all their forms.

"However…" I sink to my knees and wrap my arms around the cooler of eggs. "The day we're saving isn't over yet."

'Ohana

29.
One by One

"So, what happens now, keiki?"

The four of us jump at the sound of Tūtū's voice and turn to face her. Are we in trouble? It feels that way. Aunty and another woman are standing a few feet behind her. All three women are scowling.

"Glad to find you in one piece," Tūtū adds with an edge to her voice. "When we woke up and found you gone, we were worried *sick* about you." She rams her walking stick into the sand three times, and then tosses it aside. "Oh, come here," she cries, as she pulls us into a hug, her arms like wings. Aunty stands outside our circle, smiling but fidgety. We open our hug to make room for her, too.

Anyway.

It feels good to be held like this.

It feels good to be with friends like family.

Turns out the woman with Aunty and Tūtū is a turtle expert with a local environmental group. The police called her in when they knew what they were dealing with. Her name is Jane—a tall, thin woman wearing jeans and a green cotton shirt—and she looks like she means business which is good because she's all about getting Mama Honu's eggs back to their nest.

So are we, of course, but the police have other ideas. They write our names down, and then they ask us a bunch of questions, after which they take a ton of pictures of the cooler and the eggs and the scrunched-up iron pick. When the officer in charge says he wants to take us down to the station to question us further, Tūtū puts her foot down.

"They're *keiki*, for heaven's sake," she tells him, a finger pointed at his chest, "and they're *exhausted*. They've done enough for one night, don't you think? Now leave them alone."

There was nothing for him to say but, "Yes, Tūtū."

Keola, Nalu, Wilks, and I silently lead the way to Mama Honu's nest, the adults trailing behind. The fullness of the early morning sky casts a soft, golden glow on everything we pass, as Keola and I hold the cooler of eggs between us, taking care not to knock against it as we walk. Back at the crime scene, Jane had started to pick the cooler up, but Aunty put a hand on her arm, nodding in our direction. "Let them see this through," she said.

When we're near the pond, I signal for our procession to stop for a minute so I can let Slitherin slip off my shoulder to do whatever mo'o do this time of morning. He skitters off in the direction of camp and doesn't look back.

Half-a-dozen honu are sleeping on the black-sand beach as we continue our journey to the nest. One opens an eye to me, and I know her as one of the honu that guided me—no, *carried* me—to safety last night.

"Mahalo," I say, entering honu mind where I'm given a wordless nod.

Eventually, we're on the path that leads to the nest and then over a knoll and we're there. Sand is still kicked up and scattered where Wilks and I tussled with the bad guys. A large, round depression rimmed by a ledge of sand marks the nest that Keola just hours before knelt beside and carefully lifted egg by egg into the cooler.

The seven of us stand there, gawking at the scene where it all went down.

"Oh, my 'ohana." Tūtū looks up at us with the saddest of eyes.

With a palm frond she picked up on the way to the nest, Tūtū raises her arm like a conductor raises a baton. Her knee-length, turquoise muu-muu flutters in the morning breeze. Slowly, she moves around the nest, sweeping the frond over the sand where all the awfulness took place, as she chants what seems to be a blessing. At least it feels like a blessing, because something around us lifts.

Keola looks at me in wide-eyed wonder. "Can you feel that?"

I nod. It's as if every bad thing that happened last night suddenly got erased. And not just from this place—but also from *me*. As Tūtū holds the final note of her chant, I breathe out a long sigh of relief.

"Thank you, Creator, for these keiki," Tūtū prays, her face tilted up to the cloudless sky, "for they have shown great koa in protecting these eggs—our 'aumakua. We thank you for showing them the way." When Tūtū finishes her prayer, she steps back from the nest and nods at Jane who has been waiting patiently.

"Mahalo, Tūtū Malia," she says respectfully. "And mahalo to the four of you. Because of your bravery, thousands of honu eggs will be saved from being sold on the black market, and that's good news for all of us." She nods at Keola to bring the cooler forward. "Now let's get these eggs back where they belong!"

Jane hands Keola a pair of thin protective gloves. "I hear they call you Mr. Rogers."

Keola nods and blushes.

"Well then, I can think of no better person to do the honors."

After struggling to pull the gloves onto his enormous hands, Keola kneels by the nest in the exact same spot he knelt just hours before. This time, rather than taking the eggs out, he carefully lays them back in.

One by one.

We say our goodbyes to Jane at the nest. As we trudge up the path back to camp, we see the other Koa campers filing off to the beach in the other direction, Uncle bringing up the rear. He turns and quickly tips his cap, but he's the only one who sees us, thank goodness. I don't think any of us have the energy for an avalanche of questions right now.

Tūtū clears her throat behind us. "Something you need to know, keiki. We called your parents as soon as we knew you were missing." Tūtū's voice sounds casual, but that warm fuzzy feeling I had after watching Keola return the eggs to the nest suddenly evaporates.

Oh my gosh, my parents probably think I'm dead!

"No worries," Tūtū quickly adds. "When we heard from the police, Aunty and I came straight down to the beach, but not before I told Uncle to call your parents back and tell them you were okay. I'm sure they were all relieved."

Hopefully, that's all they were. Mom's been known to go on the attack if something she cares about is in danger. Hopefully, there wasn't enough time for that to kick in between phone calls. Anyway. All I want is to sleep for a week. Every muscle in my body aches and every inch of skin stings from all the scratches, scrapes, and bruises I got from chasing after bad guys.

We're close to camp when Uncle comes running back up the beach and whispers something in Tūtū's ear.

"Tell *her*, Uncle," Tūtū says. "She's the one who should know."

My heart sinks, I mean, it *plummets* into my stomach like an elevator with its cables cut, as Uncle turns to face me. The smile-lines on his weathered face are drawn down with worry. I think somebody has died, but no, it's worse.

"It's your Mom," Uncle says quietly. "She'll be here by dinner."

30.

Just Like That

By the time Tūtū and Aunty fuss over my wounds and I get to our hut, I'm so darn tired, I can't even think about what's going to happen when Mom gets to camp. It's like I'm one of those dolls that collapses into a heap at the exact place where it loses all its juice. In this case, it's my cot. Tūtū says we can sleep for as long as we want. Meanwhile, Slitherin is stretched out on the windowsill, Wilks pulls the sheet up over her head two cots over, and the cool morning breeze soothes my ragged skin.

Next thing I know, I'm on my balcony back home inside a make-shift pirate ship Mom helped me build. The two of us are sitting cross-legged on couch cushions with five-month-old Baby Girl wrapped in her yellow ducky blanket between us. A warm breeze flutters our sails. I'm afraid the whole thing's about to collapse, but Mom insists it will stand up to the mightiest wind. The corner of one of the sheets flaps against Baby Girl's face, making her giggle and soon, Mom and I are giggling too.

"Ahoy, maties!" Mom sings. She's back from getting us a snack, and I see her shadow behind the sheet. "Anybody on board?"

"Just me and the brat," I say in my nastiest pirate voice. "Aaaargh!"

"Aaargh!" Mom replies as she hands me a bowl of popcorn. Baby Girl wiggles her arms and legs and giggles some more.

"I think she gets what's funny," I say.

"Of course, she does," Mom says. "She's one of us girls!"

"Aaargh!" Baby Girl grunts.

It's so hilarious to hear a deep, throaty pirate's voice coming out of a tiny baby, that I wake up giggling. I lie there quietly on my cot, allowing myself to wake up slowly and leave the dream behind. It was a good dream and one that I wish were possible, if only, well … you know.

I shake my head and there's Moa, his wobbly red comb jiggling this way and that in front of my face. The sun has traveled to the other side of the hut, so most of the room is in shadow. There's still a lump on Wilk's cot although it's hard to tell if it's really her. Normally, I would push the demon rooster away, but something stops me—a clucking kind of voice inside me that pleads, "Please, look."

I get this message a lot. "Look" is often the first thing I hear when animals want to communicate with me. Aunty says they just want us to notice them.

My vision flips and I'm suddenly seeing through Moa's eyes, only I wouldn't call it seeing. In fact, I'd call it *not seeing*. Everything around us, including my own face, is super dark and fuzzy. I try to focus, but it's no use.

Can't see, Moa clucks in my head.

"Oh yeah, I can see that now," I whisper back, stroking his feathery neck. As I lean away from him, my normal vision returns. "No wonder you're always getting underfoot and clinging to Aunty all day. You're almost blind."

As sad as this news is from my point of view, I only feel waves of thanks rolling off him. Funny. He's not asking for it to be any different; he's just happy that someone finally understands. And with that, Moa waddles away, bumps into Wilk's cot, and lets out a squawk before scurrying out the door.

I'm wondering how Aunty could have missed his blindness—how you can't see the truth about someone when it's staring you in the face—when Luana sticks her head into our hut.

"Hey, Sophie Kai," she says in that gentle voice of hers. "I'm glad you're awake. Tūtū told me to come get you." With a sheepish grin, she adds, "Your mom's here and she's *huhū*—I mean, crazy mad."

As I get closer to Tūtū Malia's hut, I hear my mother's steely voice making accusations—something about "wanton endangerment." I don't know what that means, but I'm pretty sure it's lawyer-speak for "I'm going to sue you for all your worth."

I duck to the side of the hut's opening as Mom continues her rant. I can see the back of her. She's wearing one of those dark, tailored jackets she wears in court, her long, auburn hair braided tight in a bun. You can tell she tried to dress down for the island because she's wearing jeans, but the effect is still the same. All business.

"According to the police report, gunshots were fired at my daughter while she was under your care. How could you be so reckless as to let her and the other children out of your sight?!"

Sitting perfectly at ease in her favorite wicker chair, Tūtū only listens. I want to step in and say, *because everyone was asleep when we snuck out, like hundreds of kids do at summer camp every year,* but Mom rages on.

"Do you have any idea how fragile Sophie is? How devastating this must be for her?" She shakes a pointed hand at poor Tūtū like it's a gun. "It will take her years to recover from this trauma, and I'm holding you personally responsible."

I'm still tired and sore from the ordeal last night, but hearing Mom threaten Tūtū like that gives me a sudden surge of energy. "Oh, Mom, *stop*," I say, as I burst into the hut. "Please *stop!* This isn't Tūtū's fault … and I'm not fragile!"

Tūtū peers around Mom and lights up when she sees me. "Sophie Kai, there you are. Your mom's here!"

"Sophie!" Mom almost trips over a floor mat before falling into me for a hug. I hold my arms stiff to my sides. "Oh, Sophie," she breathes into my ear. "We were worried sick about you."

"Where's Dad?" I ask, turning my head away.

She frowns. "We could only get one plane ticket with such late notice. Besides, Dad knew I could handle things."

"Handle *what* things?" I snap.

"You know, what's going on at this camp." She tries to sweep a strand of hair away from my face, but I take a step back. "Sophie," she pleads. "We're talking black-market thieves with guns here. That wasn't in the brochure!" She reaches her arms out again, hoping for the hug I have yet to give, but drops them when she sees I'm not budging.

Tūtū leans forward in her chair and watches us intently. I have never seen her scowl, but there it is. Unmistakable. But is it for Mom, for me, or for the situation? After all, the fate of Camp Koa is at stake.

Man, I'd give anything to stop my mom from being, well, *Mom*.

Suddenly, I remember something Aunty said about communicating with moʻo: "First, find a way to connect. Get down on their level. Show them you understand what they're feeling, and that you feel it, too." Harder with a mom than a gecko, I'm guessing, but here goes.

"Look, Mom," I try to sound calm even though I'm trembling inside. "I get that this thing that happened with those bad guys sounds really scary."

"Scary?! You call being shot at *scary*?!" she erupts. "You act like this was some schoolyard game. What happened was terrifying, Sophie! And it happened to *you*." Mom's mouth forms a tight, grim line, and I can tell she's not backing down. But hey, my friend the shark didn't listen to me right away either.

"I get it, Mom, parts of what happened were terrifying, but none of this is Tūtū's fault. I'm the one who snuck out of my hut with my friends. I'm the one who couldn't think about anything else but saving Mama Honu's eggs. I'm the one who put myself in danger because I cared about something. Something important."

Mom's shoulders slump as she lets out a sigh. "I appreciate your taking responsibility, Sophie, I do. But don't you see? *You* are what's important here. It was *your* life on the line, and for that, somebody's got to pay." She glares at Tūtū Malia, and I scramble for something positive to tell her—like how Camp Koa has given me something she's always wanted me to have.

"Friends…" I say. "Of course, you never want to see me hurt, Mom, but did I mention that when I snuck out of camp—which I really shouldn't have done—that I snuck out with my *friends*, as in, I actually have *friends*?"

She tilts her head. Good. I've got her attention.

"Yeah. Like friends who don't care that I'm different, you know? I mean, they like my weirdness and I like theirs."

Now she's got that scrunched-up, unibrow thing going.

"Oh, Mom, you know, my *weirdness*, like how I was in Sarasota—the whole seahorse skeleton thing?"

Oh my gosh, can she really not know? It's like Aunty not knowing Moa is blind. I stare at the woven mat under my feet just in time to catch a green streak of a gecko slide under Tūtū's chair, probably one of Slitherin's cousins. *Great.* Next thing you know Mom will be calling the health department.

I take a deep breath. I might as well lay the whole thing out. Things couldn't get any worse than they already are, right?

"Okay, sooooo … I have this weirdness, see. I can talk to animals, and they can talk to me. Well, sort of." Man, it's really humid in here. Beads of sweat are trickling down my neck. I take a breath. "Actually, it's more like snapchatting between brains. I feel stuff and they show me pictures."

Mom looks from me to Tūtū. Already pale, Mom's face has gone completely white. "What have you done to my child?" she hisses.

"Oh, come on, Mom. This can't be that hard to understand." My hands are so tight-fisted, my fingernails are cutting into my palms. "I've had this weirdness long before Camp Koa. Dad must have told you about his Tūtū and her special powers. Well, it seems I've inherited them. No big deal." I uncurl my fingers, willing my hands to open. "Really, Mom, Camp Koa has been *fun*. Tūtū Malia here, Aunty Kuʻuipo, and Uncle Hanalei have all helped me see that my weirdness is a gift, that it's nothing to be afraid of." There. Mom's always telling me to believe in myself. This has *got* to score points for Camp Koa.

Unfortunately, Mom's starting to look all noodle-y, like she's about to collapse. Tūtū takes Mom gently by the arm and guides her to the chair next to hers.

"This is a lot for your mom to take in, Sophie Kai," Tūtū says gently. "Give her time."

But there is no time! I want to scream. You don't know my mother!

"Look, Sophie," Mom says, sounding weary, "your dad did say something about the possibility that you might have inherited some ... abilities, but I didn't want to believe him. Life is hard enough without having 'special gifts.'" She adds air quotes. "Here's the bottom line…"

Uh-oh. Mom's bottom lines rarely go in my favor.

But instead of steeling herself for a final verdict, she drops her head into her hands and begins to shake with tears. Like she's forgotten the bottom line altogether.

"Listen, Sophie." She raises her head and takes a breath. "I never could have imagined losing Baby Girl ... back then." She waves her hand behind her, as if that's where the past is, and gulps back a sob. "But *now*? The thought of losing you, too? It's too much. It's simply too much."

And just like that, I see how much she loves me.

I drop cross-legged onto the straw mat in front of her and reach for her hand. She grabs onto mine like she's been waiting to hold it her entire life.

"I'm so sorry, Mom. I must have really scared you…" I say, tears welling up, all the fight drained out of me. "…to come all the way out here and everything, all the time thinking I could have died. That's a *lot*." One guilty thought leads to another, and I think of that sweet baby in today's dream. "Ohhhhh, Mom … Baby Girl," I wail. "I'm so, so sorry!"

Mom freezes. "Sophie. What do you mean…*Baby Girl?*"

"You know … that *night* … how she died … how I didn't come to get you." Tears are pouring down my face now, dripping onto our hands.

Quietly, Mom slips down onto the mat beside me and folds me into her arms. There's a current pouring through her that if I had to name it something, I'd call it *fierce*, but not the kind of fierce that scares you. The kind of fierce that makes you feel safe. Loved.

"Sophie Kai," she whispers my Hawaiian name as she rocks me. "I never could have imagined that you'd blame yourself for what happened to Baby Girl." She shakes her head. "I should have known."

"But Mom…" I protest.

"Listen to me." She lifts my chin and peers into my eyes. "You are not responsible for Baby Girl's death. *None* of us are. I blamed myself at first, but the doctor said there wasn't anything anyone could do. It took me a long time to accept that, so I understand how you feel, but Baby Girl's dying is *not your fault*."

Not your fault.

Those three words begin to shimmer inside me, and just like that, I believe her.

"How could I not know this about you, my sweet girl?" Mom says, stroking my hair. "You, carrying the weight of all that guilt?" She leans back and searches my eyes. "Sophie Kai, can you ever forgive me? I'm afraid my grief over Baby Girl's death all these years has kept me from being the mother I needed to be with *you*."

"Ah, Mom ... that's okay." I'm feeling a little awkward.

"No, it's *not*," she says, then softens. "It's not okay, but..." She gently presses her forehead against mine. "I'm here with you *now*."

And just like that, it's like this wall of ice suddenly melts and evaporates all at once, and I feel so much ... *love*. We stay like that, forehead to forehead, for what seems like forever.

Tūtū clears her throat and we both jump. We forgot she was there!

"*Pono*," she whispers, moving her chair closer. "I couldn't be prouder of what the two of you have done here. We call it *hoʻoponopono*, a process of forgiveness and love, and you did it *naturally*." She taps her heart. "I'm so happy for you!"

Mom pulls me closer. I do not push her away.

"Now the three of you can move on," Tūtū says eagerly, gazing over my left shoulder—a dead giveaway for who she's including, but it makes me more than a little nervous about how Mom might react.

Sure enough, Mom looks puzzled.

"Three?"

31.
The End of the World as I Know It

Of course, Tūtū Malia knew about Baby Girl; no surprise there. After all, she's the one teaching Wilks about connecting with our ancestors. Pretty risky, though, her mentioning the "three" of us, seeing how Mom and I had just gone through hoʻoponopono and came out all peaceful and loving. What if Mom got riled up all over again, thinking I was coo-coo crazy, and that Tūtū had caused it?

Turns out hoʻoponopono works in forward, as well as reverse. When I explained who exactly made "three"—Tūtū insisted that I be the one to tell her—Mom said wistfully, "Oh, that's nice," and kept stroking my hair.

"Mom, I'm serious. Baby Girl's spirit lives on. I thought you'd be happy about that, or well, hysterical."

Mom laughed. "Oh, I don't doubt Baby Girl's spirit lives on, Sophie Kai. I've always believed that." She uses my Hawaiian name all the time now. "And it doesn't surprise me one bit that you're feeling her presence here in Hawaii, especially with your … sensitivity." She quietly looked around her. "I may not feel Baby

Girl's spirit right now, but it's enough that you do." And then she said something I never thought I'd hear her say: "I believe you."

If Tūtū is right about ho'oponopono, then maybe Baby Girl attached herself to me for more than a Hawaiian vacation, and forgiveness has released her spirit, too. She may still be hanging around us while Mom and I both are here, but I have the sense she'll stay on the island with our ancestors once we're gone. Who knows? Maybe Dad, Mom, and I will be the ones to join *her* sometime in the future. On the island, that is. I'd like that.

For the rest of the week, Mom's been renting a room at a B & B down the road so that I can "finish my commitment" at Camp Koa—her words, not mine. Oh well, once a lawyer, always a lawyer. Now that she's loosening up a bit, I'm okay with that. Thankfully, the whole lawsuit thing evaporated with our tears.

Tūtū invited her to join us at camp anytime she wants, but mainly she's only coming in the evenings for talk story. I think she doesn't want to get in the way of me hanging out with my friends. Now that I have some.

In celebration of our last day at camp, we're all heading down to South Point on the Camp Koa Express. It's a rickety ride as usual, but the mood is high. Everyone's excited about finally getting to jump off the cliff—everyone, that is, except Keola and me.

"It's not so much the fall; that's *easy*," Keola spouts back to

Honi, who's been teasing him the whole ride. "It's the climb back up. Do you have any idea how much strength it takes to lift this handsome hunk of manliness forty feet in the air? On a swinging rope ladder, no less? Are you kidding me?" Keola starts laughing that deep-bellied laugh of his, and soon, Honi and everyone else on the bus are laughing, too.

Keola's sharing the back bench of the bus with Nalu. When we all finally settle down again, he adds, "Besides, I don't need to prove anything to anybody." He puffs out his enormous chest. "I love myself just the way I am."

"Of course, you do, Mr. Rogers!" Nalu says, and everyone cracks up all over again.

I'm relieved that Keola's grabbing all the attention right now. It leaves me to wrestle quietly with my own fears. I desperately want to jump off that cliff, but I keep breaking out into a cold sweat at the thought of throwing myself into all that nothingness only to fall speedily down to the Pacific Ocean below. Sure, it's water. But it might as well be cement if I hit it the wrong way. And what if I stumble before I leap and ricochet off the rocks all the way down?

Not pretty.

I adjust the neck strap of the bathing suit I'm wearing under my T-shirt and shorts. This stupid thing has always been a little tight on me.

"You think too much." Wilks tears off a piece of beef jerky and offers me the rest.

I wave it off, disgusted. "Thanks for the vote of confidence."

"Oh, I have confidence in you," she shrugs. "I'm confident that you'll make yourself miserable wringing yourself into a knot over this decision, and then, do it anyway."

She's right, of course, except the part where I do it anyway. It's kind of nice, though, having a friend who knows you so well. I'm going to miss that girl.

Minutes later, we see a sign with an arrow that reads "South Point, the southernmost point in the United States." The Camp Koa Express turns there, hobbling onto a narrow road that cuts through acres of dry, pastureland dotted here and there by a few sad-looking cows.

I always thought Hawaii was all rainforest and waterfalls, but no, Uncle says there are ten different climate zones on this island alone—ten of thirteen climate zones *in the whole world*. When he told us that, Keola pretended like his head was exploding, making us all laugh, but geesh, this is some island.

The road curves and slopes for a few miles until it runs out at the end of the world as I know it. Underneath all this grassland is apparently rock, jutting out, out, out into thin air where it hangs forty feet above the frothing sea. Uncle parks in a grassy area about a dozen feet from the cliff's edge.

I want to throw up.

"Let's go!" Honi shouts. Already in his swim trunks, he skips barefoot off the bus. Everyone else follows happily—all, that is, except for me and Keola.

Uncle sticks his head back in. "You two comin'?"

"Yeah, man," Keola grins, giving him the shaka sign and me a hand down from the bus. "Come on, Doc. Let's do this thing ... or *not*! Nobody's gonna make us do anything we don't wanna do."

"Right," I say, but the truth is, I wish someone *would* make me do it. That way I wouldn't have to think about it.

"Keola! Sophie Kai! Over here!" It's Nalu and he's standing on the diving platform, his toes wiggling over the edge. It gives me the chicken skin just looking at him.

Keola and I join him on the platform, but as far back from the cliff as possible. Wilks is hanging out with Luana a few feet away. I can tell Wilks is trying not to meet my gaze, probably not to feed my worry, which makes me think she's worried, a thought that doesn't help at all.

She's right. I think too much.

"Sophie Kai, are you ready for this?" Nalu bobs his head in an exaggerated nod *yes* several times, encouraging me to nod, too.

I nod.

And gulp.

And nod again.

"Good," he says.

I'm vaguely aware that the other campers are stepping away

from the platform, giving us space when just minutes ago, everyone seemed to be scrambling for position—*Me next! Me next!* Their quiet is unnerving. Even Keola has backed away.

What do they think is happening?

What *is* happening?

"Now," Nalu holds my gaze. "There are just two things you need to think about before you jump."

Wait. Jump?

The word shoots ice water into my veins and the whole scene suddenly comes into focus: my friends all around me, staring; the wet, worn wood of the platform under my feet; the kūpuna—my Tūtū, Aunty, and Uncle—standing off to the side but close. The ocean below, the sky above, the sun warming my bare back.

I look down at my shimmery turquoise swimsuit—a color that's so bright, it should be blinking—and I regret not getting black. I guess at some point I must have slipped out of my T-shirt and shorts and given them to Keola because they're now draped over his arm.

"Sophie Kai?" Nalu's still looking intently at me, his last words *before you jump* still ringing in the air.

Seeing my hesitation, Keola's voice rings through the salty air. "You don't have to do this, Sophie Kai."

"That's right," Nalu says, softly. "I assumed this is what you wanted, but you don't have to. Do you still want to?"

I stare out at the wild blue yonder that waits for me on the other side of this moment, and for some reason I think of Mom flying all the way out here to protect me and how brave she was to let go of the fight against Camp Koa … and I think of how brave Baby Girl is to let go and move on to wherever *that* is … and I think, *Geesh, this is nothing*. And that ice in my veins turns to fire.

"Heck, *yeah!*" I shout to our small crowd, who Tūtū would call our *'ohana*. "I want to jump!" And to Nalu, I say, "Let's do this thing!"

He claps his hands together as everyone cheers. "Okay, *great!* Sophie Kai, listen up. I'm going to go first so you can get a picture of what this jump's supposed to look like."

"Oh, right, brah!" Honi pipes up. "You just want her looking at your scrawny backside!"

"No chance of that," I shout back, and everyone laughs.

Adrenalin surges through my veins, making my hands tingle. I shake them out, waiting for further instructions. "You said there were two things I should know?"

"Oh, *right*." Nalu claps his hands again. "First thing, commit to your run. As soon as your feet start to move, never hesitate. Run right off the edge, like you had three or five or ten more feet to go. Got that?"

"Got it."

"Good. Second thing. After you jump and you're in the air, hold your body straight as a pin: arms tight to your sides, legs together, shoulders back, chin tucked." I automatically stand at attention in exactly this way. "If anything's sticking out, well..." He winces. "It could hurt."

I gulp for the umpteenth time.

"Okay, Sophie Kai." He sets his hands on my shoulders and looks me straight in the eye. "This is going to be *fun*."

"Right!" I say, with a bit more enthusiasm than I'm feeling.

Nalu smiles and turns his back then, taking his position at the far end of the diving platform right in front of me. "Here goes something!" he yells to our 'ohana, and then to me, he whispers, "See you down below, Sophie Kai. You're going to be *great*." And off he goes at a full tilt run.

And yes, I watch, but rather than his form or his back or his speed, I see what makes him jump. I can feel it in his mid-air scream, "Yaaaaaw-hooooooooooo!"

Gosh darn, that boy is living his life.

I walk gingerly out to the end of the platform, every nerve in my body on high alert. I just need to see that he made it.

I look carefully over the edge to the waves crashing against the cliff rock a gazillion feet below. There's a rowboat tied to a buoy near where Nalu is casually treading water, grinning up at me. He looks small in that great big ocean, but more importantly, he looks very much alive. Good. This is the information I needed. People do jump off this cliff and survive.

I wave.

He waves back. "See you soon, Sophie Kai!"

I can't seem to find my voice, so I give him a thumbs-up, and then I remember how it felt to watch him jump. I return to the other end of the diving platform, face the cliff edge, and focus beyond it, where ocean meets sky.

Everybody's looking at me. Some are shouting, "Go for it, Sophie Kai!" and "We believe in you!" and "You've got this, girlfriend!" (that from Wilks) Their words fuel a new surge in me—not like ice water this time, or fire, or even adrenalin. Whatever it is, it's taking away the tingle in my hands. It's urging me forward, forward into my life.

What is this *thing*? It's like I need to know before I can jump.

"Aloha, Sophie Kai, aloha!" the voice of my Tūtū rises above all the others.

Oh. I grin and wave. *Aloha.*

It's aloha I feel streaming through my veins.

It's love. It's hello. It's welcome to the rest of your life.

Thank you, thank you, I chant to myself, feeling so much gratitude I could burst.

And then my inner voice adds: *Commit.*

And I do.

I commit and run.

32.

My 'Ohana

The fall is strangely silent.

It seems to last forever.

I've never felt so free.

I slide into the ocean, straight as a pin as Nalu coached me—nothing sticking out—then surface, breathing in deep gulps of fresh, salty air. "Easy, peasy!" I sputter as I spy Nalu a few feet away.

"You did it!" he yells, slapping at waves, spraying plumes of water every-which-way.

And then he swims over and hugs me.

It lasts only a nano-second, but long enough for our friends to see. They are all lined up at the cliff's edge forty feet above us, whooping and hollering—whether it's for the jump or the hug or both, I'm not sure. Keola and Wilks are hugging each other, too, and now waving at me with wide sweeping arms. Keola's voice booms, "Way to go, Sophie Kai!" Others are yelling, too, but the most important cheers are happening inside of me. I am so happy!

"I jumped! I jumped!" I keep shouting.

"You did! You did!" Nalu cheers, then guides me over to the rope ladder, where I climb back up to my amazing life.

Dad talks about feeling like he's "walking on air" after he finishes a huge painting that he's happy with. Well, that's what I've been feeling since coming back to camp from South Point. It's not only the thrill of jumping from a forty-foot cliff that has me floating; it's who was with me when I did it.

My 'ohana.

Tūtū talks about how 'ohana is more than your immediate family—your mom, dad, siblings, grandparents, uncles and aunts. 'Ohana can include friends or even pets. Sometimes families take in children who need extra care, like neighbor kids who become like cousins. "You know your 'ohana in here," Tūtū told us, tapping her chest. "Like aloha, 'ohana expands as we live, that is … if we live with an open heart."

Tonight, at our last talk story circle, sitting here on a log with my mom, my heart feels as big as the sky above us. I gaze at each of my friends and feel happy-sad. Happy to know them. Sad because I'll miss them.

There's Nalu and Honi across the circle jiving with each other, all elbows and pushes. Keola and Luana seem to be sharing secrets; I think they're in love. Wilks lounges contentedly on her own log until Keola and Luana jump up and join her. And, of course,

Keola says something that makes both girls laugh. Outside the circle, Tūtū Malia leans on her walking stick, while Uncle tends the fire, sending sparks flying into the night.

Meanwhile, Aunty sits on a log in front of her sister. She's cuddling Moa who is happily slumped in his sling as she clucks sweet nothings in his little rooster ears. I should tell her about his blindness, I think, and I'm about to head over there, when a thought stops me cold.

It doesn't matter.

Suddenly, their relationship makes perfect sense. Moa's being blind—much less his being a rooster—makes absolutely no difference in how Aunty and he love each other. They're 'ohana. Where Uncle fits into that is anyone's guess, but clearly, he's 'ohana, too.

"You okay?" Mom asks, placing a hand on my knee.

"Sure, Mom." I lean against her. "Couldn't be better."

"Hey, Sophie Kai." Mom nods at Keola and the girls. "Why don't you join them?"

"That's okay." I shrug. It would be nice to hang out with my friends, but I don't want to leave her alone.

"You forget, sweetheart, you're talking to a lawyer here. Reading body language is one of my superpowers." And she gently nudges me off the log.

As soon as they see me coming, Luana scoots over to Keola's other side, making room for me between him and Wilks. We've already talked about the three of us getting together when we're back on the mainland, so I don't feel anxious about leaving them. While Keola and Wilks will catch a plane in Hilo early tomorrow morning, Mom and I will leave from Kona around noon, stopping off at the seahorse farm first. I'm hoping to pick up Buddy's girlfriend on the way. That is, if she's still there.

Nalu just looked across the circle at me and smiled. Of all the island kids, I'll miss him the most, but he promises he'll text. Not sure what's happening there. I mean, he hasn't tried to kiss me or anything, unless of course you count mouth to mouth resuscitation, which I *don't*.

Keola, Wilks and I made Nalu swear to take pictures of Mama Honu's babies scrambling out of the nest if by any chance he happens to see it. Chances are he won't, the conservation lady said, but you never know.

"Friends! 'Ohana!" Tūtū sings into the circle. She's settled onto the log with my mother. "It's time to bring this chapter of our story to a close, yes?"

"No!" we echo back.

"We're not ready to leave!" Honi shouts, all sad-eyed. Really, he looks like he's about to cry. Nalu pokes him with an elbow, but he pushes him away.

"Oh, my 'ohana. You are so tender-hearted, and that's a good thing!" Tūtū laughs but then her face gets serious. "I said we're ending a chapter, not the story itself. We have many more chapters to go. New places to explore. New challenges to meet. New friendships to make. We are not done with each other yet. I can feel it in my bones!" She nods at Uncle as if that's his cue.

"That's funny. I can feel it in my backside!" Uncle proclaims, as he leaps up from his log, rubbing his bottom. "It's time to work out some of these kinks." And with that, we are treated to our last hula for the summer, as Aunty's gourd taps out a strong, warrior beat.

Keola is captivating as usual—I notice Mom is in the same trance we all are whenever we watch him dance—but it's Luana that has my wonder tonight. Sweet, gentle Luana, who usually hides her power, commands the ground she stomps on. When the dance ends, the rest of us leap up and cheer.

When Tūtū Malia told us at dinner that we wouldn't be having the usual talk story, we were all disappointed. "No worries," she said, giving us the shaka sign, "you're going to like what we have planned instead." When Uncle keeps Keola at the center of the circle as the rest of the dancers sit down, I whisper to Wilks, "This is it."

Uncle stands behind Keola with his hands on his shoulders. "Every summer, when Camp Koa ends, we choose a camper who has demonstrated the very best of aloha," he begins. "We know that all of you will agree that Keola is that one." There's a flurry of "ohs" and "yeses" and "awws," everyone clapping their agreement. "Keola is one of those helpers Tūtū talks about, right?" More clapping. "He welcomes and accepts everyone. He loves everyone. He sees beauty in everyone. Yes? Especially *himself!*"

That gets a big laugh. Keola's chuckling, too, of course.

Uncle waits for everyone to settle down. "His parents must have seen straight into the future when they named him, because Keola lives a big life—a life filled with aloha!" And with that, Uncle places a crown of ti leaves on Keola's big, beautiful head.

"The King of Aloha!" Nalu shouts, as we whoop and applaud.

Keola looks shy, maybe for the first time in his life.

After much fanfare, Uncle motions for us to quiet down. "We're not done yet, campers." And with that, Tūtū Malia stands up and joins Uncle and Keola.

"As I'm sure all of you recall during our second week of camp, we focused on *kuleana*—that is, a relationship of mutual responsibility and caring," she begins, "as in, we take care of the ocean and her creatures, and the ocean and her creatures take care of us. And while we believe all of you have grown in this important Hawaiian tradition, Aunty, Uncle, and I have chosen two campers who have demonstrated kuleana way beyond our expectations." At this point, I'm getting the chicken skin. I look over at Wilks who has no clue what's about to happen.

"Leilani—otherwise known as Wilks." Tūtū smiles and signals for Wilks to join her.

Wilks stands up stiffly, shaking her head. When she reaches the others, Tūtū takes her hand. "As most of you know, Leilani can sometimes hear the voices of our ancestors. That alone can be a huge responsibility—right, my friend?" Tūtū nudges her gently and they both laugh. "But hearing is one thing; listening is another. You, my dear, have demonstrated kuleana by setting aside your own fears to listen to our ancestors and they've responded in kind. That's the kuleana you live and breathe, Leilani. And the ancestors say, 'mahalo.'" Tūtū gives Wilks a gentle hug before placing a crown of plumeria on her head. I swear I can smell the sweet scent from here. And everyone cheers.

I want to jump up and give Wilks a big hug, but Tūtū keeps talking. "One more, my friends," Tūtū says as she invites Wilks to stay. "Remember, kuleana isn't just about talking a good talk. It's about *walking* that talk. And this camper represents that part of kuleana that is all action." She turns and looks straight at Nalu. "A behind-the-scenes kind of guy."

Nalu, who was whispering something to Honi as Tūtū was talking—*typical*—looks startled when he hears his name. You can tell he thinks he's in trouble. Everyone around the circle starts to giggle.

"Nalu?" Tūtū's holding another crown, this one made of shiny green ti leaves.

"Yes, Tūtū?"

"It's you."

"Me?" He still doesn't get it.

"Yes, dear Nalu. Get your silly, boy-self up here."

"Oh!" he says, sheepishly.

Nalu's body is shaking so hard trying not to laugh that when he finally receives his crown, the ti leaves tremble. Honestly, it's the most hilarious thing I've ever seen.

Once all the laughter dies down, Aunty rises from her log, surprisingly graceful. She seems eager to do her part, whatever that might be, which is when she walks over and extends her hand to me.

"Sophie Kai, you're next."

Oh no, oh no, oh no.

"Come on, girl. We don't have all day." Even though her voice has an edge to it, her face is all smiles.

Talk about wobbly. I slowly rise to my feet, trying to find balance. Everyone around the circle is so still, that the *snap-crack* of the fire is all I can hear. I take Aunty's hand and we join the others. Keola, Wilks, and Nalu are grinning at me. Tūtū and Uncle, too.

Aunty clears her throat. "I know, Sophie Kai, that you and I started out kind of rocky…"

Uncle coughs, stifling a laugh, but she ignores him.

"And I know we haven't always seen eye to eye. I'll admit it. I didn't think you or your friends were supposed to be here, and I knew you wanted to go home." She stares at the ground for a minute before she continues. "It was the honu that helped me see things differently."

Tūtū hands Aunty a crown of pink and yellow plumeria like the one Wilks is wearing. I still can't believe this is happening. Across the circle, Mom's eyes are glistening.

"When the honu let me into their beautiful minds," Aunty continues, "they showed me you belong here. 'Everywhere she looks, everything she touches,' the honu told me, 'ohana is all she sees.'" Aunty scans the circle. "This recognition is from everyone here, Sophie Kai, but it's also from the honu. You are 'ohana."

She nestles the crown into my hair and then leans in close. "Thank you, Sophie Kai," she says so softly only I can hear. "Thank you for teaching me we're family."

33.
Sliding into Home

Shock of all shocks, Mom and I glide through airport security like honu gliding through water, *despite* a carry-on package with way more liquid—make that saltwater—than the limit allows. I guess the TSA folks have seen packages from the Kai House go through their checkpoints before.

"Unbelievable," Mom mutters as we walk toward our gate. She's been fretting all the way from the seahorse farm to the airport about how we were never going to make it through security with a carry-on seahorse. "That was so easy." Mom casts a look over her shoulder. "When is it ever this easy?"

"When it's right," I say. "You know, like back at the seahorse farm when Buddy's new friend zoomed right over to me as soon as I stuck my hand in the tank. Easy-peasy. Like that."

Mom raises her eyebrows the same way she used to when she thought I was making stuff up, but then she bursts out laughing. "Hey, girlfriend, I'm all for easy." And then, my formerly uptight, take-no-prisoners mother gives me the shaka sign, as if it's her new mantra.

A few hours later, I wake up from a nap to the sound of the pilot's voice over the intercom. Apparently, we're cruising at thirty-two thousand feet above sea level over a thick layer of puffy-white clouds. Wrapped in the thin, blue flannel blanket the flight attendant gave her, Mom sleeps through the announcement. She looks peaceful under my crown of pink plumeria I gave her this morning at breakfast.

"This is for doing the hard thing," I had told her, nestling the crown into her auburn hair.

"And what's that?" she said, puzzled. "I thought you were the brave one."

"…for listening and believing. For letting go," I said quietly.

"Ah," she said. "Then I guess we'll share it."

I'm a mishmash of feelings right now: bored with the trip, sad about leaving Camp Koa, at peace about Baby Girl, excited about seeing Dad and Buddy. I also have to pee. But mainly, I'm burning with curiosity to see how Buddy's new friend is doing. For now, I'm calling her Mo, short for *Moʻolio*, which is Hawaiian for "seahorse."

Buddy and Mo.

It's got a nice ring to it.

I look at the box stamped with the slogan, *Kai House—Home of the Seahorse*, and underneath that, the Hawaiian, *Hale o ke kai*—and pull it out from under the seat in front of me. The seahorse people warned me not to subject Mo to bright light too quickly, but I really don't think it would hurt to take a quick peek. Besides, it will keep my mind off having to go to the bathroom.

I turn out the overhead lights and carefully pull down the shade over the window next to me before I lift the lid and peer in, through a clear plastic bag. "Hello in there," I whisper into the sloshy dark. No answer. Not that I expected one. "We'll be home before you know it." Not that she knows what "home" is.

Suddenly, I see a single white eyeball with a black speck of a pupil float to the surface, rotating up, down, sideways. Normally, that would seem a little creepy, except I know there's a seahorse body attached to it. If only I could make contact....

I clear my mind of all thoughts and replace them with an image of the aquarium back home. I focus on the clumps of seaweed waving lazily in the warm current and call up a feeling of safety and ease. *Home*, I think, allowing thoughts of Buddy to surface. I see his tail hooked around a strand of seaweed. Alone. Waiting.

Friend! I hear her think.

Yes! I think back. Could it really be that easy?

A flight attendant is walking down the aisle collecting trash, so I re-seal the box and push it gently back under the seat in the dark where it belongs.

"Hey, Sophie Kai," Mom says sleepily, waking from her nap. "What ya been doin'?"

"Not much," I say, unlatching my seatbelt. "Right now, I gotta pee."

❀ ❀ ❀

"We're sliding into home," the pilot announces as we make our approach into Seattle.

We still have about half-an-hour, though, before we touch down.

"Love the baseball metaphor," Mom says, "I bet he's a Mariner's fan. I'd rather land than slide, though." I smile, giving her the shaka sign.

I peer out the window, expecting to see the Seattle skyline. Instead, there are jagged waves rising out of a frothy sea. No, *wait*. Those are peaks of mountains breaking through a blanket of clouds. Further away but coming closer, Mt. Rainer welcomes us home.

"Sophie Kai?" Mom's voice breaks through my wonderings. "You might have been too young at the time, but do you remember when I was pregnant with Baby Girl, and I used to take your hand—like this?" She takes my hand and places it over her tummy. It's a vague memory, but I nod. "Well, Dad thinks I should be the one to tell you…" She presses my hand against her belly more firmly. It feels bigger than I expected and … kind of tight.

Oh my gosh. I jerk my hand away as if she's hot to the touch. How could I not have known this?! "Oh no, oh no, oh no, no, no…" I stutter. "I can't go through this. No, Mom. No." My heart feels like it's being pulled out to sea.

"Hold on, Sophie Kai..." Mom loosens her seatbelt so she can get closer to me. She slips an arm around my shoulder. "This is a *good* thing."

"No ... but ... *what if...*"

"I know, sweet girl. I know this is scary. That's why Dad and I waited to tell you. We wanted to make sure everything was looking good for a healthy pregnancy, and it is." She smiles, looking all glow-y.

I want to be happy. Really I do. I want to get all rowdy about it, but ...

"It's a boy, Sophie Kai."

"A boy?"

Mom nods and smiles.

Wow. A *boy*.

"Do you think Baby Girl knows? Like, maybe they've ... met?"

"I have no idea," Mom says. "But that's a wonderful thought..."

We sit quietly, as we watch the Seattle skyline come into view.

"Once 'ohana, always 'ohana," I finally whisper before we land. And then, I lean over Mom's belly.

"Aloha," I say. "I think you're going to like it here."

34.

What the Seahorse Told Me

Seahorses are usually silent, but make sounds on rare occasions. It's as if they're waiting until it really means something.*

Mom and I decide to leave our bags in the car for now, except for Mo's box, of course. It's best to greet Dad empty-handed; no telling what might happen if you don't. Luggage has been known to go flying. Dad stops for nothing when he delivers a hug and at six-foot-four with a wingspan just as wide, there's no ducking around him. Believe me, I've tried.

"Aloha, my *wāhine*! My beautiful girls!" he shouts, lumbering down the hallway from his studio with open arms. I carefully set Mo's box down inside the front hall and run to greet him.

"Daddy!" *Whomp!* And I'm in his arms.

Mom stands back a few feet, letting me have my hug, until finally she says, "Me, too! Me, too!" and Dad pulls her in beside me.

* From "Getting to Know the Seahorse," by Sophie Kai Bender

Together, we smell like the island Mom and I just left—a daddy-mix of aloe, coconut and a touch of Old Spice mixed with a strong scent of plumeria coming from the crown Mom placed back on my head at the airport. "What's this?" Dad leans back to study it, which of course unleashes the story that begins with Mama Honu and her eggs.

"Whoa, whoa, whoa!" Dad holds up his hands. "This sounds too important to be told on the fly. We have all evening for talk story. Let's get you two settled, okay?" A perfectly rational idea, which isn't like Dad at all, but then he touches Mom's arm, and I can see that he's worried about her. "You okay, Babe?" he asks.

"Couldn't be better," she says softly, gazing up at him. "We have so much to tell you."

Mom and I decided to wait until we were with Dad in person to tell him about Baby Girl. We know he'll be one big puddle of mush when he hears about her hanging out with me. Dad believes in that kind of thing.

But then I think of *everything* that happened at Camp Koa—not just with Baby Girl, but with Mama Honu and her eggs, Tūtū Pele, Aloha Dog, Moa and Slitherin, jumping off the cliff at Southpoint, and all of my amazing friends—it all suddenly moves over me like one of those king tides. It's hard to believe it's only been three weeks since I left home; it feels more like three *years*. And to think this whole thing started with Buddy telling me: "Go. Find friend."

Good thing I listened.

"Mo!" I say, remembering my mission. "Buddy needs to meet Mo!"

I'm heading for the aquarium in the living room—Mo's carrying case in hand, Mom and Dad close behind—when I stop dead in my tracks at the entrance to the living room. With the Alki beach coastline in full view, the evening's sunlit sky streams through the south-facing windows, casting an orange glow on the living room walls. Even when the décor was black, white and gray, this time of day would always make me feel more hopeful. But *now?*

It feels like a whole new life.

The whole room is a rainbow of Hawaiian landscapes, people, and creatures—a gallery of Dad's humongous canvases—lighting up the walls in bright splashes of reds, oranges, teals, and greens. "Geez, you guys have been busy."

"We wanted to surprise you," Dad says, beaming, his arm around Mom's shoulders. "Mom gave me the go-ahead after you left for Camp Koa."

"These paintings were going to waste in your dad's studio," Mom shrugs shyly, gazing up at Dad's face. "I knew it was time to bring more color back into our lives." And then she kisses him on the neck, which is about as far up as she can reach. If they were seahorses, they'd be turning colors. Speaking of which…

"Buddy!" I run over to greet him with Mo's box in hand. He's hanging out on his favorite seaweed—blending in, a brownish green. "I found you a friend," I whisper, my nose inches from the glass. His eyes rotate independently—up, down, back, forth.

I stride over to the picture window and with two long pulls on the cord, the blinds swing shut. "Sorry, but Mo needs the room to be dark," I tell my parents.

"Of course," Dad says. "We should shut off the aquarium light, too." He kneels beside me as I lift Mo from her box, and Mom leans back and watches.

When we lower Mo's bag into the water, I feel like I'm sinking with her into a shadowy new world. As her eyes adjust to the dim lighting, I imagine she feels curious about this new place and who might be here with her. She looks and looks, but the plastic bag blurs her vision.

Friend? I feel her wondering. And then she starts clicking, "Tik-tik-tik-tik-tik-tik-tik!"

Dad looks at me with big eyes. "Do you hear that?"

"Yeah, I read about it, but I'd forgotten. Mo's telling Buddy she's here!"

"Seahorses do that?"

I nod. I can feel how anxious she is. "Hang in there, Mo," I whisper.

After Dad helps me scoop aquarium water into Mo's bag, we let her float there for a while to adjust to her new environment.

When Dad finally says, "It's time," I gently pull the bag out of the water, letting Mo float free.

For a minute, I can feel her looking, looking, looking—clicking, clicking, clicking—as she takes a spin around her new home. I'm anxious to sense her first impressions—particularly when she sees Buddy for the first time—but then suddenly, *Ping!* I'm kicked out of her view. It's as if she wants her privacy for what happens next, and I'm not invited.

I'm feeling a little jealous and kind of left out, when these waves of happiness begin to wash over me, and I know … Buddy met Mo.

"I want to see! I want to see!" I tug on Dad's elbow, but he shakes his head.

"I know, sweet girl, but we should wait a little longer."

He grabs a couple of cushions from the couch, and the three of us settle back onto the thick white carpet in front of the aquarium—Dad, Mom, and me in between—gazing into the watery dark. Mom's hand is on her tummy, and I remember there's *four* of us now. And then I think about Baby Girl and I count to myself, *five*. The filter hums and gurgles as we wait.

And wait.

"Hey," Dad whispers, breaking the silence. "Want to do the honors, Sophie Kai?"

I reach over to flip the switch, and just like that, Buddy and Mo come into view.

And oh, what a view.

Buddy and Mo are facing each other snout to snout—their curved, horsey necks mirroring the shape of a heart—and they're turning colors! Buddy's shifting from his usual seaweed green to a brightening yellow, and Mo shimmers orange, her spikey mane shooting off her neck in all directions like the rays of the sun.

"Wow," Dad says, "That's one hip chick."

Buddy seems to agree. After the two seahorses bow to each other several times, Buddy floats in slow circles around her like he's checking her out. Seconds later, Mo follows suit, the two of them spiraling around each other, both clicking, "Tik-tik-tik-tik-tik-tik-tik-tik!"

"Experts call this the 'carousel dance,'" I whisper, remembering the research I did for my sixth-grade paper. "I think they like each other!"

"You *think?*" Dad chuckles.

I want to smoosh my nose against the glass to get a closer look, but Buddy and Mo are feeling safe enough to do their courtship dance in front of us, and I don't want to push it.

"Fun fact," I say. "Even after the guy-seahorse gets pregnant, a pair of seahorses will continue their courtship dance, greeting each other every morning just like Buddy and Mo are doing now."

"Smart seahorses." Dad nudges Mom on the shoulder.

She laughs, but then gets real quiet. "Is *this* what love looks like?"

I close my eyes. With a soft jolt, I can feel my empathic powers take a leap—something I've felt before—but this time, I'm not connecting with just one being, I'm joining up with many. Mom, Dad, Buddy, Mo, my little brother, the spirit of my sister, the heart of Hawaii and the heart of my home. All hearts beating as one.

When I open my eyes, I'm aware of Mom's smiling face and Dad's long arm snug across our backs. With linked tails, Buddy and Mo promenade across the length of their tank, back and forth, back and forth—as if he's showing her around—while all the while, I swear, Buddy's bulgy, white eyeballs with those tiny black pupils are riveted on *me*.

What? I think-say. *What?*

Which is when he tells me…

"Yes," I say, leaning into Mom. "This is love."

Characters
in order of appearance

Sophie Kai Bender: our protagonist

"Dad," Alika *[Ah-LEE-kah]* **Bender:** Sophie's father

Buddy: Sophie's pet seahorse

Ms. Lovejoy: Sophie's sixth-grade teacher

Baby Girl, or Mālani *[Mah-LAH-nee]***:** Sophie's baby sister

"Mom," Clare Bender: Sophie's mother

Tūtū Malia *[TOO-too mah-LEE-ah]***:** Malia Jones, Camp Koa's founder and director

Sandy: Flight attendant

Wilks, or Leilani *[Lay-LAH-nee]***:** Sophie's friend she meets on the plane

Keola *[Kay-O-lah]***:** Sophie's friend she meets on the plane

Aloha Dog: Dog … or ghost?

Uncle, or Hanalai *[Hah-nah-LAY]***:** Camp Koa elder, Aunty's husband

Aunty, or Kuʻuipo *[KOO-oo-EE-po]***:** Camp Koa elder, Uncle's wife, Tūtū Malia's sister

Moa *[MO-ah]***:** Aunty's pet rooster

Nalu *[NAH-loo]***:** Sophie's friend who climbs coconut trees

Honi *[HO-nee]***:** Camp Koa camper, a bit of a troublemaker

Luana *[Loo-AH-nah]*: Camp Koa friend, quiet but powerful

Pele, or Tūtū Pele *[PEH-leh or TOO-too PEH-leh]*: Hawaiian goddess of the volcano

Hi'iaka *[Hee-ee-AH-ka]*: Pele's egg sister

Kā-moho-ali'i: *[Kah-MO-HO-ah-LEE-EE]*: Pele's brother, king of sharks

Nā-maka-o-kaha'i *[Nah-MAH-kah-O-kah-hye]*: Pele's older sister, goddess of the sea and water

Kauila [Kow-EE-lah]: In the legend, a turtle who sometimes turns into a girl

Thugs: Turtle nest thieves

Haku *[Hah-KOO]*: Bulldozer man

Slitherin: Resident gecko or "mo'o"

Boss Man, or the Boss: Leader of the black market thieves

Jane: Turtle expert

Mo'olio, or "Mo" *[MO-oh-LEE-oh, or MO]*: Buddy's seahorse friend

Glossary

aloha	[ah-LO-ha]	--an Hawaiian greeting for hello and goodbye; love, compassion, mercy, grace
aloha 'aina	[ah-LO-ha EYE-na]	--love for the land
'aumakua	[ow-mah-COO-ah]	--ancestors, animals, or spirits that hold sacred significance to an individual or family
chicken skin		--goosebumps
hālau	[ha-LAO]	--hula group or school
hale o ke kai	[HAH-leh-O-keh-KYE]	--house of the sea
heiau	[HEH-ow]	--a sacred site
ho'oponopono	[HO-oh-PO-no-PO-no]	--a process of forgiveness and love
huhū	[hoo-HOO]	--angry
'īlio	[ee-LEE-O]	--dog
ipu	[EE-poo]	--a rhythm instrument made from a gourd, often used to accompany hula
kai	[KYE]	--from the sea
kahuna	[kah-HU-nah]	--an expert in any field, a shaman; plural, kāhuna [KAH-hu-nah]
(false) kamani	[Kah-MAH-nee]	--a kind of tree found in Hawaii
kapu	[KAH-poo]	--forbidden and/or sacred
keiki	[KAY-kee]	--child, or (colloquial) children
koa	[KOH-ah]	--courage
kuleana	[Koo-leh-AH-nah]	--responsibility
kumu	[KOO-moo]	--teacher
kūpuna	[koo-POO-nah]	--grandparents or elders

kuʻuipo	[KOO-oo-EE-po]	--sweetheart
lei	[LEH]	--a necklace of flowers, leaves, and/or shells often given as a welcoming gift or to commemorate a special occasion
mahalo	[mah-HAH-lo]	--thank you
mahalo nui loa	[mah-HAH-lo NOO-ee LOH-ah]	--thank you very much
malasada	[MAH-la-SAH-duh]	--a Portuguese-inspired donut
mana	[MAH-nah]	--power, life energy
moa	[MO-ah]	--rooster
moemoe	[MOy-MOy]	--bedtime
moʻo	[MO-oh]	--gecko
moʻolio	[MO-oh-LEE-oh]	--seahorse
ʻohana	[oh-HAH-na]	--family; referring to people or animals close to your heart, as well as your biological and extended family members
pōhaku	[poh-HA-koo]	--stone, rock
poi	[POY]	--a traditional Hawaiian food made from the taro root
pono	[POH-no]	--the rightness of something
shaka	[SHAH-kah]	--a friendly sign meaning "hang loose," relax
ti leaf	[TEE]	-- a slender plant with long, wide leaves used for lei-making, hula skirts, and wrapping food and offerings
tūtū	[TOO-too]	--grandparent; often, grandmother
wāhine	[wah-HEE-nay, or vah-HEE-nay]	--women

Acknowledgments

First and foremost, *mahalo nui loa* to my writing colleague and friend, Karen Kaimilani (Imi) Leota Sellers, for advising me during the writing process on how best to authentically represent the Hawaiian culture. Imi provided many helpful details about Hawaiian flora, fauna, geology, food, and language; translated certain passages of dialogue into pidgin; and was instrumental in creating the glossary and character page, particularly in providing pronunciations. Mahalo to Imi's mom, who also helped with pronunciations. Imi, your contribution has been immeasurable. I've especially appreciated your encouragement to tell the story that was mine to tell.

I am also grateful to the Kentucky Foundation for Women for awarding me the grant that helped in part to fund Imi as an advisor, along with the financial help to finish my novel. The Pacific Northwest Writers Association also offered a boost to this project in its early stages, awarding my novel First Place in Middle Grade Fiction.

Mahalo nui loa to Sophia Hanoa and Kūpuna Jessie Ke for meeting with me several years ago on the island of Hawaii to discuss the concepts and themes for my story. Your generous welcome, input, and encouragement meant the world to me.

Several years later, Sophia and Kūpuna Jessie met with three other native Hawaiians (ages 26 to 78) to read and comment on the final draft of my manuscript. They offered extensive notes, corrected mistakes, and made recommendations on ways the story could more accurately represent the Hawaiian culture, and most importantly, *honor* it. This team was indispensable in helping me express the love and respect I carry in my heart for Hawaii. Anything that remains that may be considered inaccurate or inauthentic, while not intended, is my responsibility alone.

Mahalo also to Karen Valentine and her friend, Leoni, who introduced me to locations around the island, answered my many questions, and taught me how to make a lei out of ti leaves.

Great gratitude to the talented staff at Middleton Books for their diligence in creating a beautiful book—particularly to Jonathan Scott for his cover and book design and to Shane DeHaven for her extraordinary proofing expertise. Professional photographer, Sarah Mullins of Sarah Mullins Creative, rendered the cover portrait of the girl exactly as envisioned, and her model, Nina McHale, perfectly expressed the spirit of our protagonist. This was obviously more than "just a book" to all of you, and that dedication shows.

Mahalo to Pete Giwojna, Ocean Ryder (www.seahorse.com) for applying his seahorse expertise to the relevant elements of the book. Your suggestions made these passages not only more accurate, but more interesting. I particularly appreciate your joy and enthusiasm for these amazing creatures—a joy that we share!

How can I ever express the depth of appreciation I have for my writing partner, Margo Buchanan, who has accompanied me every word of the way? Margo, your comments have proven invaluable, particularly in making the plot more impactful. (The shark is all yours!) This writer's journey is not nearly as lonely with *you* in it.

Heartfelt gratitude to my extraordinary beta readers: Rosie Sansalone, Jen Molitor, Jesse Fawess, Kristin Noelle Wolfgang, and Zach Knight, as well as student readers, Lizzie Hendrickson, Katarina Salisbury, Hunter Tigar, and Elsie Fricke. This is a better story because of you. Any remaining errors are mine alone!

And then there's my supporting cast of colleagues: Mahalo to all my writing buddies from the Naslund-Mann Graduate School of Writing at Spalding University, particularly Tay Berryhill who read the first few chapters in its early stages and offered invaluable comments and encouragement. Mahalo also to my colleagues from the Carnegie Center for Literacy and Learning, as well as my present and former writing students; and to all the teachers and librarians who have welcomed me into their schools for author visits throughout the years. A special shout-out to my friends at Clinton-Massie Middle School whose love and enthusiasm propelled me through the final stages of getting this book out. A special "mahalo nui loa" to all my readers who never fail to offer me deeper insights into my books and remind me of my purpose. I do this impossible work of writing novels … for *you*.

Deep heart-gratitude to my 'ohana (friends and family) who channel the love that fuels everything I do: Susan, Kate, Margo and Mike, Erin, Helen, Teresa, Soni, Megan, Laura and the "gang," Christie, Beth, Richard, Cass, Michael, Rose, Jennifer, Zach, and my grandkids Milo and Zora.

And then there's Jonathan, my angel man. Your heart and soul are everywhere present in this book and in my life. There's not enough gratitude in the universe to express what you mean to me. So, I'll leave it here with *aloha*, a word that—for me—includes *you*.

Mary Knight

Mary is the award-winning author of *Saving Wonder* (Scholastic Press) and enjoys presenting at schools and conferences around the country. She especially loves talking about writing with her middle grade readers who often give her new insights into her novels. When she's not coaching other writers on their book-length manuscripts or traveling around the country, Mary enjoys taking long walks, kayaking, and playing with her grandkids in her hometown of Lexington, Kentucky, where she lives with her sweetheart and their very polite cat.

Visit www.maryknightbooks.com.

Made in the USA
Middletown, DE
01 June 2025

76291793R00177